Dear Reader,

I am very excited to share with you Soho Teen's May 2014 title: *The A-Word: A Sweet Dead Life Novel.*

If you're already a fan of author Joy Preble, you know her for her wit, for her lovable (and flawed) characters, for the delight she takes in weaving the strange quirks of the everyday with the unseen and magical. And if you're already a fan of *The Sweet Dead Life*, then I imagine you're chomping at the bit for more Jenna Samuels, Joy's feisty teen heroine. But I'm especially eager to share *The A-Word* with the Joy Preble neophyte. I have no doubt you'll want to read *The Sweet Dead Life* as soon as you finish, but it's not essential to what you'll discover and love in these pages.

I've had the privilege of working with Joy since 2009, when I joined Sourcebooks and took over as editor for her *Anastasia* series. Before then, while at Alloy, we'd tried and failed to create a compelling YA Anastasia Romanov property. It seemed like a no-brainer, but nothing ever worked. Joy's series not only worked; it kept surprising me on successive reads. As far as I was concerned, she'd accomplished the impossible. I knew I had to work with her.

What I didn't know then—and what comes alive in this novel—is that Joy's sense of humor is as boundless as her imagination. She's a humanist with one eye on the Divine, in the vein of Libba Bray and Kurt Vonnegut. I hope this book will make you laugh and think as much I did while reading it.

Sincerely,
Daniel Ehrenhaft
Editorial Director, Soho Teen

ALSO BY JOY PREBLE

The Sweet Dead Life

THE A-WORD

A-WORD

JOY PREBLE

This is a work of fiction. Names, characters, places, and incidents either
are the product of the author's imagination or are used fictitiously, and any
resemblance to actual persons, living or dead, businesses, companies, events, or
locales is entirely coincidental.

Published in the United States in 2014 by Soho Teen
an imprint of
Soho Press, Inc.
853 Broadway
New York, NY 10003

Library of Congress Cataloging-in-Publication Data

TO COME

ISBN 978-1-61695-290-7
eISBN978-1-61695-291-4

Interior design by Janine Agro, Soho Press, Inc.

Printed in the United States of America

10 9 8 7 6 5 4 3 2 1

For Rick, who knows how important the stories are.

"Texas is a state of mind."
— John Steinbeck

THE
A-WORD

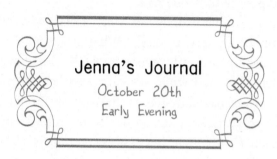

It took everything I had to convince my best friend Maggie to come to the football game. Football is not Maggie's thing. It's not mine either, even though my brother Casey played for years until that became impossible due to A-word (I still didn't like saying the word angel) circumstances out of everyone's control. But more on that later. I was going because I wanted to see Ryan Sloboda play. More accurately, I wanted Ryan Sloboda to *see me* seeing him play. Maybe that would jump-start something and he'd get off his butt and ask me out, which he'd been working up to for months. Ryan is still pretty backward in the socializing area.

Plus it was the day before my fifteenth birthday and I was feeling optimistic. Maggie's neutral about birthdays, but me—I like to do them up big. Cake-and-pony big. Well, maybe not an actual pony. But celebrate. Be happy. Tomorrow your brother might bite the dust driving you to the hospital because your mom's boss had been poisoning you (more on that later, too), and come back as your guardian angel.

Trust me. It could happen.

So eat the damn birthday cake if someone makes you one, which hopefully someone will.

But as I couldn't exactly tell Maggie that my brother was a heavenly being now, I asked, "What about the boots? Too much?" meaning my red cowboy boots that I had just shoved on my feet. I waited while she furrowed her eyebrows and thought it over, dramatic-like in that way she preferred.

We were sitting on the floor in my room, going over Appropriate Football Outfit Choices Guaranteed to Get Ryan Sloboda to Take Notice. Maggie is obsessed with finding me the perfect signature style even though I have informed her that I am more eclectic when it comes to fashion.

"Eclectic" is one of my new favorite words. It means derived from a variety of sources, which means it is perfectly fine to wear my red cowboy boots with a denim skirt instead of jeans, and also okay for Maggie to help me cover with black lace, and top it with my plaid button-down, sleeves rolled up to the elbows.

"I think you're pushing it," Maggie said in her absolutely certain tone. Maggie is Absolutely Certain about most things.

I reminded her about Ryan Sloboda's social awkwardness. Plus, even with a button or two undone, there is not much to see. But like I say, I am an optimistic girl.

"Skirt's good, though, right?"

"I guess," Mags said, kind of quiet. She poked at the black lace on the skirt, tugging it here and there. "Long as you don't go skydiving in it or something."

Maggie rarely expresses shock at what the universe spits out. Like her fashion sense, that's just how Mags is—an embrace-the-world-by-the-horns girl and proud of it. Yesterday she justified failing her Spanish II quiz by observing that

the universe probably wanted her to be more sympathetic to the plight of undocumented workers. ("Now I know how hard it is to be in a strange land and master a new language.") My opinion was that she had forgotten to study, which was also the case. But the stuff that's been happening in my universe is a tad harder to digest.

The truth is this: my brother and his angel boss, EMT/bartender Amber Velasco had spread their wings over the atrium at the Galleria Shopping Mall to save me from the evil Dr. Renfroe. When you think of comic-book bad guys, true villains, you think of them as handsome in a sinister way, just maybe not so hairy. On the other hand, Dr. Renfroe was comic-book classic in that he was charming and very good at lying. He poisoned me and experimented with memory drugs on my parents and a bunch of innocent oldsters at Oak View Convalescent. But Casey swooped in before I splattered in a public demise at the hands of Dr. Renfroe and his partners-in-crime. Amber snagged the Bad Guy. A happy . . . ending?

Here's the problem: I can't tell Mags, my best friend in the entire crazy universe, the truth. Instead I have to stick to the far-less-believable story that we attempted a crazy skydiving stunt right before Christmas. And that in the process, we accidentally helped bring down a crime ring that wanted to weaponize Dr. Renfroe's memory drugs.

Luckily, people's memories are sketchy enough on their own. That's what Casey says, and he should know, given his weed-addled brain. But I agree, what with us all watching YouTube videos and downloading Internet porn (like my brother used to before he ended up on Heaven's payroll, not that he gets paid). Besides, being famous for weird stuff only lasts so long at school. Take a deep breath and some idiot is sending a picture of herself in her underwear, and her boy-friend is forwarding it to the entire student body.

Plus Casey still looks like Casey. Not that I ever thought much about what angels would look like. But I guess if I did give it pause, I would picture them in white sparkly outfits or maybe invisible or wearing halos. Not sleeping in the room down the hall from me, passed out in a Mountain Dew T-shirt next to half-eaten Jack in the Box tacos.

I hate that I have no alternative but to lie to Maggie. Maybe someday I can tell her the truth—that Casey isn't quite Casey anymore. I'd tell her all the rest of it, too.

But if there's one thing I've learned about the angelic world, it's that there are rules. Flying under the radar is a big one. Meaning: Do. Not. Tell.

All I could do was ramble about how many buttons I should leave undone, and did Maggie think we should paint our faces red and blue in the Spring Creek colors? Which is more school spirit than I normally work myself up to, and definitely more than I had last year when I was still at Ima Hogg Junior High.

I couldn't talk about how people had basically forgotten the whole Galleria thing because there had never been a trial. Someone had paid Dr. Renfroe's bail and he'd disappeared without a trace. I couldn't talk about Manny, the owner of Manny's Real Tex Mex in Houston—the shady criminal who was blackmailing Dr. Renfroe—because Manny had also conveniently vanished. I couldn't talk about how Casey was effectively grounded from using his wings in public or that the guys who caused the whole mess weren't ever going to be dragged to justice.

It was easier to think about my boots. Which, by the way, I loved. They'd been a gift from Amber Velasco after my old

Ariats had been destroyed, since that was how Renfroe had been slipping the poison into my system.

"Ryan is going to pee his pants," Maggie said, perking up once we had declared my outfit and me a finished product.

"What's that about Ryan?" asked my brother.

There he was, in my doorway. Now that he was an A-word (I still didn't like saying angel even though sometimes I did, just not to Maggie, of course), my brother was pretty light on his feet. Pretty nosey, too.

"Get out," I told him.

"I'm taking you and Maggie to the game." He lounged against the doorpost, looking perfectly put-together in that way he had now. My brother's (mostly) previous weed habit had made him a bit fleshy. Not that it mattered then. Back before this whole mess started he was a mostly do-it-yourself operation in the romance department.

Now that he was no longer exactly human, he sported tidy hair and a toned six-pack, among other things. I found this not only annoying but also supremely unfair.

"Maggie's dad is taking us."

"Not any more. Call your dad, Mags. Tell him he can stay home in the La-Z-Boy and watch *Nat Geo*. He doesn't know jack about football."

WHAT MAGS DIDN'T know: Casey had his own reasons for taking us, aside from dogging my every step. Lanie Phelps was cheering tonight. Lanie Phelps: my brother's ex two times over. First, she dumped him after he quit football and took up weed when our family life fell into the cesspool. They made up afterwards. Of course they did. Because Lanie had no idea she was essentially dating a dead guy and that part of the reason she wanted to jump his bones was the A-word pheromones (my phrase) he put out unless he concentrated on pulling them back. Which he rarely did.

To Casey's credit, their current breakup had been his doing. He didn't talk about it, but I knew he thought he was protecting her from the inevitable.

I knew better. Breaking up wouldn't be any protection at all. I just think he figured if Lanie hated him, it might ease things when Management finally plucked him to wherever they pluck angels once they've finished their earthly duties. Not that I was such an expert on these matters. Just that I shared a bathroom with him and he drove me to school every morning. Also, I'd been his sister my entire life. My brother had never been the deepest of thinkers. It wasn't hard to follow the workings of his pea brain. Even now.

Plus everyone's favorite EMT/bartender Amber Velasco had probably insisted he sever ties with Lanie. More than once I'd heard her refer to Casey's relationship with his two-time ex as "imprudent and potentially dangerous." Which was a sophisticated way of saying that he needed to stop hooking up with her in the back of our Merc.

Bosses acted boss-like, even if they were angels.

Which brings us to the game: matters were compounded a few weeks ago when Lanie started seeing Donny Sneed, the varsity quarterback who, while not the brightest star in the sky, was basically a nice guy. Not that this made my brother any less pissy about the whole matter.

Which I totally understood.

Plus, it was football. Casey missed playing like you'd miss an arm or a kidney.

Luckily (ha, ha), our parents were currently too preoccupied trying to decide if they should stay married to notice that their son—who had helped save their lives, not that they

exactly knew that—was changed in like a million ways. On the rare occasions they did question something, he made up excuses. Like the other day when Mom looked Casey up and down and back up again, poking a finger at his muscly arm, clearly flummoxed, and finally said, "Have you been taking supplements or something? You know that Creatine is dangerous, right?"

That he still toked up now and then did not enter the discussion. Yes, it turned out that angels could do drugs if they felt like it. Drugs seemed vastly inappropriate, especially considering Casey's boss was still theoretically a member of the medical community. But who the hell knew what Amber Velasco thought? She was also a bartender. No one ever asked me. No one ever asked my opinion. No one dead, anyway.

"CAN I RIDE in front?" Mags asked.

I tried to kick her. Casey blocked my leg with his.

"We'll all sit up front," he said. "We're all skinny."

"Goodie," I told him.

"Skinny?" Mags said. "You're sweet, Casey."

"Just stating the facts, ma'am," Casey said, which made Mags blush. I shot daggers in his eyes. He shot them back.

Maybe he figured being a dickhead would work on me, too. That I would be happy to see him go. That when the inevitable happened, Lanie Phelps wouldn't be the only one who didn't miss him. I decided to focus on encouraging Ryan Sloboda out of his social awkwardness. At least it was something that had a chance in hell of coming true.

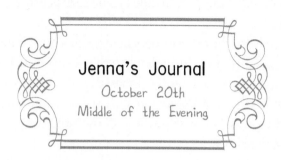

Jenna's Journal
October 20th
Middle of the Evening

By the end of the second quarter, we were winning, seventeen to seven. The coach put Ryan in at defense.

The cheerleaders, including Lanie Phelps, were chanting and tumbling and tossing themselves into the air. The band was pounding and swaying. The fancy new Jumbotron flashed: GO SPRING CREEK MUSTANGS! Followed by: TEXICON: THE OFFICIAL MUSTANG SPONSOR! My brother leaped to his feet.

"Don't forget to bull rush 'em out there, Sloboda. Show 'em what you got."

I pinched his arm—hard. "Stop it, you pissant."

Maggie, bored, grabbed me, and we hightailed it to the concession stand to stuff ourselves with Frito pie—hold the onions—and Dr. Pepper.

After halftime was over, I led Mags down to the fence by the field. "Won't Casey miss us?" Mags asked, only half-sarcastic since my brother's angel mojo was a force of nature on females. "Whatever," I told her. My brother the angel was being a jerk, even if I was the only one who understood why. "I want Ryan to see me."

"Ooooh," Maggie said. She can be sufficiently girly when she wants to.

On the field, the cheerleaders held up this huge banner that the football guys ran through when they came out. Some corporate sponsor had recently donated a ginormous blow-up mustang head and a smoke machine so that they could burst out of the smoking horse's head and onto the turf.

Quite the show.

I was still not sure how I felt about Ryan Sloboda other than I liked him enough to wear boots and a skirt and a blouse of questionable buttonage, but when he flew like a banshee out of that horse's head, my heart gave a ping. And when he waved to me—Me!—as he was trotting toward sidelines, I waved back. Except part of my mind was still on Casey and Lanie and what could possibly be going through my brother's head.

WITH THREE MINUTES left, Forest Ridge scored a touchdown and ran the ball for two extra points. Now the score was seventeen us, fifteen them. Even I knew that all Forest Ridge had to do was score a field goal and it would be all over. But we had possession. I knew that, too. Actually, I knew more than that. Unlike my brother, I am not a pea brain. I ran track until Dr. Renfroe began poisoning my boots. I figured I'd even try out again come spring.

In any case, I was fully aware that the Spring Creek Mustangs were in trouble. Ryan was back on the sidelines, pacing up and down.

"Coach won't put the pissant in, you know." My brother was now standing next to us, leaning his elbows on the low fence.

"Course not," I told him, supremely annoyed. "He plays defense. Plus he's in ninth grade."

"Put *me* in when I was a freshman. And I played both."

"That's right!" Maggie said. "I remember that." Being as she sounded like an insufferable ditz, I assumed she was trying to flirt. Then she frowned. "But you quit."

I felt momentarily bad, but only momentarily. My brother trained his sour gaze on the field. Coach Collins tapped Donny Sneed on the helmet. Coach Collins used to be my algebra teacher at Ima Hogg, as well as Casey's former junior high football coach, but was now coaching and teaching here at Spring Creek, our high school. Maybe it was a promotion. Or maybe here in Texas the same grumpy blowhards end up having the same jobs, just in different places.

Coach and Donny conferred, heads close.

My brother's eyes narrowed. He gripped the fence tighter. The list of living people Casey could talk to—namely about how it felt having to break up with his girlfriend so she wouldn't find out he was an angel—was limited. Nonexistent, in fact, unless he counted me. Now he had to watch her with Donny Sneed.

Donny was about six feet of packed muscle, light brown hair, green eyes, and a white-toothed smile. He treated Lanie like a queen. Whatever they did or didn't do together, you never heard him talk about it. He was probably good to his mother, too. According to Casey, Donny managed to postpone a midterm for everyone in his government class by arguing nonstop that if we banned guns, Congress would probably ban airplanes and the terrorists would win. The teacher gave up and left the classroom because "lunkhead idiots don't shut up." I'm still unclear about whether those were the teacher's words or Casey's. What I do know: the seniors had recently nominated Donny Sneed for class president.

Spring Creek and Forest Ridge lined up. The coaches were pacing like Ryan, talking into their headsets.

"Bootleg," my brother muttered. "Gotta be a bootleg play. Sneed can do that."

The band was wailing up a storm and the cheerleaders were chanting, "What about? What about? What about the color shout?" which I suppose they felt was helpful.

I wasn't sure what a bootleg play was. Did Donny know? Donny reared his arm back like he was going to pass left to the running back.

"Do it!" shouted my brother.

The pass was faked. Donny still had the ball. He dodged right behind the defensive linemen.

"Get down field!" my brother bellowed. "North and south!"

I guess this meant keep running toward the goal line, because that's what Donny did—right through the gap in Forest Ridge's coverage. He was almost free and clear, when number sixty-eight from Forest Ridge broke free and sped after him. He was fast. Faster than the track guys I used to watch. Too fast. He dove for Donny. It was all over. I knew it.

"Uh-oh," Maggie said.

"Aw, shit," said my brother. "Idiot."

Number sixty-eight lunged.

Casey leaned across the fence, stretching out an arm. He blew a breath.

Later, number sixty-eight would tell everyone that some jerk from our school had somehow sabotaged him, messed with his cleats when he wasn't looking, and that's why he tripped. But anyone with eyes could see that both his shoelaces

came undone only while he was closing in—undone in such a lace-flapping frenzy that there was no way you could miss it. And trip he did. He fell at Donny's heels.

The impact must have set Donny off-balance, because he started stumbling, too.

"Jesus Christ," my brother muttered.

Out on the field, Lanie Phelps gave a girlie yelp.

Donny righted himself—the crowd cheered like wild people— and then he was running across the goal line.

Touchdown. Victory. The score was twenty-three to fifteen. We kicked the extra point to twenty-four and not long after that the buzzer sounded. I eyeballed my brother.

"Thought you hated him," I whispered in Casey's ear. Not that I had to lower my voice. No one could hear me with all the joyful shouting.

"I do," he said. "Fuck."

Then everyone rushed the field even though it wasn't allowed, and we pushed on through the gate with them, across the cinder track to the turf, the crowd hooting and hollering about how great Donny had done. How he'd won the game by himself.

But he hadn't done it by himself. Casey had used his angel mojo to help him.

Lanie Phelps ran toward Donny. He grabbed her up in a celebratory hug, her blonde, pink-ribboned ponytail flying behind her.

Casey started walking toward them. My heart flung itself into my neck, beating like crazy. What was he up to? Maybe I didn't want to find out. If it were me, I'd want to pound the guy's face. But *I* wasn't an angel. On the other hand, even angelized, my brother was an unpredictable sort.

I dashed after him, tugging his arm. "Let's go," I said.

Which was when Maggie, scurrying at my side, elbowed me in the ribs. "Look at Casey," she whispered.

His skin wasn't just radiant, it was glowing. He didn't have the same shifting shadows on his face as the rest of us did. There were *no* shadows. Just an invisible sun fixed solely on him, illuminating every feature.

"Those new stadium lights are amazing," I hollered in case anyone else was looking, which other than my best friend, they were not. They were too busy congratulating Donny for something he hadn't exactly done. Donny hugged Lanie closer. He pulled off his helmet and kissed her rumpled, blonde, sweaty cheerleading hair.

I tugged at Casey's hand again, agitated. He must have gotten the hint because the glow vanished. But then that angelic calm of his flowed through me, even though I didn't want it to. Touching him was warm. It was a good warmth, like settling back into a beach chair at sunset. I could almost feel that invisible sun on my face. Everything faded comfortably. Even Maggie, blinking at Casey, befuddled.

And then the world came rushing back. My brother slipped from my grasp and strode quickly to Donny and Lanie—who turned to Casey with so many emotions in her eyes I needed a calculator to keep up with them.

I held my breath. All the calmness I'd felt had become panic, now that Casey had let me go. He clapped Donny on the shoulder pads.

"Good job, Sneed," he said. His lips twitched, but he kept a straight face. "You won the game for us. You're the man."

My shoulders sagged.

Okay, it wasn't that funny. But it was sort of funny.

Then a voice to my left said, "Jenna."

My heart stopped in mid-beat. Ryan Sloboda.

"Thanks for coming," he said. He was sweaty. His hair was standing up every which way. There was a huge smudge of dirt on his cheek. But he was looking at me. Not at the coaches or Donny or anyone else. At me.

He grinned.

My mouth went dry. The Frito pie congealed in my belly.

"I'm going to call you, okay?" Ryan said. He was calm and matter-of-fact about it.

"Okay," I told Ryan. My heart pranced around my chest like one of those show ponies.

My brother continued telling Donny Sneed what a hotshot player he was, while Lanie looked on, discombobulated. Why was her ex being nice? I had the same question, but screw it: Ryan Sloboda was going to call me!

Of course then Coach Collins stomped up and told Ryan he needed to get his ass to the field house. "You too, Sneed," he added.

"Hey, Casey," Ryan said to my brother as he hustled off. "Good game, huh?"

Casey's face went blank. Then he frowned. Bad sign.

"I gotta pee," Maggie announced, which definitely broke the already breaking mood. Casey told her we'd meet her at the car.

WE WALKED BRISKLY toward the Merc, not because we were rushing, but I think because it made Casey feel like we were doing something normal people would do. He avoided my eyes. The glow was long gone. We lounged under the parking lot lights while people searched out their cars and the knots of traffic wound to the street. I wanted to think about Ryan Sloboda. But Casey had made that impossible.

"Why did you help him?" I asked. "Donny I mean. You did, right?" Maybe I was wrong.

My brother heaved a sigh, like an old man. He looked tired, even though I knew he would never be either old or tired again.

"What am I supposed to do? Let Lanie be saddled with a loser? She's top-of-the-class. Already accepted to UT. Then vet school, if she gets in, which I know she will. Did I tell you that? That she wants to be a vet? He's Sneed. But he's good to her. He's *good*. Better him than most of the other numbnuts around here . . ." His voice faded. "She'll see that when she's in vet school."

A million sharp-tongued comments froze on my tongue.

Casey nudged me with a smirk. "Least it's funny for me, right? Knowing he would have fallen flat on his face?"

"Ha ha," I said, not laughing.

He didn't respond, just rubbed at his back where I knew his retracted wings sat. Something tightened inside me.

"Do you always know they're there?" I whispered.

Casey's gaze shot to mine.

We didn't talk about it much. Or at all. Maybe since I knew he was grounded because he'd used his earthly flight to save me. Crazy angel rules.

"I guess," he said after a bit. "Yeah. I do. I guess that's part of it. Of being—"

"How did it feel?" I interrupted. "Flying?" So much had happened since last year that it had felt like just one more thing to talk about. But suddenly I needed to know.

"Amazing," he said, and it surprised me. His voice was deep and sincere in the way he wasn't always with me, even now. "I could feel them stretch out and become part of me. Like my body welcomed them or something. Does that make sense? And then there I was—in the air flying toward you. I'd

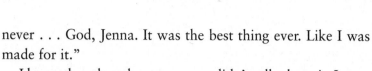

never . . . God, Jenna. It was the best thing ever. Like I was made for it."

I knew then the other reason we didn't talk about it. It was just another thing he loved and couldn't have, another thing he now had to miss forever.

Across the parking lot, I spied Maggie hurrying toward us. I waved my arm and she waved back. Somewhere in those two short motions, my brother's smile faded.

"I'm not ever gonna be good enough, am I?" he asked, looking everywhere but my face. "That's the real reason I'm still here, isn't it? They turned me into . . . this." He gestured down his body with his hands. "And I saved you. What the hell was I supposed to do? Let you die? They sent me back and made me your guardian, and when you needed me I was there. And now what? I'm stuck here forever. That's what I think. Me but not me. Able to look and not touch. Wings I can't use. Screw this, Jenna. Screw it all."

I started to reach for him and stopped, knowing that if I touched him I wouldn't feel normal, here, present. "You'll figure it out."

We both knew I was lying, but what else could I say?

My brother tilted his face toward the top of the light pole at the end of the aisle. The florescent glow increased its brightness, flooding the parking lot with fake light, stronger and stronger.

"Stop it," I said.

"Why? What difference will it make? What difference will I make? Isn't that the whole point? For me to make a difference?"

"There's a reason," I said, lying again.

But by then Maggie had arrived, and he gave up and drove us all home.

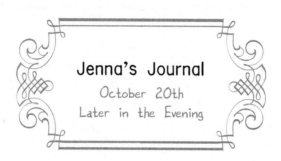

Jenna's Journal

October 20th
Later in the Evening

Mom was in the kitchen, busy with speech therapist paperwork (she always seemed to be working these days) when we trooped in the door. Also, talking on her cell.

"Your father won't be here for your birthday," she said, glancing up. "He's staying in Austin." She waved the phone at me like a baton.

"Happy Birthday, sweetheart," my father sing-songed in my ear.

"It's tomorrow, Dad."

"So I'm the first one to tell you."

That was one way of looking at it.

"Lot going on here," he said when I stayed quiet.

I almost laughed. A lot going on here, too, Dad. I wondered what he meant. Our father was a reporter who split his time between the *Houston Chronicle* and the *Austin American-Statesman*, sports writing mostly, but he'd branched out to politics, among other things. He'd recently published a piece in the *Sunday Statesman* about this group of people who wanted Texas to secede from the Union. Texas had been its own country once, so this was not as odd as it seemed.

"Crazies plotting to overthrow the government again?" I asked him.

My father grunted. "That's not what it's about, Jenna."

"Then what's keeping you from coming home?"

This stumped him enough that we said our goodbyes, and he promised—ha!— he would try for the following weekend.

Here is what neither of us said but understood completely: that odds were, he would have left us years ago, anyway. Even if Mom's boss Dr. Renfroe hadn't given him a megadose of memory-losing drugs because Dad started investigating Renfroe's nefarious activities. (Nefarious is not a favorite word of mine, but it is on the SAT list, and it means evil and conniving. Like a person who'd keep drugging ailing oldsters and justify it in the name of scientific research.) Because what father would admit to his children that their life together actually had never been enough? Sometimes your family is falling apart even before the cracks are evident.

"You sleeping over?" Mom asked Maggie while Dad was telling me he loved me.

"If that's okay," Maggie said, even though of course it was.

"It's Jenna's birthday in a few hours," Mom told her. "She gets to have whatever she wants."

This was more optimistic than even I could manage.

"How was the game?" Mom directed this to Casey. What she probably wanted to say but didn't: Why don't you go back to playing football now that you look so great and you've quit one of your jobs since I'm working again and not comatose? Followed by the part where she might ask why that nice Lanie Phelps wasn't coming around anymore like she had been a few months back.

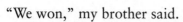

"We won," my brother said.

"Jenna's outfit was a hit," Maggie observed.

Mom's eyes narrowed. She scanned me up and down and up again. "Hmm," she said, then cut her glance to Casey as his cell vibrated like a fire alarm in his pocket.

"It's fine," he hissed into the phone. "Don't you worry."

On the other end, loud enough that we could hear it, Amber Velasco was saying something in the annoyed, high-pitched, East Texas drawl she slips into when she's peeved.

Lately, with my brother, it had been her normal tone.

Even Maggie recognized it. "What's up with her and your brother?" she whispered. Mom went back to the mess of documents in front of her. "Is there something going on that you aren't telling me?"

"You want to order pizza?" I asked her. Maggie still thought Amber was just the wacky EMT who pulled us out of our Prius wreck. And that was all she was ever allowed to think, for her own good. "Cause if you're waiting for my brother to make sense, you'll be waiting 'til the Second Coming."

This seemed to satisfy Mags, who started rattling off topping choices. As for me, I was sorry I'd put it that way. Our family had never been what you would call religious, but let's face it: once your brother comes back from the dead as your guardian angel, you begin to wonder about things. Like what would happen if I brought my brother to Maggie's Sunday school class for show and tell.

"I'm going out," Casey said, shoving his phone in his pocket.

Mom looked up. "It's almost midnight."

Casey strode toward the back door. "Won't be long. Bryce needs me to help close over at BJ's. Someone went home sick."

At the kitchen table, Mom steepled her fingers. "You work too many hours," she said.

"You want Dominos?" I asked Maggie. "Or Papa Johns?"

Casey slammed the door behind him.

"You want me to order for you, too?" I asked Mom. She shook her head.

"I'll get one with pineapple and Canadian bacon," I said. "Just in case."

Mom was looking at her hands. "He wouldn't have to work so many hours if your father were here."

I stood there. On the one hand, I knew full well Casey wasn't going to work. He was going to meet Amber somewhere or do something that Amber had told him needed doing. On the other hand, my father was being a douchebag even if he was providing income again. He was still renting an apartment in Austin. That wasn't coming cheap.

It was Maggie who saved us. "So who invented pineapple pizza anyway?" she asked. "Not the Italians, right?"

"I'll ask the delivery guy," I said.

Mom smiled. Then her forehead wrinkled. "Did you leave this house with your blouse unbuttoned like that?"

My cell phone buzzed in my pocket. "Gotta check this," I said, and her wrinkle deepened.

It was Ryan texting. '*Call u tomorrow?*'

My heart leapt.

'*K*' I typed back.

He texted again with a smiley face. The winky-eyed one. This time my heart waved its jazz hands. It hadn't done jazz hands in a long time.

BY THE TIME we crawled into bed—Maggie on one side and me on the other—I was ready to puke. We had consumed most of a pineapple pizza (the Dominos guy did *not* know who invented it) and half a cheese. Also chocolate chip

cookie dough sundaes. My mother had taken one thin slice of pineapple to her room.

My brother was still not home.

"Jenna," Maggie said as I turned off the light. "Something weird is going on with Casey, isn't it?" She leaned up on an elbow and peered at me in the dark. "Is he in some kind of trouble?"

I didn't answer. What could I say?

Then: "Are you?"

"Everything's fine," I lied.

Maggie burped. Not long after that she passed out in a food coma.

This is the fortunate thing about having a best friend who, in her own words, "Treats her body like a temple." Load the temple's altar with Frito pie and Hawaiian pizza and ice cream and you don't have to tell her much of anything. The temple's too busy digesting. But I had stretched my own personal limits getting her there.

I lay awake for a long time rubbing my overindulged belly and listening until finally, sometime after three, I heard my brother's footsteps on the stairs.

I tiptoed into the hallway. "Where have you been?" I whispered.

"Go to sleep," Casey said. He opened the door to his room, started to step inside.

"That's not fair," I said. I was no longer feeling sorry for him.

"That's the way it is."

He closed the door behind him.

Then he opened it again. "Hey. It's Saturday. Happy Birthday." He winced. "And brush your damn teeth. If you're gonna have a boyfriend, you can't have pineapple pizza breath."

"Don't talk to me about personal habits. Listen, I can get my learner's permit now." If he wasn't going to tell me the truth, then I needed to focus on something he *could* do. "You can take me Monday, right?"

"You? On the road?"

"Drive better than you."

Casey shrugged. He'd been letting me circle the Merc around the mall parking lot on Sunday mornings when it was empty. I'd been overjoyed until that stupid niggling voice in my head asked if maybe he was rushing things so that if he got yanked away by Management, I'd be ahead of the game.

"Where were you?" I asked again. "Talking with Amber, right?"

Sometimes he went other places, I knew. Spring Creek was a rumor mill like that. I tried to ignore it, but still in the hallways I'd hear how crazy Casey Samuels was driving that POS Merc like it was a race car down the feeder road 'til it almost shimmied in half. Or that they had seen someone who looked like him standing on top of the water tower by the high school, and how the hell did he get up there?

"Yeah," he said.

"And?"

"And I was with Amber." He stepped back into his room, hand on the door. He did not often elaborate about what he and his angel boss/still-EMT-as-her-cover-job discussed when I wasn't around. My birthday was no exception. It was three in the morning and the fifth slice of pineapple pizza was too big in my gut, but I was a tough girl. I waited.

Eventually he said, "That little pissant Sloboda better be nice to you."

"Like you were nice to Donny?"

We gave each other a prolonged stink eye.

"I got you a birthday present," Casey said then. "You want it now?"

"Hell yeah."

He disappeared into his room again and returned with a pink gift bag. I could tell he'd done it up himself: the tissue was randomly stuffed inside and the ribbons tied on the handle were drooping straight, not curling. I dug in.

It was one of those makeup combination kits from Sephora. This one had like a zillion eye shadow colors and lip glosses and a bunch of brushes including a pointy one that I wasn't quite sure what to do with.

"The lady said this would be good for someone fifteen," he said. "Course she doesn't know you, but . . . if you don't like it, we can go back there. Pick out better colors or something. But I showed her a picture and she said these would be good with your complexion . . ." He'd clearly used up his knowledge about feminine beauty products.

I didn't know much more, myself. Except I knew this: my brother had gone to Sephora in the mall to buy me a gift. I hugged him hard. "I love it," I said.

"Me, too," he whispered.

We stood together in the dark hallway like that. Here is what I wondered: Did all angels have the same adjustment issues? Or was it just Casey? I hurried back to bed and tried to fall asleep, Maggie snoring next to me. The Bible thumpers all talked about that Better Place. But my brother, although he was acting like a dick these days, had been brought back to save me. Now he was stuck until Management saw fit to move him. And worse, I knew he liked it here.

I bet the thumpers never would have predicted that.

Then again, I liked this world, too. I liked Casey in it. Taking him away from me was no one's reward.

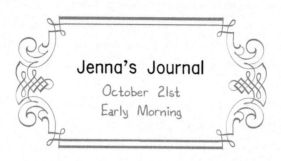

"You think they're done yet?" I peered through the foggy glass on the oven door. I had given up on signature outfits for today and was wearing navy athletic shorts and my pink *This Ain't My First Rodeo* T-shirt, the one I'd loaned to Amber once in an emergency back when I had just discovered that she was more than the EMT who'd pulled us from our wreck of a Prius.

Also, I was wearing flip flops because the temperature had shot up outside. It was pushing over eighty already at just after nine in the morning. My hair, which I'd been growing out some, was in a French braid. On my eyelids I'd swiped plum shadow from my new kit. Also black mascara on my lashes.

Maggie was in cutoffs and tank top and an ancient pair of black sparkly Ugg boots. She called them her "concession to popular fashion trends." Maggie can be quite intellectual when she wants to be.

We were making kolaches. Attempting, anyway.

Mom had left early for the weekend shift at Texas Children's, but her birthday gift to me was on the kitchen table: a note that said *Happy Birthday* and an IOU for dinner out at the new sushi place near the mall. Also a gift card to Forever 21 with another note that said: *I don't know what you like these days. Get yourself something fun. xoxo Mom*

Casey was gone again. No great surprise there.

"What's that smell?" Amber Velasco sashayed through the kitchen door, a sizeable box wrapped in Happy Birthday paper in her hands. Amber did not believe in knocking.

My brother stomped in behind her lugging a plastic grocery sack.

"Are those kolaches?" Amber set the box on the kitchen table and strode over to where Maggie was hauling the tray out of the oven. She was wearing jeans with bling on the ass and one of those black button-downs that she favored. The jeans looked good on her, I had to admit. Even though she still wore her EMT outfit much of the time, Amber had definitely nailed her own signature outfits. My brother (since I am listing everyone's clothing) was wearing jeans and a tidy looking black polo shirt. His skin looked smooth and tan like it always did now.

I eyeballed the birthday gift box. I couldn't quite believe it.

AMBER PEERED AT the kolaches.

"Pretty impressive, right?" Maggie looked proud, even though all we'd done was pop open a can of Pillsbury and unwrap some generic mini-sausages from H-E-B.

Amber snagged one, holding it between her thumb and forefinger while she nibbled a bite. "If you really want to make some good ones, then you need to mix your own yeast

dough from scratch. You know the German immigrant bakers, they'd call these pigs in blankets. But the ones with cheese and fruit filling, now those are the ones that—"

My brother flicked the rest of the kolache out of her hand. "Let her have her damn breakfast."

For a few seconds, all four of us were silent. The bitten kolache oozed sausage grease on the floor.

Maybe last night he'd been all angel-generous with that touchdown assistance. Today he was in a mood. I waited. *One. Two. Three.*

The arguing began full steam. With shouting. And references to Management. And in front of Mags. That was what froze me up, especially when Amber said to Casey: "I never should have fought for them to send you back. You've been trouble since the second they slapped those wings on you."

So much for opening my present.

Here were my options:

1. I could let the two of them throw down right here in the kitchen while Maggie and I took bets as to who would win. In which case I would have to explain why they were fighting and about what. Which I'd have to do, anyway.

2. I could fake death. Unfortunately, Amber and Casey would probably revive me. In which case I would still have to explain. (See #1 again.)

3. I could ruin my birthday and tell Maggie I felt a stomach virus coming on, whisper to my brother that he should put a hand on her shoulder and switch on the happy calm angel vibe, shove her to the door and tell her that it was only a half-mile walk home.

While I was deciding, my cell phone started vibrating. I should have ignored it. But I was new to phone ownership. It was still like crack to me. I peeked at the caller ID while Maggie nattered something about wings and what the hell was going on. *Ryan!* He had kept his promise! I clicked TALK.

"Hello," I said in my quiet, peaceful lady-like voice.

"Jenna?"

"Yeah."

"I can barely hear you," Ryan said.

I grabbed Maggie by the arm and hustled us out to the back yard. "That better?"

It was. Except that Maggie's eyes were popping out of her head and I could see she had a million questions, none of which I was prepared to answer.

"Happy Birthday," Ryan told me. His voice made my insides liquefy like a smoothie. "You still want me to come over, right?" Here his voiced kind of squeaked. "I've got a present for you. Okay?"

Okay? Of course it was okay. I told him so. "But later," I had to clarify. "Like tonight, maybe? Before dinner? Unless you have plans." I was not one to babble, but there I was. Babbling.

Ryan didn't seem to notice. We established that five o'clock would be fine. I figured I could solve my domestic issues by then, or at least figure out a way to fake solving them.

"Seriously, Jenna, what is with your brother and the EMT girl?" Maggie's hands were planted on her hips. "Why does she talk about his wings? Is that a drug metaphor?"

"Maybe." I wondered what the thumpers would have to say about *that* little lie.

SOMEHOW IN THE next fifteen minutes. I managed to get her packed up. "Casey can drive you," I said, knowing she'd

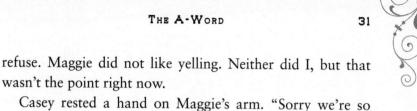

refuse. Maggie did not like yelling. Neither did I, but that wasn't the point right now.

Casey rested a hand on Maggie's arm. "Sorry we're so rambunctious today," he said. "Birthdays bring out the worst in us. You have a good one, Mags."

It took a minute—Maggie is not an easily suggestible girl— but all at once, there she was, smiling big as day and telling him that it was fine. She'd talk to me later. And for once, I was relieved that Casey could do whatever it is he could do.

"Thanks for sleeping over," I told her. "And for the kolaches."

She dug into her messenger bag. "Almost forgot." She handed me a small square package wrapped in brown paper with little red berries stamped on it. If you have ever wondered who makes their own wrapping paper with ink pad stamps and butcher paper, Maggie is your girl.

I unwrapped it. It was little silver charm on a thin chain—a mustang head on which she'd put a hot pink Sharpied 76— Ryan's number.

"For luck," Maggie said. "You and Sloboda—I think it could be the real thing. Just don't show it to him until it is. Otherwise you look like a desperate stalker chick."

"Got it," I told her. I wanted to hug her. I would have, if I could tell her the truth. So I didn't.

"I hope you two are satisfied," I said to Amber and Casey once Maggie was out of earshot. I flopped into a kitchen chair, the silver mustang charm still clutched in my sweaty hand.

Neither of them apologized.

Amber's gift sat at my elbow. I ignored it. Mostly.

Casey said, "I'll make you some breakfast tacos. You like that." He opened the drawer under the oven and pulled out a frying pan.

From the grocery sack, he extracted flour tortillas and eggs and salsa, and onion and a bell pepper—even a couple of potatoes that he began chopping efficiently with one of our kitchen knives.

I was pissed off, but I watched his hands as he cut and chopped and sectioned everything out on the cutting board: neat little piles of taco ingredients. When he was done, he cracked five eggs in a bowl and whisked them around with a fork, then swished some oil in the pan and started it to heating and added the chopped-up onion and pepper and potato. The light from the kitchen window angled against his face as he worked.

I slumped at the kitchen table with Amber and thought: *I am the only one in this room who actually has to eat. I am the only one in this room who actually has to sleep. I am the only who has an actual birthday anymore.* Not that it was going so well.

"I'm sorry," Casey said, but not to me. "I guess I've been thinking that there's some other way. I know that's stupid. I know it. But I have."

Amber pursed her lips.

My stomach went knotty. Something was about to happen. I could feel it in every molecule of my body. Like last year, just before I seized up and Casey raced me to the hospital and we crashed. I knew something was very wrong. Of course I never could have predicted that my passing out would domino into everything that had happened to Casey since.

He turned the flame off under the frying pan. "I just keep thinking that we can't be the only ones. Only then I tell myself that I'd know by now, wouldn't I? I mean if someone else had the answers: why we're stuck here and if there's a loophole

for this whole grounding business and what it is I'm supposed to do next—you'd have told me by now. But you haven't. So the way I figure it, you don't know anymore than I do. Just like it's been since I . . . well, you know."

Amber's gaze locked on mine. I stared back. She knew that I felt something was wrong, and she looked like *she* felt it, too.

Casey laughed—a harsh ha ha sound. "Management must be having a good chuckle, huh? Waiting for me to realize that this is it. My fate. My place in the big scheme of things. The guardian angel who worked at BJ's BBQ for eternity and drove his little sister to school."

"Least til they notice you keep looking the same," I said and then felt bad I'd thrown that in there. "Plus I'm getting my permit. Another year and I'll drive myself. Unless you want to let me get my hardship license. Cause that would speed things up." I felt bad about saying that too, but it slipped out.

"What I mean is, it can't be just you and me that this ever happened to," Casey said to Amber, ignoring my comments. "Guess I was wrong about that, too."

He dumped the fried stuff in a bowl and then scraped the beaten eggs in the pan and turned the flame back on, stirring with the whisk. I noticed for now the millionth time how capable his hands looked. How even if he was confused as all get out, he was something more than he had ever been. Something I could count on.

Amber cleared her throat. "You weren't wrong."

If the clock over our stove wasn't already broken, it would have stopped ticking.

"We're not the only ones," she said.

That was when Amber said a name. Bo Shivers.

How many other angels were hanging around that we didn't know about? Was Houston a hot spot for this kind of thing? It was possible, I supposed. Low cost of living. Good housing market. Maybe the Realtors were in on it. Maybe all those new downtown condos were filled with heavenly beings wanting access to good restaurants and major sporting events.

"You knew this and didn't tell me?" Casey shoved his hands through his hair. Of course it didn't stay mussed up, but he did add a slight sheen of frying pan grease to his bangs. "Why? Who is this Bo person, anyway? Besides one of us? What's he got on you, that you wouldn't tell me? Incriminating photos or something?"

I had to give it to my brother. His brain was calculating this news in a more logical way than mine.

"No." Amber paused. Blew out a breath. "Bo's not . . . well, Bo's difficult."

"Hell." Casey glowered at her. "I'm difficult. You're difficult. My damn sister's difficult. That's no excuse."

Maybe to distract him, Amber shoved the gift box at me. "Open it."

Casey scowled, but I was not one to look a gift angel in the mouth. So to speak.

Here is what Amber gave me: a pair of jeans a lot like hers—the fancy nice dark wash ones with embroidered leather and crystal crosses on the back pockets. Also, a white long sleeve fitted button-down with slick looking pearl snaps.

"*This*," Amber said with a toss of her pony tail, "is a signature outfit."

My pulse ticked in surprise.

"I pay attention," she said. "It'll go with your boots."

"You're an advanced heavenly creature," my brother grumped. "You need to be using your super powers to help the universe, not getting boys to look at my sister's ass."

"That," said Amber Velasco, flashing a mischievous grin, "is exactly the point."

A BRIEF DISCUSSION later and it was settled. We were going to Houston. Midtown. To meet this Bo Shivers, whoever he was. Casey said he'd drive and Amber told him no, she'd take us in her Camaro, but she gave in quickly. I suspected this was to distract my brother. When he was driving the Merc, he was in charge—whether that was actually true or not.

Our neighbors the Gilroys were putting up Halloween decorations as we backed out of the driveway. This was new for them. In the past, they'd concentrated on Christmas. But now they were doing it up with spider webs and gravestones and black cats and the like. Plus orange lights wrapped around the trunks of their pine trees.

"Hey y'all," Mrs. Gilroy waved. She was spray painting an epitaph on one of the tombstones. *REST IN PEA* was as far as she had gotten. I wished she'd leave it that way.

"Snazzy graveyard," I called to her. Her cheeks pinked at the compliment.

"I'm giving out Hershey bars this year," she hollered back. "Y'all be sure to stop by."

Mrs. Gilroy was pleasant like that.

"SO HERE'S WHAT else I need to tell you," Amber said. She was riding shotgun like usual and I was lounging in the backseat. Also like usual.

"I need to be back before five," I interrupted. "Ryan is coming over with a birthday present."

"Pissant will probably get you something lame," muttered my brother.

"Jealous." That was Amber's observation. A lowdown one. I knew she did not mean that Casey was jealous of Ryan, but that Casey was jealous I had a significant other and that this was no longer an option for him. Amber could be a jerk like that. But instead of calling her on it, the word made my brain fire this: *I have a boyfriend!* At least that's what it looked like.

"Amber heaved a sigh. "Like I was saying. I might have put off going to Bo for longer, but, well I've been sensing something lately. Even just now, at y'all's house. Something's coming. Something's here, maybe."

I admit, it was nice to hear that it wasn't my imagination. She and I were on the same page with that one.

"And Bo?" Casey's tone darkened. He was still looking at the highway.

She blushed. Light red, then deeper. "Bo is my boss."

"Boss?" my brother and I squawked in unison.

"Yeah. Not that he . . . I told you," Amber stammered, maybe for the first time ever. "Bo is difficult. You'll see for yourself soon enough." She sounded . . . nervous. Except Amber was not the nervous type. More the nerves-of-steel-pull-you-from-a-crashed-Prius-EMT type. Either way, why keep him a secret?

"Whatever," Casey groaned. "Hope he bosses you around like you do me." He signaled a lane change. The freeway was packed but moving steadily. "You said something's coming. What? And how do you know?"

"It's going to sound weird," Amber said after a few beats of silence.

"Ha!" That was my response.

"It's like a sixth sense," she said. "But not exactly."

"Like you see dead people?" My brother's face was dead serious. Then he bit his lip and burst out laughing.

"Like you probably have it, too," Amber snapped. "Like—"

"Like a Spidey sense?" I asked. It seemed to be what she was nervously stumbling for. My brother was not the only one who got his information from Hollywood. "You know. Like in those movies. Like your Spidey sense is tingling."

I expected her to roll her eyes. Instead she said, "Yeah. Like that."

I thought about how I felt lately. And I wasn't even one of them. Maybe it was just common sense. Maybe she was being ridiculous. "Do you feel something's wrong, too?" I shoved myself through the gap in the seats to Casey. He batted me away, smacking me in the nose. Hopefully not on purpose.

"Ow," I said. "Asswipe."

"Sit back" he muttered. "And no. Well, maybe. I don't know."

"Concentrate," I directed him. "Do you see something wacky coming with someone named Bo Shivers?" I'd have told him to close his eyes, but that seemed reckless.

"We'll talk about it at Bo's," Amber said, and not a word more.

Were they insane? No way could Amber drop all these bombshells—*Bo Shivers? She has a boss? Angels have Spidey senses that tingle? And I might have them, too?*—and then clam up. This did not settle well with me. Or the breakfast tacos in my belly. So I did the only thing I could think of that would make at least one of them acknowledge I was sitting back here, waiting for real answers. I pulled out my cell phone and began to act swoony and girly. If there was one thing I knew it was this: like my brother, Amber was permanently single and lonely and pissed off about it. I bet I could press her buttons that way. Maybe something would slip out. Plus I had a cell phone now. With video of Ryan Sloboda! Who was coming over later to bring me a birthday present! The day was weird and getting weirder, but I was accumulating gifts like nobody's business.

"Look," I said, scrolling to the video I'd taken last night of Ryan out on the field. It was shaky, but clear enough. I shoved my phone at her. "See how good he was playing? And without any special help." I air-quoted the last two words even though I was not normally an air-quote girl.

"Jenna," Casey began.

Amber snatched my phone. She pressed pause and eyeballed the screen.

"Ryan's too young for you," I deadpanned.

She almost smiled. Except she wasn't looking at Ryan. She was looking above his head at that crazy big Jumbotron. "Is this new?" Amber asked. She flicked her fingers to enlarge the picture. The words *Sponsored by Texicon* filled the screen.

"I guess, yeah." I fell back in the seat.

"Texicon's sponsoring a whole bunch of stuff now," Casey said, suddenly perking up. "The football programs with all the guys' pictures and stats, new flat screens in the locker room. Other stuff, too. Sloboda and them are lucky to be playing now."

Who cared about Texicon Jumbotrons? Even Amber wasn't that weird. So why . . .

My thoughts whirred and clicked. *Oh.*

"Amber," I said, leading with her name while my brain sorted itself out. "Isn't Texicon where your friend Terry works? The lab guy? You know—the one who analyzed Mom's blood and all."

Amber, her gaze still glued to my phone, didn't answer. She looked lonely and sad and curious all at the same time. Were those tears in her eyes? No way. But that's what it looked like. Maybe this was *more* than her being weird. Maybe not. I mean, we had already established that she lied like a rug to us when she felt like it. I did not have high hopes that she was imparting every crucial detail about her personal life.

Amber chewed her bottom lip. Eventually, she tossed me the phone.

"Yeah," she said slowly. "Same guy."

There was a note in her voice—one that made me wonder: was it Terry who'd been Amber's boyfriend back before she was an angel, back before she was killed? We didn't know about all that either, did we? Was this another item in the growing pile of Things Amber Wasn't Choosing to Share?

"Yeah?" I said, encouraging her to spill.

But she didn't say anything more. Maybe she would have,

but it was at that moment that Casey pulled up in front of a high rise that read Taft Street Lofts, with a banner that announced: Units Still Available. Best Views in Houston.

"We're here," Casey said, in case Amber and I hadn't noticed.

THE BUILDING HAD a doorman and valet parking. We had to tell the guy who we were visiting. Upon hearing the name Bo Shivers, he became suddenly gracious and gave Casey a ticket to redeem the Merc once we were done. The lobby was huge and pretty. Slick tile floors and a desk with another doorman guy and there were even some tasteful Halloween decorations: an artsy metal tree with little black cats and pumpkins hanging from it was my favorite. I made a mental note to tell Mrs. Gilroy about this. She was always looking for new ideas.

The elevator was glassed in. I could see all of downtown as we rode to the top. Yes. Bo Shivers, whoever he was, lived on the top floor. Penthouse. Like in the movies.

"I love this place," I blurted, surprised that I did. "It's amazing."

It was. The higher we rode in the elevator, the more amazing it felt. On top of the city. Sleek and clean and—something else I couldn't put my finger on. Not money, although obviously it took money to make something like this. Maybe the settled feeling you get when there isn't anything to worry about. Not that I had experienced that lately.

Or maybe ever. But I knew that if I did, this was what it felt like.

The elevator doors opened at the twentieth floor. I figured my pulse would be hopping, but it beat in my veins all normal like. Smooth. Even. Maybe a little excited—but the good kind, like when you're about to open a present on your birthday (which, hey, it was) and you know by the shape and feel of the box that it is going to be exactly what you wished for.

We walked down the fancy, well-lit hallway. There was only one apartment up here that I could see. With its own private entrance. I guess it was no different than our house having its own door. But it was. Money did that, I knew—although not from personal experience.

"So how come this guy's so loaded?" Casey asked, frowning.

Amber didn't answer, just waved her hand like she was shooing flies. Her jaw was tight.

We stood at the tall metal door now, me in the middle, Casey on my left, and Amber on my right.

She raised her hand to knock. But the door swung open before her hand could reach it.

He was tall. Muscular, too. More cowboy-type than gym rat, but his dark jeans fit smoothly as did the olive-colored, long-sleeved, V-neck sweater he was wearing. His boots, like Amber's, were worn in and scuffed. His skin was bronzy and his hair—longish, falling to the bottom of his neck—was mostly dark with a few strands of silver. His face was lined, but in a way that said, *I've lived through stuff.* Like whatever he'd done, he'd done it hard and fully and it showed. Which is not the same as getting old. Not at all.

"Ms. Velasco," said the man who could only be Bo Shivers. "What a delightful surprise."

"I'm Bo," he said, extending his right hand. His left toted a squat glass of what smelled like Jack Daniels. Not that I'd ever imbibed, but I'd smelled it on Casey's breath more than once so I knew it when I sniffed it. His voice was deep and low and when he said his name, I felt it in my chest like you do when someone has their car stereo on too loud. He gripped the glass loosely now, thumb and first two fingers only—low, dangling close to knee level. I kept waiting for him to drop it.

"I won't bite, Jenna. I promise." His gaze locked on mine in a way that managed to be comforting and unsettling at the same time. "Especially not on your birthday. Fifteen is a fine age, isn't it?"

My brain was pinging so fast that I could barely keep up with all the thoughts. *Had Amber told him it was my birthday? How often did she talk to this guy, anyway?* This guy she'd never mentioned even existed, living in this ritzy place with some kind of soft jazz playing in the background from an invisible speaker system.

"You know her name?" Casey straightened, tall and con-frontational-like, which I did not believe was the best idea right now. We had barely said hello. In fact, we hadn't at all. I couldn't tear my eyes from Bo Shivers.

He *was* old, wasn't he? But he was interesting. And not just because he was showing off that he knew about me, which maybe he did and maybe he didn't. Maybe he was saying it just to get under our skin, which if he was Amber's boss, I sort of understood.

Funny: Mom's Uncle Gene who lived up in Colleyville used to sneak nips from a flask all the time. That just made me roll my eyes, not pique my interest like this man and that glass of whiskey.

"Nice to meet you." I extended my right hand, deciding to go for it.

We shook. He had a firm grip, and his palm was warm and calloused. A long but faint scar etched the top of his hand from the middle knuckle to his wrist and maybe higher, but the sweater sleeve covered it. More scars wound around his wrists, again faint, but there. Again, I couldn't help staring. How did you get scars like that? I bit back the impulse to ask him.

He withdrew his hand. Took a long sip of his drink.

"I'm Casey," my brother said. We were still standing in the entry way.

"I'm aware." Bo swallowed, then met my brother's gaze. "Been aware, in fact. Although I take it the awareness hasn't been mutual." Here he cut his eyes to Amber.

I figured they were going to have it out. He was obviously pissed that we hadn't known about him.

"Bo," Amber began, sounding anxious and peevish all at once, but Casey cut her off.

"You gonna invite us in, or we gonna stand out here for eternity?"

Here's the thing: I knew he didn't mean it to be funny. But it was. I couldn't help myself. I chuckled.

Bo Shivers tilted his head. His eyes went dark, then crinkled at the edges, and then he was laughing, a full out belly laugh. He stepped aside, gesturing with the glass of Jack for us to enter.

"You got a nice place here," I told him. Our mutual sense of humor had made me bold.

"Eternity has allowed me time to decorate," he observed dryly.

So, he was smart and funny. In addition to being rich. I liked smart and funny. Even in an old guy. Or maybe not that old. I was finding it hard to tell. And the loft kicked ass. Not that I was an expert on interior design, but I knew what I liked. Dark wood floors all polished and shiny. Shelves of books positioned here and there. Bo was quite the reader, it seemed. On the walls, what walls existed, there were paintings—real ones, not poster art from Big Lots or the ones from that store they opened in the mall around Christmas when people found themselves inspired to purchase pictures of Marilyn Monroe or Jim Morrison or other dead celebrities. Fancy grey stone on the kitchen counter that I could see from here because it was mostly all one huge open space. A wall of windows that looked over downtown.

We followed Bo toward the couches over by the windows. I could see now that one was actually a glass door. It led out to a balcony that skirted the entire side of the loft.

I knew people lived like this. I had just never experienced that life close up.

Off to the right, a set of panels partially blocked what must be his sleeping nook. I could make out a big bed against one of the few walls, and a plush-looking comforter. On the wall behind the bed, there was a smallish painting of a woman's face, done in chalk or water color or some such.

"So," Bo Shivers said, whipping my attention back to him. We settled on the squishy leather sofas. "To what do I owe this visit?"

"We've got some questions," my brother said. "About this whole grounding business." He was out of sorts, I could tell. Nervous. Sitting on the edge of the sofa, hands clasping on his knees, like he was ready to take off. Could he? I wondered suddenly. Could he fly again like he did that day last Christmas to save my life? Or did it just look like that because I knew he was tired of all this endless waiting for something to change, even now, sitting way up high here with all this pretty stuff around us.

Casey went on and on: prattling about losing his earthly flight—and wasn't that unfair, and had it happened to anyone else, and if so what had that angel done about it? Amber put in her two cents about her Spidey sense and how she thought something was coming and was Bo maybe having the same feelings . . . which it seemed to me he kind of was, although between Amber and my brother it's not like he was getting too many words in. Or maybe he was staying quiet and watching on purpose. Probably that was it.

Except me, I was still remembering. I saw those wings of Casey's in mind's eye: all white and fully unfurled and so magnificent that they hurt my eyes with their glory even as I was tumbling to my doom. He had leaped without thinking,

caught me in his arms, and hauled me to safety. He had known what would happen, but he hadn't hesitated. Just like that night when he'd rushed me to the hospital and crashed our beat up Prius. Just like that moment when everything in our world changed.

I came back fast, he'd told me. *I came back for you.*

Now he was hanging out at football games watching all the things he could never really have again, his wing nubs hiding—retracted and unused.

Here is what happened then: I looked up, or maybe I was looking up all the time. But now I focused back in from all my remembering. And Bo Shivers was watching me, eyes neutral and dark as night. Something crawled up my spine and back down. For a moment it was like what happened when Casey laid a hand on my shoulder. I'd feel all calm and peaceful until he lifted it away and the worry seeped back in, all the more intense for its brief absence. But it was different. More like Bo Shivers trying to mine through to my soul or something, which I know sounds all dramatic, but that's how it felt. An itch so deep inside me that I was never going to reach it. I stared back.

"Take a picture," I told him. "It'll last longer."

"Jenna!" Amber squawked.

Bo didn't so much as blink. "I apologize if my honesty is startling. I don't find that lying gets us anywhere, do you?" Which was strange since he hadn't said anything to me that I could take for truth *or* lie.

His brows drew into a slight frown. I felt momentarily in the dark, like an eclipse of the sun. Was he doing that? It was possible, I knew. I was still categorizing what Casey and Amber could and couldn't do, but this was something new. Something intense.

At which point Mr. Bo Shivers set his drink on the coffee table, rose to his feet, and strode over to the glass door. He opened it, stepped out on the balcony. He walked steadily, posture perfect. If the Jack had made him drunk, there was no sign. The wind had picked up outside, and I could hear it. Everything in the loft wavered in the sudden breeze. Chill bumps raised on my arms.

With that, Bo Shivers walked to the railing, slung one long leg over it and then the other, graceful as a gymnast and jumped.

Time froze.

The breath stopped in my body as he fell out of sight—arms stretched wide, palms up. Like a yoga position. Like falling was a meditation.

No. Not that. More like useless wings.

"Holy shit!" my brother said. Amber tore to the balcony.

I sat where I was, mouth gaping, stomach clenching, heart beating like a hummingbird on crack.

Behind us in the kitchen area, I heard the sound of ice clinking into a glass and then something being poured.

All three of us whipped around.

"I have a little problem with a death wish," said Bo Shivers, solid and in one piece. He strode from the kitchen with a freshly poured glass of Jack. "I apologize for that, too."

My heart was still lodged in my throat, but I managed, "Thought you didn't lie." I didn't know if I was angry or relieved or both.

"What the hell?" was Casey's response. "Can I do that, too?" He sounded simultaneously hopeful and flummoxed. Did falling count as flying?

"No," Amber said, banging the balcony door behind her.

"You could try," said Bo pleasantly, swirling his drink.

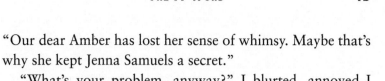

"Our dear Amber has lost her sense of whimsy. Maybe that's why she kept Jenna Samuels a secret."

"What's your problem, anyway?" I blurted, annoyed I found him so fascinating. Was this how Mags felt when she got all swoony around my brother, even though he was the last person she would normally go goofy about? That she wasn't sure if the emotion actually belonged to her?

I didn't expect Bo to answer, but he did. And I didn't expect to hear any truth. But I think I did.

"The problem, my dear," he said slowly, "is that Amber and your brother and I have something in common. We're all stuck here against our will. I just like to experiment with it, is all. So far, I have found no way to beat the system. But I am ever hopeful."

Did this mean he jumped off balconies on the hour? Or worse? How long had he been doing this? Weeks? Years? Longer? I tried to formulate the right way to pose the question. But what came out of my mouth cut a different way.

"You save someone too?" I asked.

Bo Shivers shrugged and took a long sip of whiskey. He did not meet my eyes.

I took that as a possible yes.

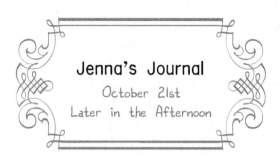

After that, I expected the angel contingent to remove me from the discussion, but Bo said, "I really am sorry if I scared you."

"Didn't scare me," I told him. I folded my legs on the leather couch, trying to look calm and collected, like I was lounging at home. I flashed him a toothy grin. Did he know that my heart was bumping against my uvula? (For the vocabulary-challenged, your uvula is that little punching bag in the back of your throat.) "Guess you're closer to Management up here," I added. Like Casey and his "waiting-for-eternity" comment," I hadn't meant it to be funny, but I guess it was.

Bo smirked, even though something serious fluttered behind his eyes. "I like you, Jenna Samuels."

I didn't respond. I had not yet formed my opinion of Bo Shivers other than that he was a person who could walk off balconies and be none the worse for it and who, when he used both my names to refer to me, made it sound pleasant. He also could have hid the truth that his former self was dead and gone, like Amber had for so long, and pretended whatever he wanted. But he hadn't. He might turn out to be the world's biggest liar. Maybe he already was, and more, too. Bo was not, I suspected, always a nice guy. But I had heard one important truth, even if it was the only truth he ever told: he was trapped here, just like Casey and Amber. Which meant that whatever he'd done, Management wasn't moving him forward. But most of all, I knew he was sad. I could smell it and taste it—like the juices from an overripe peach that's crossed into rotten. Sadness lay shallow under his skin, criss-crossing him like those scars on his hands.

Who had he saved? Why had he done it? Where was that person now?

He could say what he wanted. I'd always know it was there. Did I know this because I'd spent almost a year hanging out with two angels? Maybe? Or maybe it was all those years of it being just me and Casey while our parents drifted for one reason or another. Maybe I was just the type who could feel things like that. Either way, I was as sure of it as I was sure of the outfit that Amber had given me this morning. It was the best damn signature look yet. If Ryan Sloboda ever actually asked me out, I would wear it for him. Knock him out of his boots.

Jenna Samuels, he would say, *I am your love slave for life.*

Or at least ask me to Homecoming. He might even kiss me. And I might even kiss him back. If he was lucky.

This was what I was thinking here among my personal team of angels. Mags would have been proud. But I listened to them so that eventually I could write it all down. That way I could remember. If there was one thing I'd learned from all this, it was that memory is a precious thing.

Here is the short version:

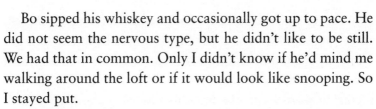

Bo sipped his whiskey and occasionally got up to pace. He did not seem the nervous type, but he didn't like to be still. We had that in common. Only I didn't know if he'd mind me walking around the loft or if it would look like snooping. So I stayed put.

Amber and Casey did, too. Casey sat at the edge of his seat, hands on his knees. Occasionally he glanced over at me like if he didn't, I might do something crazy. Somewhere in between all the fidgeting and pacing and Jack-sipping, the following was established:

- Bo was in charge. Casey brought up Management again, not so subtle-like, and Amber shot him down with, "Let Bo talk."

- Bo had a thing for chaos. "It attracts me. I attract it." Amber had used the same chaos theory, right down to the letter, in explaining our accident last year. Casey had loaned our Prius to stoner Dave who smashed it in the Jack in the Box sign and made it unstable and thus we'd had our accident. I felt now what I'd felt then: This was the fancy angel way of saying "shit happens." And in Bo's case, that was just fine.

"Meaning what?" I finally piped up. "You like to jump off roofs?"

"Meaning I can tell when something's coming," he said. A hint of a smile curved the corners of his mouth. "Things shift and I feel it."

"We *know* something's coming," my brother groused. "We told you that when we walked in here."

A breeze whipped up in the room even though Amber had

shut the door to the balcony. The muscles in Bo's arms tensed, then rippled, veins rising. My first thought: he must work out a lot. My second thought: he was causing the wind. My third thought: he knew way more than he was saying and he was trying to pass it off like he was playing games. My fourth thought: why?

"You told me what you think you know," Bo said. "If you knew it all, you wouldn't be here. You and Ms. Velasco are quite the team."

"They are," I snapped even though no way was it true.

Bo's brow furrowed, even though the hint of the smile remained. The wind settled, but not all the way. "You know that Oak View is up and running again?" It was a statement more than a question. He walked to the windows again and placed his hand on the balcony door, swigging Jack with the other.

Again, something flickered in his eye.

"I put a Google Alert on it," Casey said, meaning Oak View. "On Renfroe, too." I know he must have thought this would sound proactive. Mostly, its sounded geeky.

"Did you now?" Bo sighed like the teachers at Ima Hogg used to when Corey Chambers asked idiotic questions just to get us all off topic because he was high on weed and hadn't done his homework. "Did your alert tell you that it was owned by a European conglomerate now?"

It had not.

"Is that a problem?" Amber asked.. "This conglomerate?"

"Don't think so," Bo said. "But there's something."

"*What*?" I eyeballed Bo as hard as I could. "If I hear the word 'something' again I'm gonna scream. All that Spidey sense stuff is starting to seem like bull. We drove all the way down here for nothing, didn't we?" I stood. "I bet you know. Can't you just tell us?"

"There are rules, Jenna," Amber started, as if I wasn't fully aware of all the stupid angel rules. As if I didn't already spend a large chunk of time with two dead people. As if I weren't the only living person in this ridiculous fancy loft. I kept my glare on Bo Shivers.

"It works the same as it's worked for centuries," he said.

"Centuries? How the hell old are you?"

"Jenna!" Casey grabbed my arm.

"Old enough to know what people are capable of. And what they're not." Bo cut his gaze to Casey. "Let her go."

My brother removed his hand. What had Bo Shivers done? Maybe Houston was where you went for punishment. It was hot enough in the summer, that was for sure.

So maybe he was being punished.

Maybe, a voice inside me whispered, he was punishing himself.

"The human condition is nothing but repetitious." Bo's voice was a low growl. "Follow the power. Follow the riches. One or the other or both. That's the way it works. The way it's always worked. If we do it enough, then maybe . . ." He glanced at Amber. Then his eyes flicked to the balcony, going distant, like he was remembering something.

"How long you been trying to beat the system, anyway?" Casey asked.

"Longer than you've been hiding in your room beating your dick."

I tried not to laugh. I really, really did. I would never be disloyal to my brother. Not ever. This is the one absolute truth in my life right now. Maybe the only absolute truth I'll ever have. Not just because he was my guardian angel. But because he was, even in life, good and solid and as true as north on a compass. Even with his bad habits.

But here is what was on my tongue, almost sliding off: *"I like you, Bo Shivers."*

I did not say the words. First of all, I wasn't sure they were true. The whole angel pheromone thing messed with people's minds. That's why folks had no clue my brother and Amber weren't exactly human. It was entirely possible that's all it was. I was generally immune to my brother's appeal. But I had no idea if that carried over like a protective device—an angel immunization because I was related to one. I knew what was going on behind the curtain.

Either way, I started thinking that this visit hadn't been a waste. Bo tickled my funny bone. In that darker way. Not like people's uncles or grandpas who asked you to pull their fingers or flicked loose change from behind your ear and expected you to believe that you were sprouting quarters from your head. Those types looked right past you. Not Bo. Maybe to change the subject to safer territory—something that wouldn't make my brother's eyes gleam dark—or maybe because I wanted to know, my mouth flapped: "You paint all these pictures?"

"That I did," said Bo Shivers. His eyes cut to that painting of the lady over by his bed on the far side of the loft. Just for an instant. If I hadn't been so focused on him, I would have missed it.

"Bo?" Amber asked, "When you said, follow the riches—"

"Darlin'," Bo drawled, the accent sounding pure West Texas even though I was positive he was not from here, not really. "We've talked enough. You need to do what you need to do."

"Follow the money trail, right?" Casey pressed. His voice was calm and controlled, which I knew he was not. "Like what? Manny's cartel? There's money there. Least there was.

Maybe still with those memory drugs. But we solved that whole thing, didn't we? Police are dealing with it now, right? Maybe even the FBI. Even if Renfroe's on the run. I mean it's not like he can hurt my family any more. We'd see it coming."

I had to give my brother props: he was a stubborn cuss. Of course let him get a whiff of Lanie Phelps—even now that he seemed resigned to let that moron Donny Sneed have her—and the whole thing went to hell. It was odd, though. The Lanie Phelps thing made a secret part of me happy. Not because he was a horn dog. Just that at those times he was thinking about her, I could pretend that none of this had ever happened. Forgetting to protect me because he was leading with his nether regions was a comfort. *That* Casey was still the old Casey. Unlike now.

Bo shrugged. "Amber's in charge of you. This is your issue, not mine."

"Well, this was useless." Casey's mouth drew into a line. He glanced around, all judgy now, like he was sniffing milk gone bad. I followed his gaze as he lighted on something I hadn't noticed before, a pile of typed papers on a pretty wooden desk near the bed. There was a laptop there, too. And a printer and some other tech stuff.

"So what?" Casey went on. "You writing a book or something? You planning to get rich, yourself?"

"Bo teaches history at St. Thomas," Amber said. I'd almost forgotten she was there, what with all the testosterone in the air.

"That your cover job?" I asked.

"Ancient Civilization through Medieval Times," Bo confirmed.

I decided not to ask if maybe he'd experienced any of this firsthand.

"*Coaches* teach history at our school," Casey said with a dismissive sneer.

"And what do *you* do, Casey?" Bo asked.

"He takes care of me," I said.

My brother's face turned red. And not in a good way.

"It's a big job," I added. "I'm quite the handful."

Bo laughed. "Casey's got his hands full in all kinds of ways."

It probably goes without saying that we left soon after that.

If Bo Shivers had a functioning Spidey sense—if it were real and not just some of Amber's hopeful bullshit that my brother seemed willing to believe— he wasn't going to tell us today.

"Y'all come back real soon if you discover anything," he said as he shut the door behind us. "I'll be around."

Jenna's Journal

October 21st

Much Later in the Afternoon

"**C**an I practice driving on the way home?" I asked as we rode the elevator down.

It *was* still my birthday. Wasn't I supposed to be calling the shots? Of course Casey said no, and we piled into the Merc—angels in front, me in back—and chugged our way through a construction traffic jam on I-45.

"So what, then, Amber? You've known Bo since you . . ." Casey trailed off. Usually he didn't pussyfoot around death. Bo Shivers had thrown him off his game. He'd thrown all of us off.

"Since then, yeah." Amber looked out the passenger window rather than at Casey.

"He's really a professor?"

"Yes. Cover job, but yes. You have a problem with that?"

"Did you meet him right away?" I asked, joining in because if it was up to my brother, he'd dance around the right questions.

In my head, I had a vague recollection of Amber's face as

she pulled me from the wreck. The night Casey died. The night they sent him back. She had been there from the beginning. I figured she'd tell me that she didn't remember or she didn't want to talk about it. Instead she said, "Pretty much," which for Amber was a Rare Personal Revelation.

"But he teaches history," I said. "So how did that work? I mean you're an EMT. It made sense that you were there with the ambulance. And after, at the hospital. But what he'd do? Walk in and tell you about the Lincoln Assassination and then say, hey, you got sent back. Let me explain?"

"Doesn't work that way," Casey interjected.

The Number One Classic Angel Excuse For Everything, I thought, sulking in the backseat. I wasn't even going to answer him. But a thought bloomed, like a tiny plant popping from a very muddy soil: *Bo* had never said those words. If I was one-on-one with Bo Shivers and asked him how things worked, he would tell me. He might tell me in a weird way, like by flinging himself off a balcony. But if he lied—because his secrets were too big or too old or too sad—I'd know. He wouldn't give me a pathetic non-answer because he thought I was too young or too innocent or too alive to handle the truth.

Amber cleared her throat. "I thought I'd dreamed him at first. Because I saw him when I . . . well, I saw him after I was gone. I told you, I was living in Austin."

"With your boyfriend," I prompted her.

She sighed. "Yes. With my boyfriend. And I was alone in the apartment that night. Someone broke in. I remember that much. I remember that I struggled. That it hurt. I . . . you know what? I don't want to talk about this now. It's not what you asked, anyway. You asked about Bo. So here's what I can tell you. He was part of, let's call it my greeting committee. I heard him in my head. He said that they were sending

me back. That I was a guardian now. That he would be in charge of me. And then I woke up in my apartment, the place trashed to hell, and he was sitting on the couch with me like he'd come to visit."

 "And then?" I leaned forward, shoving my head between the front seats. My brother swatted at me, but I stayed put.

"And then we went on from there," Amber said, shutting the confession down. "He told me what I was. I realized it was the truth. I pulled myself together. Moved here. Started the EMT gig. The bartending. And I waited. There's a lot of waiting, which you already know. I watched people in a way I never had. I saw what made them happy and miserable and scared. And then last year he gave my first assignment: You." She jerked her shoulder toward Casey.

I chuckled. My brother did not. And I wondered why it had taken almost a year for her to say these things. Or maybe she had. Just not to me.

"But you don't see him all the time like I see you." Casey said it as a statement not a question.

"No. I—I told you. Bo's different. He's difficult. He does things his way. I saw him more at first when I was learning the ropes. Now, not as much."

"But you talk to him," Casey pushed. "You've been talking to him all this time."

"I thought we had established that," Amber grumbled. "Look, he's stuck here. I don't know why. He won't say. He's *never* said. He keeps testing Management, though. The balcony thing is his favorite party trick. But he's tried it other ways." Amber turned to us with a tired smile, which surprised me. "Leaped off Congress Street Bridge while the bats were flying one time in Austin. Scared the pee out of the tourists."

"He let people know what he was?" Casey swerved. The Merc shuddered when he yanked the wheel.

More Amber quiet time. "Yes and no. He did, but they don't remember. Like at the Galleria last year. There are clean up procedures. Y'all know that. Bo's . . . older. Powerful." She sighed again. "But he wants what we all want. To move on. Management won't let him. So he jacks with them. Acting like he has a death wish just puts an ironic spin on it. Simple."

I got the irony; he was already dead. But I didn't think it was simple.

"But it's not flight, is it?" This came from Casey. "What he did back there. Falling without wings . . ."

I pondered the crazy angel physics of it.

Amber repeated that Bo was powerful. Different. Falling and reappearing wasn't flying. It was all she would say on the matter.

"What about your boyfriend?" I said, partly because I wanted to know and partly because I believed she was holding something back, like always.

"We broke things off," Amber said. "I didn't—" Her cell buzzed then, loud enough to make us all jump.

I peered over the seat while she pulled the phone from her pocket. It was a number I didn't recognize. She said "well," a couple dozen times and added an "I don't know," in there, while her eyes got bright and her cheeks pinked up and the worry line in the middle of her forehead scrunched. "Okay," she murmured. She bit her lower lip. "But only a few minutes." She clicked off and slid the phone back into her pocket, all business again. "We need to make a stop. Won't take long." After which she shook her head—at what I had no idea—her cheeks still rosy.

IN THE NEXT half-hour, I learned the following:

1. We were going to Chateau Hills Subdivision to Terry the lab guy's house.

2. Terry the lab guy *was* her boyfriend. I knew it! The guy she'd lived with in Austin. The guy who didn't know his girlfriend had come back from the dead as an angel. "I moved out the next morning," Amber said. "Bo thought it would be for the best." (*But what about you?* I wondered. *Did you think it was for the best?* Casey hadn't moved out like that. On the other hand, Amber had not been sent back for Terry.)

3. Those Management folks had emotional flaws in their system. If ever met them, I would tell them so.

4. Bryce happened to live near Terry. (I learned this after my brother went off about how Amber should have told us the truth about Terry considering she'd trusted him with our mother's blood sample.) Bryce was the assistant manager at BJ's BBQ where Casey waited tables—the chubby guy with the dorky sense of humor and an alphabetized collection of comic books, Dark Horse being his favorite. He lived in a double-wide on his parents' property. It was Bryce who had hooked us up with his pinball wizard pal Zeke at Manny's Real Tex Mex. Zeke was one of the last people to see our father before he disappeared and it was because of him that we had found some clues to help us solve the whole mystery last year. In short: there were coincidences piling up, and I couldn't tell what mattered and what didn't. Which stank.

5. Additionally Amber told us, her voice firm, her East Texas twang pitching high, we absolutely, positively under no f-ing circumstances (Amber used the actual word, by the way. Just to be clear here.) were NOT going to let any angel stuff slip out. Or anything personal, for that matter. She had broken up with him five years ago. He didn't know what she was now. End of story.

"MOUTH ZIPPED," AMBER said as we pulled up to a one-story ranch house. "Or I will tell Ryan Sloboda that you are planning your damn wedding already."

This was a bit over the top for her. But she didn't have to tell me twice. Also, this made me decide to change into my new outfit once we got home. No sense waiting until Ryan asked me out. I would wear it to make *sure* he asked me out.

"So how come this Terry guy's so desperate to see you all of a sudden?" My brother asked. Silence filled the Merc. We idled. We waited.

"He said he missed me," she admitted.

"You believe that?" My brother drummed his fingers on the steering wheel.

"No."

"Ah," said Casey. "Well, good."

Amber primped at her hair.

My brother turned off the ignition. "Don't worry," he told her. "You look like an angel."

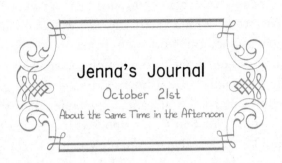

Terry McClain had curly dark brown hair and pale skin and a dusting of freckles on a nicely straight nose. He was medium tall and lanky, like that Mark Zuckerberg Facebook guy. Or at least like Jesse whatshisface, the actor who played him in the movie. Only cuter. He wore thin, black glasses, the square hipster type. And his smile—at least when he opened the door and saw Amber, before he registered that she had a posse with her—struck me as genuine.

Maybe she was wrong. Maybe he had really missed her.

"Hey," he said tentatively, eyeballing Casey and me. "I'm Terry."

"Hey," we both said.

Amber flashed an apologetic smile. "This is Casey and Jenna. Casey's, um, shadowing me at work. Jenna's his sister."

"Want to be an EMT, huh?" Terry asked. "Or you want to go pre-med? You're what? A senior? Good move. Internships look good on a résumé."

Casey shrugged. I could see Amber being in love with

Terry, I supposed. Yeah, I could. He was kind of geeky but smart—he had to be if he worked at the lab and could figure out if people were being poisoned by crazy idiots. Amber would have to be with a smart guy. She was close-mouthed, but there was a lot going on in her head. She'd wanted to be a doctor. So of course she'd go out with someone into science.

I didn't officially have a boyfriend yet—although maybe by tonight—but I knew I wanted someone I had things in common with. Not that I was opposed to making out like Casey and Lanie. Just that eventually you had to come up for air and it was best if you had something to talk about when you did. But Lanie *was* Casey's type. Even without the angel pheromones, she was what he wanted: blonde and pretty and girly and willing to laugh at his stupid jokes and maybe actually think he was funny. Was Ryan my type? He was sturdy and athletic and funny and smart. And cute. More than cute. His face. His eyes. How he swaggered—just the right amount—when he walked. The way his thumbs crooked into the pockets of his jeans. His . . . everything. When I thought about him, my knees turned to jelly and my stomach went quivery. I wondered what it would be like when he finally kissed me.

"Y'all want coffees?" Terry gestured toward the kitchen. "I got this new machine. Makes like a million different types of coffee. Tea, even.

Terry's house was small, or maybe it felt that way because Bo's loft had been so roomy. But a nice-sized Ikea-type desk sat against the far wall of the family room, with a new-looking Apple desktop set up—one of those big ass monitors with a normal-sized keyboard. A fancy printer, too. And a top of the line iPad sitting next to it. Terry liked his tech stuff up to date, I guess. Made sense.

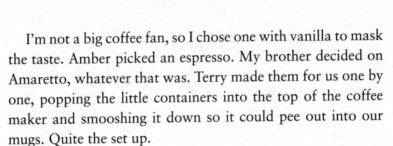

I'm not a big coffee fan, so I chose one with vanilla to mask the taste. Amber picked an espresso. My brother decided on Amaretto, whatever that was. Terry made them for us one by one, popping the little containers into the top of the coffee maker and smooshing it down so it could pee out into our mugs. Quite the set up.

"So." Terry said once we were all sipping politely. He traced a finger over the top rim of his hipster glasses. "How's that lady doing whose blood I tested for you? That was the craziest thing, Amber. I'd never seen anything like it. What ever happened with all that?"

The vanilla coffee lodged in my esophagus. I realized that he had no idea who Casey and I were other than our names. He did not connect us to "that lady"—our mother. Why would he? Even with what had been reported in the papers after Renfroe's arrest, it would be impossible to put it all together. We had not charged Renfroe with trying to destroy our family. We had our own secrets to deal with now.

"She's fine," Amber said.

"Good to hear." Then he said, "I'll be right back. Y'all enjoy." His gaze lingered on Amber for a few extra seconds until he turned and disappeared down the hallway to the other part of the house.

"Guess he wants you caffeinated before he jumps your bones," my brother loud-whispered.

I'd have thrown in my two cents, but Terry was back in a rush, a wrapped box in his hand—blue paper, bow, ribbon, the whole shebang.

"Can we talk for a second?" he asked Amber.

"I'm right here," Amber told him firmly, but there was something in her voice that made me take notice. Something that said that a part of her maybe still wanted to be alone with him. And the way he kept looking at her like she was a princess—well, I could see how that would be hard to give up.

Terry hesitated some, clutching the box like maybe if he stood there long enough Casey and I would disappear. When that didn't happen, he handed it over. "I know we're not . . . well, you know . . . But ever since you asked me to help you last year with that blood sample, well, I . . . I saw this and I wanted you to have it. It looked like something you would . . . it looked like you."

When Amber didn't make a move, he added, "Open it. Go ahead."

Her face was serious, and I could tell she was torn, but she ripped off the paper and bow and opened the box. Out came a pretty silver and turquoise cross, hanging on a sizeable silver chain. Terry had given some thought to Amber's signature style. I was impressed.

"Terry," she said softly. "It's beautiful. Thank you." She hooked the necklace around her neck, but even though she smiled at Terry, her expression was unreadable.

In my pocket, my cell vibrated loudly. While Amber and Terry ogled each other and my brother rolled his eyes, I sneaked a peek at the phone. A text from Ryan. My heart thumped.

Coming over in an hr. K?

"We need to go soon." I tugged on Casey's arm.

He gave me the stink eye when he saw the name. "Pissant can wait."

"No. He. Can't."

We'd have sniped at each other some more, but suddenly Amber announced, "We're going."

We set our coffee cups on the kitchen counter and said our

goodbyes. Terry looked like he wanted to hug Amber, but she made no move to let him do so, which was hugely awkward and took up a minute or so with the bobbing and weaving.

Why had we stopped here, anyway? This Terry guy could have mailed her the damn gift. But if there was one thing I'd learned lately, it was that nothing is ever what it seems. People have agendas. Even if it takes them awhile to spit it out. *My* agenda was to get home before Ryan landed on my doorstep so I could change into my new blingy jeans. I guess you can only lie to someone's face for so long before it gets uncomfortable. Here was this nice, kind-of-cute guy with a fancy-ass computer and a sophisticated coffee machine and money to buy jewelry. She used to be with him, and now he was calling again and offering her a gift. And she had to blow him off because she was an angel and he didn't know it. Hadn't known when she broke up with him five years ago right after she died. Didn't know a damn thing.

That had to suck. For both of them.

I watched Terry look at the necklace on Amber's neck and I thought about types again: Terry and Amber. Casey and Lanie. Me and Ryan. (I hoped.) Not that you had to have someone like animals in the ark, but the world was a crazy place. It was easier to pair up than go it alone.

I thought about Bo Shivers in that penthouse loft.

Mostly I thought: *Let's go. We're done here.*

"I'm still at Texicon," he said to Amber at the door. "Head of research now."

"That's great," Amber said, but she was on autopilot.

Back in the Merc, I wanted to text Maggie and tell her everything that was going on because that's what friends do, but I couldn't. Too many secrets. I did text her: *Ryan's coming over!* To which she responded: *I want details.* Followed by a series of red hearts. Maggie sometimes went overboard with the emoticons.

It was getting dark by the time we got home, but our cul de sac was nice and lit up because of Gilroy's bright orange Halloween lights. She hadn't gotten much farther with the tombstones, though. She finished the one: *REST IN PEACE, BUBBA.* Guess they were going for a Southern atmosphere.

That was when I saw him riding up the street on his bicycle. (Ryan was also not old enough to drive yet. His birthday wasn't until November, I knew, so he also didn't have a learner's permit, either. Yes, this made me the older woman in our relationship. But only by less than a month. So not quite cougar territory.) My heart bumped hard. *You are being such a girl, Jenna Samuels,* I told myself. *Stop it.* But even the buzz cut he'd gotten for football made me happy and I was not typically a fan of the buzz cut.

I opened the back door even before we were fully stopped. Ryan was pedaling closer now.

Amber whipped around. "You want to kill yourself? Wait til the damn car isn't moving." She scowled as Casey cut the ignition. "Why don't you *both* try not to do anything stupid while I'm at work?" She boot-smacked the door and stomped to her Camaro without so much as a "Happy Birthday, Jenna." Not that she hadn't already said it and given me my gift. But now I couldn't change into it. Ryan was *here.*

"Go on," my brother said quietly. "Just try not to look so damn obvious. Guys like it when you play hard to get."

It was good advice.

I took my time sashaying over.

Jenna's Journal

October 21st
Evening

"You want to come inside?" I asked Ryan, heart thumping. What if he said no?

But he nodded and parked his bike, re-adjusted his backpack on one shoulder, and in we went. Mom was in the kitchen drinking coffee.

"Mom, Ryan; Ryan, Mom," I said, then grabbed his arm and hustled him up to my room before Casey could get a word in. This was both bold and risky: I had never had a boy in my room before. Was my room even *presentable?* I was not one to leave underwear and such lying around, but that possibility seemed preferable to sitting in the kitchen with my mother and brother while Ryan and I attempted awkward small talk.

"Leave the door open," Mom hollered after us.

Which I had to hand it to her was decent motherly advice.

Once we were in my room and I had thrown my comforter over my bed and kicked some dirty clothes into the closet, Ryan carefully opened his backpack. Out came a box with five pink-frosted cupcakes, each one with a letter of my name. J E N N A. The frosting was a tad squashed, but they looked otherwise quite tasty. My eyes bulged, a big stupid smile on my face. It felt very quiet all of a sudden.

"I baked them," he said, looking proud. He dug in the backpack again and pulled out an envelope. I set the cupcake box on my bed so I could open it. I tried to will my fingers to stop trembling. This was more than my already overloaded system could handle. "Morris jumped on me while I was packing them up," he added.

My words rushed out in an awkward jumble. "You bake? Who's Morris?"

He laughed. "Pit bull/lab mix. And yeah, I do. Bake, I mean. Mostly homemade pizza. These are my first cupcakes."

I was still clutching the note. My heart was beating fast but not crazy. Subtly, I gave him the once over, noting his jeans and Spring Creek Mustang T-shirt. Also he was wearing multi-colored Vans, probably because he had biked here. I knew he favored boots like I did. The shirt fit him nice and the jeans were a straight, slim cut that made him look absolutely fine, including his butt which I'd sneaked a peek at while we were climbing the stairs. He smelled like cologne—Ax maybe—but not too much of it and the cupcake smell was under there, too.

I fumbled with the envelope and pulled out a birthday card with a picture of a cupcake and Happy Birthday inside. Pretty generic and safe, which relieved me. But inside, in neat and tidy handwriting that was part cursive and part print and sort of manly looking, he had written: *I'm bringing the party to you. Hope you like the cupcakes!* Ryan S.

I smiled to myself. Like I wouldn't know which Ryan!

"It's a Tony Stark quote," he said, to the question I was

working up to ask. "You know—Iron Man. From *The Avengers?*"

Did he like those Avenger movies? And how much? Just
in general or full-on Comic Con like? Not that it was a deal
breaker or anything, but suddenly my brain whirred into
overdrive, wanting to know EVERYTHING about him.

My mouth said, "You write nicely."

I wanted to slap myself. I could be clever around Bo Shivers, but I sounded like a ditz in front of Ryan Sloboda. No
wonder angels didn't know squat about the universe. It was
a freaking mystery.

He shrugged. "I want to be a writer. After college. I'm
going out to California to write for TV. I've researched it and
do you know the WB channel offers a writer's workshop?
You get to apprentice with them. Learn the ropes on how to
write for shows. You have to do what they call a spec script
to get in. So I've been taking notes when I watch TV—about
how all the shows are set up."

"California?" I said. I had been only once. We'd done one
of those studio tours when we were in LA. Hadn't thought
about it since our family's implosion and downward mobility. Now I was thinking that my life could be a TV show and
Ryan could write it, only who would believe it? Mostly I was
thinking, *Don't move to California.*

"My parents—well, they love Texas. And I love it, too. But
I want—"

"More," I said, not meaning to finish his sentence but out
it popped, and I was nervous until he grinned real wide.

"Exactly!" he said.

After I figured we had done enough talking and I decided
to eat one of the cupcakes, specifically the J. The frosting
might have been squashed because of Morris—which was a

great name for a dog—but the chocolate cupcake part tasted good and the frosting was this cream-cheesy stuff that I love. I offered the E to Ryan.

"Happy Birthday, Jenna," Ryan said, his mouth half full.

"You played well last night," I told him. "Real well."

"Wasn't out there that much. But God, that Sneed. Did you see that miracle play at the end? That was too much, right?"

I choked a little on my last bit of cupcake. He patted me on the back until I stopped coughing. Then there I was, going from nervous to tingly because he looked me in the eyes and said, "I'm glad you were there."

I am not a girl who is easily dazzled. But here was what danced in my brain: I have a boy in my room! I have Ryan Sloboda in my room! He brought me birthday cupcakes and wrote me a note with an Avengers quote! He has PLANS and a dog. I could stand here like this, with him, forever.

Of course Mom chose that moment to pay attention to my life and call up the stairs that we would be leaving for the sushi restaurant in a bit and did Ryan want to join us? Which he did but couldn't, so he said. This was fine with me. After the whole afternoon with Bo, I was not sure I had the fortitude for a night with Ryan.

Still, I took another risk. I told Ryan I would meet him downstairs, and could he take the rest of the cupcakes to the kitchen, but if he didn't mind, I was sweaty and needed to change for dinner first so that we could take our time talking some more before he left.

Then I raced into the bathroom and threw on my new signature jeans and white button-down that Amber had given me, and slipped the silver mustang #76 charm from Maggie into my pocket—and after I swiped more purple eyeshadow

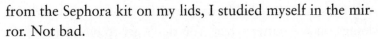

from the Sephora kit on my lids, I studied myself in the mirror. Not bad.

I sashayed downstairs, all casual like.

Ryan's eyes popped nicely at the outfit. Good to go.

I did not ask what Ryan and Mom had talked about while I was gone, but both the N cupcakes were missing, so I figured there'd been more eating than talking. I did not ask where Casey had disappeared to. Nor did I particularly care. I'd had had enough of my brother's angel shenanigans for one day.

Ryan said he needed to pedal back home.

And then it was the best part of my day. Actually it was the best part of any day I've had EVER.

IT'S FUNNY THAT I remember the conversation so clearly, considering it was so dumb. We stood at the curb, backlit by the Gilroy's Halloween lights.

"Thank you for my cupcakes," I told him.

"Sorry they were squashed," he said.

"They were awesome," I said. "You're like those cupcake bakers on that show."

He shrugged, and then we stood eyeballing each other awkwardly until I blurted, "Why the Avengers?" maybe because I was the teensiest bit concerned about the comic book thing and mostly because I LOVED that he had taken the time to quote something that he had picked JUST FOR ME.

Ryan blushed again, just a little, and my stomach clenched, also just a little. Was it too personal a question? I was new to the whole potential boyfriend thing.

"It's funny—the movie with all of them, I mean. The dialogue—like with Hulk and Loki. It cracks me up, and . . . they're superheroes. See, that's the thing I like about Tony Stark. He isn't supernatural. He's just a guy in a suit who's totally smart. But he's committed to saving the world. He hangs on no matter what. You don't get to have that in the real world, you know. You don't just wake up the next day and have powers. I mean the closest I ever come to feeling like that is in football."

This is what came rushing out of Ryan like a river of words. It could have flummoxed me because I could certainly tell him stories about someone who had woken up with powers, but instead it made me feel happier than I had in a very long time.

"Or this one time when I was little," he went on. "My grandpa Dale in Fort Worth entered me in Mutton Busting at the rodeo. I hung on to that damn sheep for my life. I didn't let go even after the buzzer rang. And they were picking me up and parading me around and I know it's just a stupid kid's thing, but that feeling . . . I was just five but I knew I wanted to grow up and have things that I just didn't let go of, you know? Important things. I guess it reminds me of that."

I was fumbling for something to say when Ryan leaned in, closing the space between us. "Jenna," he said. "Can I kiss you?"

My heart thrashed like a fish on a line. I nodded. "Yeah. I mean yes."

A million thoughts had been dancing in my brain: Did he like me? Was my breath fresh? Was that really Ax he'd spritzed on himself?

Now there was only one. He was going to kiss me. He had *asked* to kiss me.

He dipped his head and our foreheads bumped. My pulse was doing Nascar laps. Ryan reached out and rested his hands on my shoulders. Had he done this before? How many girls had he kissed? I knew he'd made out with that Mia Ross

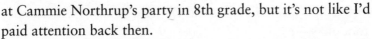

at Cammie Northrup's party in 8th grade, but it's not like I'd paid attention back then.

His face hovered over me. I had never thought there was any amount of Ax cologne that was good, but now I did. It was the perfect amount. My nostrils filled with boy. With Ryan Sloboda who was about to kiss me, his hands warm and firm on my shoulders. Then his lips touched mine. The lightest of kisses at first, like he wasn't quite sure it was okay even though I knew he was because he HAD ASKED and I had said YES. Then his hands moved, trailing down my back, setting electrical fires on my skin, pulling me closer.

Holy hell.

His lips were soft and solid at the same time, which was a wonderful thing. He tasted like cupcake frosting, or maybe he always tasted sweet—only I hadn't known until now. His lips opened a little and I did the same. It was like warm butterflies everywhere. I moved my hands up to cup the back of his neck, felt the stubble of his haircut with my fingertips while his hands rested, warmed and pressure-y, at the small of my back.

I'd never been kissed at all. I used to feel backward about that, like I wasn't keeping up with the pack. But now my brain announced: you were just waiting for the boy who would kiss you the right way. I thought I would die of nerves and pleasure right there on our driveway in the orange light from the Gilroy's fake Halloween graveyard.

I opened my eyes, and he backed away enough that I could pay attention. He swallowed. I watched, dizzy. Did he know it was my first real kiss? Could he tell? My general impression was that once I kissed him back, I could have had a third eyeball in the middle of my head and he might not have noticed.

"Will you go out with me?" he asked. His voice was firm

about it, which I liked. "And I'll take you to Homecoming, too, okay—?"

"Jesus Christ!"

That one wasn't me. It wasn't Ryan, either.

"What do you think you're doing, Jenna?" My brother advanced across our lawn at a fast clip, eyes on me, like Ryan wasn't even standing there. "We're going to dinner soon," he said. He looked me up and down. My lips were still in full tingle from the kissing, and my signature shirt had come untucked from my signature jeans. I contemplated all the ways I could kill him. Unfortunately, he was already dead.

Ryan just smiled. "I'll call you later," he said. "Keep your phone on. Okay? Happy Birthday." And waited until I mumbled some agreeing sound before he swaggered off, all Tony Stark quippy-like, tossing a "See you later, Samuels," to my brother as he went.

I swear I heard him whistle.

"Jesus Christ," my brother said again. It seemed to be his go-to response.

I wondered vaguely if he was getting angel demerits. Then I figured Management had enough on its hands with Bo Shivers and all his damn balcony leaping. Bo Shivers probably kissed a bunch of girls in his day and didn't care if he left them wondering.

After that, we drove to Sake City and ate California rolls and Mexico rolls (which had jalapeno) and something called a torpedo roll which had pretty much everything including avocado. My lips tingled from the kissing and the wasabi.

The waiters got together and sang "Happy Birthday" and put a candle in a bowl of edamame. Nice touch, Mom.

Ryan texted while we were eating. I had my phone on silent on my lap. He wanted to meet me at break time Monday in the Commons area.

Hope you like the last cupcake. ~R

I did let slip that Ryan was taking me to Homecoming. Mom allowed that maybe we should buy me a dress, and did Forever 21 have something that would work since that's where my gift card was from? I said I would look into it. Casey was texting through this discussion. I wondered if it was to Lanie.

After that we went home. Or rather, Casey dropped us

off and said he had something to do. He did not elaborate. If it was angel business he couldn't say it in front of Mom. Of course, Mom didn't blink about this, which pissed me off even though I should have just let it go. So I stood on the driveway after she'd gone inside, thinking that my birthday was almost over and that all told it had been a good one. Also, my lips were remembering Ryan's.

Mrs. Gilroy was out front, perusing her fake graveyard. Her paint cans and brushes were stacked against a pine tree.

"Looking spooky," I told her.

"Having trouble finishing," she said. "MJ's been under the weather, and my arthritis is acting up. The rest of those grave-stones will have to wait til tomorrow."

I nodded, not knowing what else to say. A thought flut-tered: Mrs. Gilroy was old. Bo Shivers was older. This disturbed me in more ways than my brain could handle.

Eventually, I went inside.

I showered. I got in bed. I texted Maggie. She called and I told her everything about Ryan's kissing. It made me feel less bad about not telling her all the other stuff.

Here is what I did not do: Fall asleep. My brain was whirring with Ryan and his lips and the fact that I had a BOYFRIEND now.

By midnight I was pretty sure I wasn't going to sleep.

By 2 A.M. I was positive.

I got up. I peeked into Casey's room. He was still gone.

This is how I decided that I would sneak outside and sur-prise Mrs. Gilroy by painting the rest of those tombstones. She'd left the Halloween lights on so it was pretty damn bright out there.

This was where I was, putting the finishing touches on *BELOVED AUNT MATILDA, FELLED BY AN OAK*

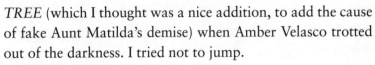

TREE (which I thought was a nice addition, to add the cause of fake Aunt Matilda's demise) when Amber Velasco trotted out of the darkness. I tried not to jump.

"What are you doing?" she asked.

"Painting gravestones," I said. *Wasn't it obvious?* "It's two in the morning. So now I'll ask you the same question."

Amber glanced at Mrs. Gilroy's yard, then back at me. She didn't answer.

"Where's Casey?" I demanded.

She didn't know. At least that's what she said. Suddenly, I suspected that he might be at Bo's. There was more to Bo's role in things, I knew, and so did Casey, and there was only so much he could take before he went and did something dumb. Since there was nothing I could do about it, I decided not to obsess over it.

Amber chewed on her lip for a bit, then said, "Sorry I left . . . like that." She stopped there. Apologies weren't Amber's strong suit. "I hope it went well with Ryan."

"He brought cupcakes," I said. "We're going out now." I added. I left out the kissing. She hadn't apologized enough for that.

"Oh," said Amber. "Well, good." She looked at her boots.

"Want to do one?" I held out the second paint brush. Terry's necklace was framed on her chest in the V from the open buttons of her shirt.

We painted in silence for awhile. Amber came up with: *SULLY ANDERSON: GONE BUT NOT FORGOTTEN.*

I did one that said: *FIDO. BEST DOG IN HEAVEN.*

Every now and then, Amber would reach up and touch that silver and turquoise cross, as if to make sure it was still there.

"You know," I said, dipping my brush in the paint to start

another stone. "Just because someone gives you something, doesn't mean you have to keep it. Doesn't mean you owe them anything."

Amber moved to the last unpainted tombstone. "Your brother gave you your life," she said, so soft I almost didn't hear her. "But you're absolutely right. I need you to remember what you just told me."

It took a minute for all that to sink in. Because she had just told *me* that I didn't owe Casey anything. "You ever gonna tell me what really happened to you?" I whispered. The words were out and I had no way of pulling them back in. Truth: I didn't want it.

Amber was silent again, for so long that I began to think that either she hadn't heard me or she was not going to answer, which amounted to the same thing.

But then she said, "I can't," after which she added, "Because I don't know." And the way she said it, I knew she was telling the truth.

"Bo knows," she said.

Jenna's Journal

October 22nd
Morning

I had never been one for schemes. Before the AI (Angel Incident), I didn't have a need for plotting and planning. I went to school. I hung out with Maggie. I watched TV, and I listened to music, and I annoyed my brother—and a long time ago I went with my dad to taste food at restaurants when he was writing his BBQ trail book.

Even after things went bad and then worse, even after he disappeared and Mom spaced out and stopped working or caring, I didn't think "Hey, I'm going to dig into this. I'm going to solve this." (Not even when I first got so sick because of the poison. Granted, I could barely function.) We looked for Dad, of course. We hoped that he would come back. It's not like we didn't DO THINGS. But eventually, I moved on. He was still missing, but I put it in the back of my head where it whirred like the guts in Casey's laptop—eating up brain space and making me feel sad. But really what could I do about it? Then I was dying, and Mom was fading, and Casey was hanging out with Dave and smoking weed and working two jobs and actively failing most of his classes even though he was whip smart. That's just the way it was.

Until the AI, I kept things on automatic. I got myself up. I got myself to school. I kept up my grades. I kept up appearances that we WERE FINE. Since we definitely were NOT, that particular job took a damn lot of energy. I ate the occasional stray snickerdoodle from Dave's Mamaw Nell. Things like high school—or a social life or a boyfriend—seemed far off, like Mars or Uranus, or Pluto, which wasn't even a planet anymore. If I thought about the future, it was this fuzzy thing, like static on a broken TV.

Now, thanks to my brother, there was a future. Except that he was technically dead and there was this ENTIRE WORLD that no one else knew existed except for me. A world of glowing dead folk with Spidey senses that might work and wings that *did* work and an Angel Management System that had more loopholes and secret rules than the US tax system.

Maybe that's why right now, I felt different. I might not have my learner's permit yet—although hopefully Casey would cart me over there on Monday—but I had helped catch an actual bad guy last year. It hadn't gone that well, but I had done it. I had helped my brother solve the mystery of what had happened to our family. I had always been a strong Texan girl, but I was stronger now because of it. Now when I took care of myself, it was conscious, not just going through the motions. I knew what was out there. And I knew that I had to BE AWARE. Plus, I had kissed Ryan Sloboda like I'd always imagined a kiss should be! Better, even!

If I could manage all those things, I could certainly help Amber Velasco figure out what had happened to her five years ago. Because no one should be in the dark about their own truths. Even people who sometimes annoy the hell out

of you. That is what I figured when I woke up, after Amber had left and after I heard Casey stomp into his room around four. And that's why I needed a scheme. So:

- I would spend some quality time researching newspaper reports from the day five years ago when Amber had her own life-changing AI. This would be a little tricky. Yes, there had been a break-in, but technically nobody was hurt. When Terry came home, she was sitting in the mess. (Of course she was dead. And Bo had already talked to her. But Terry didn't know.) That was the problem: no living person but me knew.

- If I figured out something, I would get Casey to take me to Austin to follow up. My opinion was this: Amber didn't know because she didn't *want* to know. Or she was afraid of knowing, which I totally understood. I wasn't sure what was going on between her and Bo Shivers, but she was afraid of him, too. Maybe because he had been there when her whole life turned into something else.

- Whatever the truth was, I needed to find it. There were problems I couldn't solve. I couldn't put my family back together unless my father decided he wanted to come home full time. I couldn't have my brother the way he used to be. I couldn't stop him from getting worked up over Lanie Phelps. I was hard-pressed to find a way to track down Renfroe and Manny again. But Amber's death? That was doable.

By one in the afternoon, here is what I had discovered about Amber:

- The only mention of the robbery was a small article in the local news section of the *Austin American-Statesman*. She was referred to as a student named A. Velasco. Her full first name was not given. But it had to be her.
- The article also named the address—and after digging some more, I discovered a record of the sale of the apartment building two months later. I guess it had been notable because it was by the UT campus and not far from all the hip places on Guadalupe and Lamar and 6th Street—so it was worth a bucket of money.
- Amber Velasco had no other mention on line from that time or any other.

This did not surprise me, since both Casey and I had tried looking her up before on personal stuff like Facebook or Tumblr. Casey said Management did their best to wipe out reference once you were no longer exactly human. I guess the A. Velasco had slipped by them somehow. I had no problem believing this was possible. My brother still appreciated a toke of weed now and then to settle himself, so I knew the A-word community wasn't all-knowing.

Terry McClain, on the other hand, was all over the web. For starters, there was his blog: *Of Mice and Men*. He hadn't posted in over a year, but back five years ago he was writing up a storm. Stuff about Comic Con—he favored Star Trek over Battlestar Galactica, although he rattled on for so long that I think I fell asleep with my eyes open—

and a series of posts that talked about his work testing drugs on mice.

This gave me pause. I remembered how he experimented with the tainted vitamins that Renfroe was giving Mom. He fed them to his mice, and they forgot to look for cheese. Of course that hadn't happened yet when he was blogging.

Another series proclaimed his undying love for the South Congress doughnut truck. For each day that week, he talked about doughnuts. Sweet. Savory. Weird. In Houston we had normal doughnuts: glazed or jellies or what have you. But in Austin you could get doughnuts with fried chicken on them. Or ones with habanero peppers. Terry's favorite was a maple frosting and bacon doughnut which sounded disgusting, but who was I to judge people's food preferences?

Only one article about the robbery quoted him. "My girlfriend was terrified," he said. Once again, Amber's name was left out.

I wondered if I could ask her about that. Was it Bo who'd

finagled the silence? Or did the police want to protect her identity because the criminals were still at large?

All I could say for sure was that I was now craving dough- nuts in the worst way. It was time to take a break. Plus, Maggie was coming over to discuss wardrobe options for Homecom- ing. I figured this would be quite the project. Especially since she had requested a more detailed play-by-play of the kissing with Ryan. Which I was more than happy to recollect.

U let him put his tongue in ur mouth? she'd texted.

Maybe, I'd texted back.

Unfortunately I couldn't mention my specific craving to her when I opened the door. Because how could I explain about the doughnuts if I didn't tell her about Terry and Amber and everything else including that my brother was an angel now? I had never been good at keeping things bottled up. Now I was the world's biggest expert. It sucked.

"You hungry?" I asked instead, generic like, a picture of that maple bacon doughnut wandering my brain. I was begin- ning to think it was less disgusting and more potentially tasty.

"I think you are compensating for wanting to kiss Sloboda some more," Maggie informed me.

I had to laugh. I remembered how he slipped his hands in my back pockets and set off rockets in my brain. It also distracted me from the secrets. Also it was probably true. Kissing Ryan Sloboda was better than any doughnut I could imagine. Maggie had a read on things like that.

She tugged at the hem of her grey sweater dress. It was really more sweater than dress, except she was wearing tights so that took care of the peekaboo factor. Maggie was a churchgoer on Sundays. I'd gone with her now and then, mostly to get out of the house, but not since the accident. I, on the other hand, was wearing my Sunday morning pointless

Internet research sweat pants and an old Ima Hogg T-shirt. Not exactly signature outfit material. The #76 mustang head necklace Maggie had given me did give things a certain flare, though. At least in my opinion.

"So how good a kisser is he?" Mags asked, waggling an eyebrow. I'd barely shut the door behind us.

"I'd give him an A plus. Higher even. Two plusses."

Maggie laughed. Followed by me turning red in the face.

"You really like him." She nudged me with her elbow.

I blushed some more. I really *did* like him—Ryan Sloboda, who played football and once hung onto a sheep for dear life and liked *The Avengers* and his dog and baking me cupcakes and telling me how he was headed to Hollywood to write stories for TV. But did he really like *me*? I was pretty sure he did. On the other hand, I'd grown up with my brother. I knew how it was with boys. Put a pair of willing lips in front of one and he'll latch on to them like lip-glossed life preservers.

"Is he taking you to the Bonfire?"

"Don't know," I said, wondering if I should. This boyfriend thing was feeling a lot like a test I hadn't studied for.

"Of course he is." Mags frowned. "Probably he's gonna meet you there. He's on the football team so I bet he has to do that skit."

For a non-school spirit girl, Maggie knew a lot about this kind of thing. Then again, Bonfire was big at Spring Creek High. Casey used to love it. Maybe he still did. A couple days before Homecoming, there was a parade with red-wagon floats from all the student organizations. After that, there was a pep rally. The football guys cross-dressed like cheerleaders and the cheerleaders cross-dressed like the football guys and everyone generally made happy fools of themselves.

Then came the bonfire in the student parking lot: a flaming heap topped with a dummy of the other team's mascot so we could burn it and cheer. It was kind of violent and pointless, but that was Texas football.

"I went last year," Maggie said. "You were sick, remember?"

Of course I remembered. Renfroe had been poisoning me. I could barely put one boot in front of the other. "How about those Homecoming dresses?" I said, changing the subject. I flashed her my Forever 21 gift card from Mom. "I'm flush with cash."

I snuck into Casey's room to swipe his laptop, then we sat side-by-side on my bed. We settled on high-low dresses, which meant that they were short in the front and longer in the back. There was one with a red corset top that Mags favored. I was a subtler girl and perused one with a blue sequined top.

"Hell no," said my brother's voice.

There he was again, sneaking up on us all stealthy, glaring at the laptop.

"You been taking spy lessons?" Maggie grumped at him.

"You are NOT wearing that," Casey said, scowling at the red corset dress.

"That one's mine," Mags informed him.

"You showed that to your mother?" Casey glanced from the screen to Mags to the screen to some place over our heads.

"Get out," I said, pointing to the door. Here he was acting all high and mighty and constipated, like I hadn't Lysoled the keyboard, averting my eyes a million times while I deleted all the links to large-chested women doing things a lot racier than wearing a corset top. But here was the problem: I also wanted to know where he'd been. I wanted to tell him my plan. I couldn't do this while Maggie was here.

"I brought home Chinese from Bei Jing Bistro," Casey announced. "Mom's on her way back from Texas Children's."

I didn't tell him that I hadn't even noticed she wasn't here.

"You don't have to always bring us food anymore," I said. "They still give me a discount," he said, like that explained it. He turned back to Mags. "You want to eat with us?" Now he sounded all adult, asking her to dinner. Like a parent. I felt safe and sad and angry all at once.

"Where else you been?" I held his gaze, trying to figure it out. I knew he wouldn't answer or if he did it wouldn't be the whole story. It was déjà vu all over again— like last night and the night before that. And then the oddest thing: I could have sworn that I heard Bo Shivers' chuckling somewhere in the air. I knew he wasn't here. But the hair stood up on the back of my neck anyway. For a second, I though I smelled his whiskey. Casey's eyes locked on mine. Did he hear it, too? I tried to read his expression, but it was like reading a blank screen. One with perfect skin tone.

Maggie shivered. "Cold in here," she said. She narrowed her eyes at Casey and asked, "You been drinking? I smell Jack Daniels."

I squeezed my eyes shut for a second. I didn't want to lie to Maggie anymore. But I couldn't exactly be honest, either.

"Mags," I said slowly, my brain testing the waters. "I think I need to call it a night. We looked at so many dresses that my head hurts."

It wasn't a lie. Also, it wasn't the truth. I swore I heard another Bo chuckle. His image flashed in my head: That long hair with strands of gray, the scars on his hands and wrists that spoke to something unspeakable. Those shining dark eyes. This time *I* shivered. Was he watching us? Or really here somehow, trailing a scent of Jack? What if Casey developed

that ability? There I'd be, kissing Ryan Sloboda and hear my brother's voice in my head. (Or worse, Ryan would hear it.) My brother would backslide like he did with the weed because he was cranky and disgruntled and tell Ryan about the time I ate a jumbo bag of Corn Nuts and my breath stank for a week.

I told my brain to stop imagining this because it was making me want to puke.

"Be an angel and pack her up some eggrolls," I told him.

He seemed to let my lame A-word joke go. "You need me to drive you home?" Then he reached out toward Maggie's shoulder.

"Don't!"

They both stared at me like I was a loony.

"Don't forget the duck sauce for her eggrolls," I amended. "You know Bei Jing."

My brain ran out of lies, so I left it at that. What I was thinking was: I wanted my best friend in the world to feel whatever she was feeling. Not get hopeful happiness if it wasn't hers. But there was only more awkward silence. Eventually, Maggie stood and I said I'd walk her out and she said that she wasn't in the mood for Chinese. I allowed that probably no one was, but that was the way things worked around here these days.

My brother stalked after us, muttering something. Then Maggie announced that she was accepting Casey's offer of a ride, but he needed to hold his horses because she and I had THINGS TO DISCUSS. I have put this in all caps because that is how it sounded coming out of her mouth. Shouty and pissed off. Which I totally understood. Her best friend had just hollered "Duck sauce" like it was the end of the world.

I wrenched open the door to find Mom lugging a bag of

groceries. She was wearing tan slacks and a white blouse with a navy sweater. That, and her Texas Children's hang tags printed with Holly Samuels, SLP, which stood for Licensed Speech-Language Pathologist. Her hair was in a half pony tail. She looked tired but otherwise okay. I realized that checking her health was second nature to me now. I wondered if I'd ever slip up and forget that less than a year ago, she'd been almost comatose.

What I also wondered: if she would ever remember to check on me that much, her daughter who almost bit the dust from her boss's boot poison.

Probably not.

"Maggie?" Mom said, making it a question for no good reason I could think of.

"I'm leaving," Mags told her. "But hi."

Casey scooped up the grocery bag. "Heavy," he said. I assumed he meant the groceries and not our moods. Maybe it was both.

"What a day," Mom said to none of us in particular. "Lots of swallowing therapies. Cancer kids."

She let that hang there along with everything else. Our house faced west and the sun was setting behind her head, lighting up the frizzies in her hair. Suddenly I felt like we were all standing too close together. Casey, still holding the groceries, cleared his throat. I could feel the million things he had bottled up because he couldn't or wouldn't say them.

But nothing happened except that he told Mom he'd help her put the groceries away. She looked at him like she couldn't quite place why he was so nice these days. When she kissed him on the cheek, he squirmed, but she smiled big and didn't look as tired any more. My brain squirmed. Had Casey's angel powers soothed her? Was maybe that why she

wasn't worried about me? Why had she never mentioned Renfroe or Manny or the memory drugs and poison we'd been plied with? And here was what I didn't want to think about: That my brother had chosen to protect me from Mom's worry by taking it away from her. Which also took *her* away from *me*.

I let Maggie drag me outside.

"For the millionth time, what the h is going on?" Maggie had still not developed a colorful vocabulary so this is exactly how she said it. "You know you keep kicking me out, right?"

I *did* know. I had hoped *she* hadn't noticed.

Suddenly I was even more desperate to tell Casey my plan for solving what had happened to Amber. Because right now, all we were doing was swirling in the same dizzy circle over and over. What a kick in the pants for the Bible-thumper crowd if they ever discovered that guardian angels had about as much say in their jobs as Wal-Mart greeters. Maybe less since the greeters could at least pick which basket they shoved at you even if they had to do it wearing those ugly vests.

Maggie was waiting for an answer that made sense. My heart felt like a stone.

"There's stuff," I said. "Weird stuff."

Mags pressed her lips together in a line. "You already told me that."

"My parents are separating." This wasn't definitely true. Also it made me think of them like two pieces of paper coming unglued.

"Figured as much."

My eyebrows shot up. "You did?"

"Um, yeah. Is he staying in Austin then? Your dad? Makes sense though. That's why your brother has been such a bone-head, right? Cause he's all overprotective?"

"Yeah," I said. "That's it." Then added: "He's like my personal guardian. Gets himself all worked up."

"Fancy way of saying nitwit."

We stood there digesting my parents' impending break-up which I wasn't even sure was actually happening. I had managed to both lie and tell the truth. This made me feel worse.

"You can tell me whatever you want," Mags said, scuffing her foot on the driveway like she was trying to erase something. "You don't have to keep it inside."

"I know."

"Promise?"

"Promise," I lied.

But I was not surprised when she announced she would walk home with her eggrolls rather than taking up Casey on his offer of a ride.

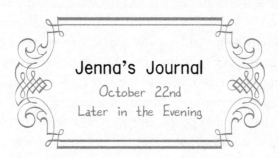

After that, my mother, brother, and I ate lukewarm moo shu pork and shrimp-fried rice. We shoveled food in our mouths while Mom told us more about the cancer kids and their swallowing issues. I stole glances at Casey. If I solved Amber's murder, maybe Management would promote her and leave my brother the hell alone. He'd be upset, but he'd work through it. He was a tough guy. He could pal around with Bo! Probably a bad idea, given Bo's desire to fling himself off balconies, guzzle Jack, and look at me like he saw every single secret inside including this one.

If Bo took a stance on the matter of Amber's murder, I suspected it would be for his own self-interest. But I was doing the same thing, wasn't I? The A-word community had gone to all that trouble to bring my brother back, spruce him up, and assign him to guard me. As I was still alive and a minor and without an actual driver's license, it made no sense for him to move on. Was it weird that I felt like Bo and I had things in common? Maybe. But I couldn't stop thinking about it. That picture of a lady he'd painted—the one on the far wall by his bed. What had she been to him?

Easier to solve Amber's death than dig into the secrets of Bo Shivers.

Especially when all I really wanted to think about was Ryan Sloboda's lips and how they felt on mine. I wasn't one of those simpering types, but I wanted to linger on it for a while. More than a while. I deserved as much, didn't I? Because that is what normal people did with wonderful things. They memorized the shape of them, the taste and sound of them. That's what got you through the tough times. That's what kicked your heart up and made you feel that anything was possible. But I was only a normal girl part of the time. The rest of the time, I was stuck in A-word land.

I picked up a fortune cookie from the pile Casey had scattered on the table. Cracked it open and pulled out the little white slip.

One man's lie is another man's truth.

I would have called Casey on it—pressed to see if he'd used angel mojo to give me some crap fortune. But it was at that exact moment that his cell rang like a five-alarm-fire warning. He grimaced. Eyeballed the screen while I craned my neck trying to read the text or whatever it was. Then he shoved away from the table, chopsticks clattering to his plate, one landing on my last bite of moo shu.

"Gotta go," he said.

Mom gaped at him. So did I.

"BJ's. Bryce. Sorry. Three people called in sick." He was at the door while I was still processing.

Hey. I was going to tell him my genius plan. The door slammed.

I leaped to my feet.

"I'm going with him," I told Mom. I had no idea what I could say by way of explanation, so I didn't even try.

"It's Sunday night," Mom said. Her chopsticks—crisscrossed over a fat shrimp— were pointed at her mouth, frozen right where they'd been when Casey's cell had gone off. "Family night."

We hadn't been a real family in a very long time. But the look on her face made me sad. Not sad enough to stop walking.

"We'll hang out later," I said. "Maybe watch a cable movie. You can leave the food. I'll clean it up when I get home."

I heard her chair scrape and knew she was following me so I hustled faster. Out the door. Down the driveway like the house was on fire. Casey was already backing up the Merc. "Wait!" I hollered. "Casey. Wait!" I raced forward, catching up with him, pounding my hand on the Merc's hood. Bam. Bam.

My brother slammed on the brakes.

"What the hell, Jenna?" he bellowed, and I could hear him even though the windows were shut. "Go back inside."

But he hadn't pressed the gas again so I yanked open the passenger door and flung myself in. Casey rammed the gear shift into park.

"No."

"Go," he said.

"What part of no didn't you understand?"

Casey pushed at me. "Get out."

I was puffing up to holler at him some more when out of the corner of my eye, I spied Mrs. Gilroy standing in the middle of her fake graveyard, crying.

I did not have time for this. I seriously did not.

But out of the car I went. Why? I wasn't exactly sure. But

if I had to say, it would be this: Mrs. Gilroy was nice. She made us Christmas fudge. And my family had been hurt by Dr. Renfroe—a man who had hurt old folks like her in the name of science. The way I looked at it, what else could I do?

"If you leave without me," I hollered back to Casey, "I will post all your naked baby pictures on the Spring Creek High website and Photoshop Lanie Phelps into them." I raced over to her yard.

"How did this happen?" Mrs. Gilroy had dropped to her knees in front of the *SULLY ANDERSON* tombstone.

"It's okay," I said, bending to pat her back. "I finished it for you. Last night."

"What?" she said.

"I painted your tombstones." I did not add that Amber had helped, had in fact painted the *SULLY ANDERSON* stone. She looked confused enough. Maybe she figured it was a Halloween miracle or something.

"I'm sorry," I added when she kept looking miserable. "I can fix them, if you want. Did you have other names picked out?"

Maybe the Fido one offended her. Maybe she had an Aunt Matilda who actually *had* been conked on the cranium by an oak tree. Things happened. My family was certainly proof of that.

"You don't have to cry," I said. I stood then and held out a hand to haul her up.

"She needs to go home," I heard my brother say from across the driveway.

I swiveled my head. Mom had joined him. Wonderful. They were standing together next to the Merc. I hated when people talked about me like I was invisible.

I turned back to Mrs. Gilroy. Her mouth kept moving, but

nothing else came out. Her glasses had slipped down on their beaded chain and were now guarding her chin. Her eyes—a faded blue—were spilling over. One tear got stuck in a wrinkle on her cheek. It was not a pretty picture, but what is when you're bawling?

All of a sudden, Casey was standing there with us.

I whipped around. Mom was walking back toward the house.

"Let her go," Casey said. I did. I didn't even argue about it.

He sat down on the grass next to Mrs. Gilroy. He took both her hands in his, calm and slow like he had all the time in the world. Like he hadn't just raced out with some secret agenda. The air around them lit bright, then brighter. Stronger even than those Halloween lights strung on the Gilroy's trees.

"What's wrong?" he asked her, his voice strong but gentle as a breeze. "It's MJ, isn't it?" The hairs on the back of my neck rose one by one. My brain kicked into overdrive, processing. Thinking. Realizing. MJ was Mr. Gilroy, who had liver-colored age spots on his jowly cheeks and favored one piece Dickey overalls and who was getting too elderly to climb the ladder stringing lights at Christmas.

Mrs. Gilroy nodded.

"Betsy," my brother said, using her first name that I didn't even remember she had. "MJ's been short of breath lately. He's telling you it's allergies. But maybe he's not right about that. You know us guys, Betsy. We're pigheaded sometimes. Here's what I think: his heart isn't pumping like it should be. You probably need to take him to the doctor. That St. Anthony's Emergency Center's open on Sundays if you're worried about waiting at Houston Northside. But the hospital's a good place, too. They fixed me and Jenna right up after our accident, remember? You think you could get him in the car and take him? Or Jenna and I could cart you. If MJ'll let us."

My mouth was hanging open now. Full-on fly-catching jaw drop.

Helping Donny Sneed win the football game was one thing. A funny thing—sort of. This was . . . My pulse slammed, my skin was prickled, and I thought: I am stupid. I am stupid. How did I not know? Casey was helping Mrs. Gilroy stand now and then patting her back, a 'there there' kind of pat.

"I'll take him," she said, her voice thin but determined. "You're right. You're right. He's been taking those Claritin. You can buy them over the counter now, did you know? But he's so tired. And I thought it was his hip. But you're right."

"Take him tonight, Betsy. You promise you'll take him tonight? Now?"

Mrs. Gilroy nodded again. "Let me walk you inside," Casey said. "I'll be in the Merc," I said, more to myself than anybody else. I climbed into the passenger seat, cut the engine because the car was still running, and sat and thought. Ryan's fabulous lips didn't even enter the picture. Which was a shame.

Less than a minute later, my brother reappeared.

"You painted her fake tombstones?" He stared at me hard, like this was a crime.

I shrugged. "Me and Amber." I stared right back. "You're an angel," I said. Which sounded stupid, but that's how it came out.

"Amber? When the hell was Amber here?"

"Last night. And don't change the topic."

"Jenna," Casey said and then sighed. "You know what I am."

"No," I said. "I don't. Not like this."

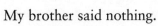

My brother said nothing.

"It's that Spidey sense thing, isn't it?" I asked when the silence got boring, and Casey had begun fiddling with the car keys and peeking at his cell phone which was blinking like crazy because he was running late to wherever he was going.

"But you can't read people's minds, right?" I said, having the conversation with myself. "Y'all keep telling me it doesn't work like that."

Another sigh. His cell rang, loudly, even though I could see he had it on silent. After like ten rings it stopped.

I tried to collect my thoughts. "You toke up still. You bitch and moan over Lanie. You—"

"I don't . . . I don't need the full replay." Casey sounded peeved. Somehow this made me perkier. He brushed a hand over my shoulder and I scooted away.

"Explain," I said.

He pursed his lips. Turned the key and revved up the Merc but did not shove it in gear. "It's you," he said. "At least mostly."

Something hard lodged in my throat. "What?" I tried to swallow around the boulder or whatever it was, but my mouth was too dry. MSG in the fried rice, probably.

"I'm your guardian, Jenna. You care about Mrs. Gilroy. And don't deny it. You painted her damn fake tombstones. I think . . . no, I don't think. I know. Amber says it comes from that. Bo agrees with her I think, although right now . . . I don't understand the physics exactly, but that's the short of it. I can read her, sort of, because of you."

He looked at me even harder, serious as I'd ever seen him. Plus he'd referenced physics, which was freaking me out. Even after he'd pulled himself together last year, he had still failed Teen Leadership—which he was now re-taking. And more troubling, he was talking to Amber about me. He was talking to Bo about me.

"Me?" I squeaked.

Casey backed the Merc down the driveway, eyes on the rearview now. "Yeah. Crazy, right?"

"Well," I said as he shoved the car in drive and floored it. We lurched, then sped down the block. Maybe tomorrow, after he finally, finally took me for my permit, I would practice. I would drive slower than this, that was for sure.

"Well, what?"

"Prove it."

He glared at the road. "It's true. You don't have to do a test for it."

I almost laughed. He was trying to turn the tables on me, referring to my Angel Test, the one I'd come up with when I was having trouble believing that my brother was not the same as he'd been before our car accident. I'd even dyed his hair Champagne Blonde with Mom's Clairol products just to see if I could change his looks—which of course I couldn't. Also, I had no idea where we were going.

"If it's true, then you can prove it."

We hung a right out of our neighborhood, heading west, then over the railroad tracks. He screeched to halt as the light turned red.

"Is Mr. Gilroy really sick?" I pressed.

"I think so, yes."

"Is he going to die?"

Casey tapped his fingers on the steering wheel. Checked the mirrors even though we were stopped. "You need to look in that rearview regularly," he informed me. "You never know what kind of lunatic might be speeding up to rear-end you cause he's yakking on his phone."

"Casey."

"Don't know. I can't know. But he's sick and she was scared and he was stubborn. I think she'll take him now. If she does, it could be okay."

"But I don't even think about them," I said. "They don't matter to me like . . . well they don't."

The light turned green and Casey floored it again, hanging a left under the bridge, onto the feeder and then onto I-45 headed south. Toward Houston. Joining the stream of head-lights as the sun dropped out of sight.

"Bo?" I asked, nodding toward his phone.

"Bo," he said. He drove with his left, called on his cell with his right. "You still there?" he said into the phone after a couple seconds. "I'm coming. There was a—I'll be there quick as I can." He tossed the phone into the cup holder. Sig-naled a lane change and passed a pick up with its blinkers on. He didn't explain further. I didn't ask.

"You care about everybody, Jenna," Casey blurted out. "You do. It's around you. It's *in* you. It's . . . you. I never knew it before. Never cared to know it. I know it now. I see it and feel it even if I want to ignore it, which I can't. It's like—energy. Yours. Theirs. And it feeds into me. So I can tell what you need, Amber says. It's not like at first, when I . . . It's different now. It's constant."

I stared at him, trying to understand. "But you don't know what your purpose is?"

"Nope. But I know this. I know it all the damn time. It's—it's loud."

"Like me," I said, not even meaning to.

Casey almost smiled. "Yeah. But not always accurate. I guess I'm not that good at it yet or something. Or maybe everyone you know has loud problems."

That was entirely possible.

"Truth?" I asked.

"Truth," he said. "For real."

I gave him the stink eye. "You still haven't proved it."

"You don't want to believe me, that's your problem."

"You don't have to be such a dick about it."

He laughed then. "Of course I do."

Did I believe him? Mostly. I believed there was more to his A-word-ishness than I had thought. I believed that he knew when I was upset about something, but he was my brother. If he paid attention, he didn't have to be an angel to know that. Same with the Gilroys. They were older than Moses. No big surprise if they were feeling poorly.

"What about Amber and Bo?" I asked. "Can you read them?"

That would make the whole thing easier. I cared about Amber, sort of. Bo . . . I wasn't sure. But maybe Casey could use that energy or whatever to find out what Amber's damage was all about. Maybe they'd reward him by giving him his flight back. Something. The downtown skyline loomed closer—all those tall buildings. In my head, I imagined Bo Shivers leaping off each of them in slow motion. I still had no idea exactly where we were going. With anything, not just this particular car ride.

"Nope," Casey said. "With other angels it's different."

I pondered this. What if someone *could* read Bo? What would that someone see in his head? "Casey," I said, drawing out his name while I formulated my question. "What do you think it feels like for Bo to fall like that? You haven't . . . I mean.."

Casey's eyes stayed on the road. "Don't know," he said. But the way he said it, I wondered if he did.

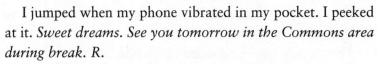

I jumped when my phone vibrated in my pocket. I peeked at it. *Sweet dreams. See you tomorrow in the Commons area during break. R.*

See you I texted back, spelling out *you* like he had.

I liked that he had taken the time to use the whole word. I guess that was the writer in him. It made me feel special. I rubbed my thumb over my mustang head necklace. If I had not been in A-word land, my heart would have flailed its jazz hands again. Instead, I thought: This stuff Casey was trying to explain . . . was it like hearing Bo chuckle in my head— only more? What if he knew when things were wrong with my friends? Would I want to know?

"What about Ryan? Is he okay?" I felt momentarily bad that I hadn't looped Maggie in there, too. But she was my best friend. If she was fixing to have a coronary, she'd at least text me that she was feeling out of sorts. Probably blabber about how the universe had some grand plan. I loved that about Maggie, who knew I would be there for her no matter what. And that she would be there for me. But Ryan was another story. One I wanted to continue.

"Wait," I said, as Casey opened his mouth. "Don't tell me. If you're in his head, get out of there!"

Turn signal again. We were getting off the freeway. Midtown.

"Ryan's fine," Casey said. "The pissant."

"La la la," I told him, holding my ears. "I am not listening." Even if I was, it was hard to focus. So much happening all at once. "I have a plan," I blurted because telling him this was something I could control.

"Oh?" Casey turned left down some street I didn't know. Tall office buildings surrounded us, a canyon of concrete and glass.

"I'm going to figure out how Amber died," I said. "And you can take the credit."

That wasn't how it sounded in my head, but that's how it popped out.

"Jenna," Casey said, making another turn. "How's that gonna work?"

"Gonna work fine. Need to go to Austin, though. For research. Maybe I can even drive as long as you're in the front seat with me."

He made a grumbling sound in his throat, but I could see in his face that he was actually mulling it over.

"We could get her promoted," I added. "Be good all around."

"Jenna," Casey said. "I don't know if—"

"Why do you act like you can't do angel things?" I exploded. "Like you're not as good as Amber?" It was, I figured, what I really wanted to know.

One beat. Two. We turned again. This part of town was deserted. It was Sunday. It was night. No one was at work.

"If I pretend," Casey said, and I knew he was telling the truth, "I can pretend the whole thing. That I'm me. That nothing is changed."

And in that moment, I knew that's why he was pretending, beyond just protecting me.

We were barreling down Main Street now, up against the light rail tracks and speed bumps, the only barriers between the cars and trains. People regularly bashed into trains they swore they hadn't seen coming. That was Houston for you; everyone treated their personal vehicles like horses and the rest was just obstacles to get around as fast as you could.

"Casey, if we figure out who killed Amber, she'll move on. It's why she's stuck. Maybe they won't send someone else to boss you."

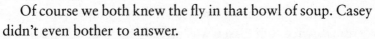

Of course we both knew the fly in that bowl of soup. Casey didn't even bother to answer.

"Um," I said as we pulled up to what looked to be a dance club. *Wild Horses*, read the sign. Country music bar probably. A bunch of people were milling around outside, guys and girls both in jeans and boots. Girls in those skimpy cute tops that I wanted to start wearing. "What are we doing here anyway?"

Out ambled the fly in our own A-word bowl of soup. Bo Shivers weaved his way down the sidewalk, possibly drunk. He was duded up in jeans and boots—snakeskin it looked like, which made me shudder remembering the juiced-up snake poison Dr. Renfroe had used to taint *my* boots. Also a white pearl-snap shirt untucked, flashing a bit of flat tanned belly as he walked.

I was not opposed to the fact that he looked damn good. But it was disturbing. There was an age limit for sexy, and he was definitely breaking the curve. And maybe not as drunk as I thought when he first burst out of the bar.

Casey hopped out and chased him down. I guessed I had to tag along.

"Where is she?" Casey asked.

"Tried to get her to go home," Bo said. "She just hopped on that mechanical bull and told me screw off. In quite the mood, our Amber. Worse I've seen actually. Something set her off. She hasn't been like this since that first year."

If the universe had wanted to flummox me some more, it was doing a fine job. Because I had sudden feeling I knew exactly who they were talking about.

Bo narrowed his eyes at me. "Why is she here?"

"Long story," my brother said.

Bo cleared his throat. "C'mon, Casey." Then to me: "Stay put. This shouldn't take long."

Casey grabbed me by the arm. "She's coming with us."

Bo scowled, but Casey was already hauling me inside. He clapped the bouncer on the arm as we went. The guy smiled and let us pass. Bo smiled, too.

"See what I mean?" He pointed to toward the center of the place.

We craned our necks.

There was Amber Velasco, dancing on top of the bar. Her jeans were tight and she wore a skimpy low-cut white tank top and those boots of hers, her EMT belt hooked below her waist. Her hair was loose and out of its normal ponytail. She had a beer in one hand and a cowboy type in the other. The sound system was pumping *Copperhead Road*.

She and the cowboy bent low at the appropriate boot stomps. The bar was shaking with each stomp. The crowd was cheering. Also, she was glowing, and not from the hazy bar lights. No doubt the wasted crowd thought someone had trained a spotlight on her

"Holy shit," I said.

My brother said, "Language, Jenna."

"Like I told you," said Bo Shivers. "I think she's depressed."

His lips curled, slight but wicked-seeming, like this amused him.

Things went downhill from there.

Jenna's Journal

October 24th

Somewhere After Three in the Morning

"The Camaro's out back. I can drive." Amber insisted.

It wasn't easy getting her out of there, but Bo (suddenly not tipsy in the least) convinced her it was time to go. Even in this state, she bended to his will. We were catching our breaths on the sidewalk. Amber was swaying her Badonkadonk to the muted strains of Trace Adkins filtering from the club. Bo's look was a thing of darkness. My brother's wasn't much better.

"You should move along," I told the cowboy, who had followed us—bad choice on his part. In the light of the street lamps, he looked more insurance salesman with a big belt buckle and tight jeans than bull-riding hottie. "Sooner would be good."

He looked like he might move, only then Amber pulled him to her—she was quick about it, half-lifting him off the sidewalk—and locked her lips on his. It was a sloppy kiss, not that I was now a kissing expert, just that it seemed random and wet and focused mostly on pissing off Bo and my brother.

The cowboy didn't seem to care. Or notice that Amber was freakishly strong.

Bo placed a hand on the guy's shoulder. His shirt sleeve pulled back some and I saw those deep scars of his.

All of a sudden I felt a rush. How was it that Bo's scars were still there? Casey had come back from our car accident all prettied up and perfect, zits gone and flabby-too-many-tacos belly miraculously flat and ab-tastic. All those cuts from the windshield, that long gash that I'd seen as I was trying not to die—they were gone. And when I cut him during my stupid Angel Test, it healed right away.

But Bo had his scars.

Why?

Like at Bo's loft, something crawled up my spine and took its time flickering back down.

"Amber," Bo said, his voice slow. "I have faith that you can do better than this."

Amber turned her head briefly to mumble, "You don't have faith in anything, remember? Least of all love."

"Do we really need to do this, darlin'?"

Slurpy-kissing Cowboy turned to Bo, and their eyes locked.

"Go home," Bo said.

The Cowboy blinked with a dangerous grin. I held my breath, expecting a brawl. But then the grin faded. He drew back from Bo, swallowing, and muttered something under his breath. (It sounded like "crazy freak" but could have been anything.) Without another word, he wandered across the street, stumbling a few times over the big white speed bumps that lined the Light Rail tracks.

"Watch out for trains," I hollered.

"I'll drive you home," Bo said.

Amber gave him the stink eye. She fished an elastic band

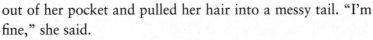

out of her pocket and pulled her hair into a messy tail. "I'm fine," she said.

Suddenly, she was. Standing up straight and steady. Eyes clearing. Color back in her face. And her usual firmly neutral look that gave no clue what she was thinking. Or what the hell she and Bo were actually talking about with that whole faith conversation. I knew angels recovered from their excesses with lightning speed, but Amber and Bo were both quicker at it than Casey. Or maybe my brother liked to wallow in it because it made him feel like he used to. I suspected that was how it was with him.

Bo told Amber it wasn't up for discussion and that he'd deal with the damn Camaro if that's what Amber was worried about.

"Don't forget to hydrate," I advised Amber helpfully. "You're my back up tomorrow if Casey can't take me for me permit, remember?"

This time Amber gave *me* the stink eye.

"Thanks for helping her with those tombstones," Casey said. Was he really thanking her? Maybe.

"Mr. Gilroy's not doing well," I announced because now Bo was staring at me and someone had to say something.

"Your neighbors are quite the handful," said Bo.

"Something like that," I told him, feeling about as cranky and tired and confused as that Cowboy must have felt. The way he had just described the Gilroys, wasn't that how I had described myself to him back at his loft? He could pick his own vocabulary. He didn't get to use mine. I rolled my eyes and hoped he got the message.

Casey dragged me toward the Merc.

"What is it with those two," I grumped. "He knows stuff about her that we don't, doesn't he? About lots of things,

I bet. The way he looks sometimes, like he's seen it all and done it all, too. Gives me the willies."

Casey gave a noncommittal grunt.

"You're not going to tell me, are you?

"Don't have anything to tell."

And here was the problem: I had a feeling he really didn't.

HALFWAY HOME, ONE question was still poking at me.

"Casey," I said, as the Merc zipped along on the mostly empty freeway. "Why did Bo call you?"

He made a tsking sound like I was an idiot. "Cause Amber was out of control."

"No, she wasn't."

"Did you not see her on that bar?"

"Y'all can turn your drunk on and off at will, Casey. Least that's what it seems to me. She was blowing off steam. You blow off steam all the time and I don't have to call her. And *I'm* not one of you. Even that thing with Donny was . . . well . . . Bo's powerful, right? He's been in charge of her for five years. Why is it that he couldn't haul her off the bar and away from some cowboy wannabe?"

Casey didn't answer right away, just gripped the steering wheel, his eyes on the road. The Merc thumped along in the darkness.

"I needed to know what was going on," he said eventually, not looking over at me. "Amber's my boss."

More driving in the dark. More quiet. We rarely played the crappy radio when we were in this car. It was fuzzy sounding and we generally had some sort of crisis to deal with. I didn't even miss it much, except now when it was just both of us breathing. My brain whirred. *You don't have faith in anything*, Amber had told Bo. *Least of all love.*

"I think she's hurting," I said. "I think it's that Terry guy. Maybe she misses him. I think if we figured out what happened to her then—"

"Enough, Jenna." Casey's voice was sharp.

Well, fine then. I decided to let it go. I was not in the mood to argue matters of romance with my permanently single brother. So I closed my eyes and thought about Ryan instead.

WE MADE IT home. We checked on Mom, asleep in her bed. I showered. I changed into shorts and T-shirt. I checked my phone for texts. None. Got into bed. Set my alarm so I could shower in the morning. I was new to this boyfriend thing, but I figured clean hair was a plus. Tomorrow I'd put on some of that purple shadow again. Maybe try my hand at the eyeliner thing, too, if I woke up early enough to deal with it. And one of the glosses—maybe Dewberry, which I thought would go good with the shadow.

I didn't feel myself fall asleep.

I mention this because I wasn't sure if I was dreaming when I heard Bo Shivers laugh again. Not a chuckle this time, but something skin-prickling, deep and dark and dismissive. The kind of laugh you never want to hear from someone. I sat up but I couldn't find my nightstand lamp and I couldn't see because the curtains were pulled tight. There was no light from outside, not even hallway light seeping under my door.

"Bo?" I called, my voice shaky, but trying to be brave. The laugh echoed around me again, the sound feeling tight and close—seeping into my eardrums and traveling down to my chest where it wrapped around my heart.

What the hell? Was that really him I heard? What was he laughing at?

My heart seized: was he laughing at me?

Jenna Samuels, I told myself. *Don't be a baby. You are having a nightmare. You need to wake up. Your life has not been a bed of roses lately. Some old angel with a death wish cackling in your head is no big deal.*

Which was when I heard the scream. Loud. Shrill. Female. Amber Velasco.

I fumbled for the light again. Couldn't find it. Tried to leap out of bed but my feet tangled in the covers.   "No!" the Amber voice screamed. And then I could see her. I had to be dreaming. I had to be. She was standing with Bo just beyond the foot of my bed, a reddish glow surrounding them, all of which I knew was impossible but there they were in the darkness. "Jenna!" Amber hollered, but she wasn't looking at me, just peering into the pitch black. "No! Bo! No!"

I opened my mouth, but fear was lodged too sharp in my throat.

And then light was shining in my eyes.

I blinked.

I was lying in my bed. My heart was galloping. I shivered, even though I was hot. The sheets were damp. Casey was standing over me, his hand on my shoulder.

"Jenna? You were screaming." His hand whipped to my forehead like he was checking for fever. "What's wrong?" He bent over me, face close to mine.

He smelled clean and crisp, like air and eucalyptus and fresh sheets, hand cool on my head. I didn't push it away, just let the soothing feeling seep in. But it was working at half-force or something, and the calm wasn't coming fast enough.

"I think I was dreaming," I said, not positive at all, heart still thumping way too hard, my throat dry as sand.

"About what?"

I swallowed. "About Amber. I don't know what else.

Bo maybe? I heard him laugh. She was hollering my name, Casey. She sounded so scared. She was yelling at Bo. Telling him 'no.'"

Casey sat next me then and stroked the top of my head. The light from my lamp drifted across his face, illuminating his eyes and that forever perfect skin of his—no zits, no scratches, just smooth and tan and nice.

"Why does Bo have scars on his wrists?" I asked, the question coming out of nowhere and everywhere. Bo's laugh kept ringing in my ears. Why had I dreamt that? Why had it felt so real?

My brother looked startled. He removed his hand from my head. "What do you mean?"

"Bo's wrist scars. Why does he have them if you and Amber are so perfect?"

He grinned. "You think I'm perfect, huh? Can I quote you on that later?"

I socked him on the arm, which settled my heart and stomach some even though I knew he barely felt it.

"It was only a dream, Jenna. You're okay."

I collapsed back against the headboard, yanking my comforter with me. The dream wasn't about me, even though she'd called my name.

"It was real," I said. "More than a dream."

"No such thing."

"And there's no such thing as your brother coming back as your guardian angel. With wings. We have to find out what happened to Amber. Whatever it is, Bo's not telling her on purpose. That's what I think. He knows and he won't say and she doesn't want to know."

"Does it matter?" But I could tell from his voice that he thought maybe it did.

"Take me tomorrow," I said. "To Austin. Where she lived . . . then." I couldn't bring myself to say *when she died*. I just couldn't.

Casey was quiet for a few seconds. My heart was beating normally now. I wasn't freezing anymore. "Thought you were going to meet the pissant during break," he said.

"You are seriously an asswipe." But I heaved a sigh, feeling torn. "This is important," I said, even though my brain filled up again with lips and hands and cupcakes and other wonderful things.

This time Casey was silent for much longer.

"We'll leave early," I said, taking this as a yes. "Be home in time to take me to the DPS for my permit." No way was I letting him off the hook for this part. Even if we had a mystery to solve.

"We're not gonna find anything."

"You don't know that."

Another silence, not as long. After which he allowed that maybe I was right. "Bo's a guardian angel, Jenna," he said, as if I didn't know this. "No matter what else you—what else we— don't know, that's the truth of it." Then he added: "If you didn't know me like you do, you wouldn't trust me, would you? Especially the way I was before . . . Even if I was always trustworthy. You wouldn't have thought I was someone you could count on, would you?"

"You're not Bo."

"Answer the question."

I snorted, attempting to sound snotty. It didn't work.

"I'll take you to Austin," Casey said. "But we'll stop at school first so you can tell the pissant face-to-face that you've got family business to take care of. Guys like stuff like that, when you tell them face-to-face."

Was Casey a secret romantic? I would not normally have taken love advice my brother, but nothing felt normal right now. Nothing had been normal for a long time. Besides, it was a good idea, not that I would tell him I thought so. He knew the truth, anyway. I would trust him no matter what. Weed or no weed. Behaving like a nitwit or not. Always and always.

"So you think he's a good guy, then? Ryan?"

"Don't push it."

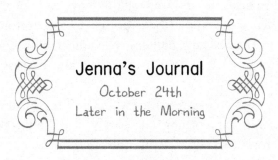

I was in high spirits by the time we chugged up to Spring Creek High. In spite of my nightmare (if that's what it was). In spite of not sleeping. In spite of ditching my boyfriend. (My boyfriend! I could say that!) We were finally DOING SOMETHING. It might not be the right thing, but it was SOMETHING. I knew down deep that Casey wouldn't have agreed to this Austin road trip unless he felt it was important or possible. Or that it might make Management see the error of their ways.

I don't know why I was so convinced about this. But I was.

Wishful thinking, maybe. Still, every angel player in my weird little world was either hiding something or worried about something or sad about something or all three. Getting to the source of where this whole thing had started felt IMPORTANT—the chain of events that led from Amber's murder to Bo showing her the ropes to Amber pulling me and Casey from our wreck and everything that had happened since.

What I tried *not* to think about: why me?

If I hadn't had a seizure that day last year, Casey wouldn't have had to drive me and we wouldn't have had the accident. Except then we wouldn't have gotten to the bottom—sort of—of why the bad guys had destroyed our family. Of course Dad might have left us anyway, I realize now. Honestly, it all made my head hurt.

"Don't take your sweet time about it," my brother said. It was 6:53 in the morning, sun barely rising in the sky. The plan was for me to talk to Ryan, then race out before the first bell rang so no one caught me cutting class.

Casey would stay in the Merc. He'd be missing school, too, but that was how it was these days. He was passing everything now, but just barely except for the repeat of Teen Leadership and his science class, which was Forensics. I'd nosed around those college websites he'd bookmarked, just to see what he was up to. But I hadn't been sure until I overheard him a few months ago with his friend Dave, talking about how forensic scientists solve crimes. How it's pathology and DNA and trace evidence and even odontology, which he told Dave meant forensic dentistry. And how maybe that's what he might want to do, be a cop or a detective.

Of course Dave had jerked around about it, saying how Casey might ought to be taking more chemistry so he could make a good drug dealer, which in Dave's opinion he would not because he was too soft. Casey stopped hanging around with Dave after that. As Casey put it, it was a choice of either avoiding him or punching him in the face. Good riddance, as far as I was concerned. Soon after, Dave vanished in a cloud of weed smoke and went to live with his parents again. The last time we'd heard about him was when his grandma, Mamaw Nell, called to say we could keep the Merc. She no

longer needed it, now that she had bought some fancy sports car with her slot machine winnings.

The point was: even as an A-word my brother wanted something real. Something legitimate. Something other than what he was. Of course that was impossible, right?

I shoved those thoughts from my brain as I rushed in to find Ryan.

He was standing by his locker. He looked beautiful and perfect. His buzzed-but- growing hair stuck up in a maybe random and maybe on-purpose-but-nice way.

I wondered how I looked after not sleeping. I was wearing my #76 mustang necklace and my regular jeans and double T-shirts—dark and light blue, the light one underneath, hanging a little longer than the dark. I'd swiped on purple shadow again and the berry lip gloss and almost poked my eye out between the pointy liner brush and the mascara wand, but it was all on there and not too gloppy, either. My hair was in a medium-length French braid. My cowgirl boots added the finishing flair.

It must have looked decent because Ryan's eyes lit up when he saw me.

He smelled like Ax again, a little too much this morning. I figured there was no polite way to tell him this so I pretended not to notice. What I did notice: he kissed me on the lips—just a quick peck—before I could even tell him what I had to say. I stopped noticing the Ax. Funny how that worked. Funny how dumb conversation can be, too.

Me: "Hi."

Ryan: "Hi."

Me: "I'm not going to be here today."

Ryan: "You're not?" (Here he looked confused, not that I blamed him since I was standing there.)

Me: "My, um, dad couldn't come home from Austin so Casey is taking me to have lunch with him."

Ryan: "Oh. We have a bio quiz, right?"

We were in the same class. My stomach got knotty. We'd been going out for like a day and here I was, lying to him.

Me: "Yeah. But . . ."

We looked at each other. I scuffed my boots on the floor.

Ryan: "Family's tricky sometimes." He twitched his lips like he was pondering. "You do what you have to do. I've got practice till late but after that. You call. I'll answer."

This made me happy and nervous all at once, but I said, "Okay." Then added, "That would be great." Which sounded lame, but I guess it was enough because he tapped a finger on the mustang necklace with his number on it —which had been inside my shirt and now was somehow not—and then grinned the cutest grin.

My pulse zinged. "Maggie gave it to me," I said. "She . . . well, she's Maggie. You know."

Did that even make sense to him? My face felt warm. I hadn't meant for him to see the necklace. Like Mags said, I didn't want him to think I was being a stalker or whatever.

"Cool," Ryan said. He nodded, like a chin exclamation point. People were coming and going and the hall was packed, but I barely felt or saw them.

My heart was beating up a storm and then it beat even faster because he said, "You can wear that to the bonfire. At least I'll have one fan who's not my dad." He looked modest when he said it. But we both knew that he was a freshman on varsity and that he could have a swelled head about that if he wanted to. I liked that he didn't seem to want to. I liked almost everything that he'd done or said in the last minute. More than liked.

Still, I said, "So you're asking me to go? Cause I might have other plans, you know." I glanced into the air, like I couldn't care less. When I glanced back, he was frowning.

"Do you?" His eyes were wide and he was fidgeting.

I said, "I'll be there."

Maybe I'd said it a little too quickly. But there was no question. For a second I thought we might kiss again, but we didn't. Which was a shame for obvious reasons, but also if I'd been kissing him then maybe I'd have closed my eyes and not seen stupid Lanie Phelps chatting up Donny Sneed over by the library.

He was wearing his letter jacket with all his football play-off patches from last year, leaning against the glass wall and looking pleased with himself. Lanie was smiling and gesturing, her hands fluttering around like pale little birds. She must have sensed me looking because she glanced over and, after a few awkward seconds, she waved. I waved back, mostly out of obligation. Here was another problem with Lanie Phelps: She seemed to believe that I could somehow help put her and my brother back together again. And that maybe I wanted to. Which I *did not*. Even if I had once overheard her tell Casey that he was what people called a diamond in a rough. That no matter what people thought *she* knew he would be someone special someday. *Was* special, in fact.

Well, if only she knew, right?

I didn't have time to stew over it because I needed to hustle out before I ran into Maggie. At least I could lie to her in a text and not face-to-face.

I told Ryan goodbye and ran back to the entrance, pounding past Principal Baker's office, where I heard a lot of giggling. Girlish giggling. So I paused.

And then I about fell to the floor with apoplexy—which

for the vocabulary challenged means a stroke—because there, in Principal Baker's office, was Bo Shivers.

BO WAS WEARING khakis and a button-down and expensive looking shoes. He was talking to Principal Baker and a gaggle of junior and senior girls who couldn't take their eyes off him. (Bo, that is. Not Principal Baker, who used to coach football and still wore Sansabelt slacks even with his sport coat, which was doing nobody a favor in the fashion department.) Goosebumps prickled my arms so hard it hurt. I sucked in a steadying breath and burst into the office.

Here is the short version of what happened next:

Principal Baker looked annoyed, like adults do when ninth graders interrupt them. (My personal opinion was that anyone who didn't like teenagers probably shouldn't be working in the public school system, but that horse had left the barn a long time ago.) Then he recovered and introduced me. "This is Mr. Shivers. He's going to be the new ninth grade Pre-AP World History teacher."

Then I asked what had become of that nice Mrs. Parnell, who had a fondness for map lessons and an unfortunate upper arm jiggle when she wrote on the board. I was informed that she had taken a sudden leave of absence due to family matters, and also informed that I shouldn't ask personal questions, but Principal Baker would make an exception since he was glad I cared. Then Baker told me and the cheerleaders to go to class, but of course I kept standing there, glaring at Bo, who said, "Nice to meet you. Jenna, is it?"

I forced myself to keep my boots on the ground and not smacked against his shins. Bo patted Mr. Baker on the shoulder and said some nonsense about how I looked like a good student and if Baker didn't mind, he'd like to chat me up

about how class had been going. Get a student's perspective. My brain was whirling on what to do next. Then who should appear in the front foyer but my brother, looking from me to Bo and back again like a wild man, his mouthing opening and closing like he couldn't find the right words. For which I didn't blame him.

The rest of our conversation—once we managed to be just the three of us standing outside the front door—went like this:

Casey: "What the hell are you doing here, Bo?"

Me: "He's my new World History teacher."

Bo: "Get yourself under control. If Management wanted your input on this, they'd have asked you."

Me (because seriously?): "Management wants you to quit your college job so you can teach me what color map pencils to use?"

Bo: "Map pencils?"

Casey: "I don't need you minding my business. I don't need you in my sister's business."

Bo: "Something's coming. You can't be everywhere at once. I'm sure that isn't a surprise to you. Or perhaps you've been too occupied trying to find answers for something that doesn't need answering. There is nothing new to learn and nothing new to see. So you can go park your car where it belongs and come on in."

Casey: "You were there when she came back. You must know what happened to her. I think if you won't say, it must be something with power connected to it. That's what your big thing is, right? Follow the power. Way I figure it, you must believe there's something in it for you if you keep quiet. But she deserves to know."

Bo: "You think you know what's best for her, Mr. Samuels?"

Casey: "Yeah. And Mr. Samuels is my deadbeat father. You're talking to me."

Bo: "Some things are better left alone. I've got more experience on this. Trust me. Things I've seen—"

Casey: "You're old. I get it. Here's what you need to get: My sister wants to go to Austin. That's where I'm taking her. This is now a family matter. And *you* are not our family."

After that, Bo held Casey's gaze so long it made me squirm. But he didn't push matters, which surprised me. Bo didn't strike me as the giving-in type—more the 'let's be a jackass to piss off Casey type.' Then again, Casey had been moping around so much, I wouldn't have figured him for taking a stand. Or for calling out our dad for what he was now.

"Truth's a good thing," I added, hoping to break the tension.

It hung there between us with the other lies we'd all told.

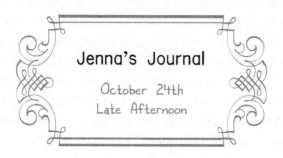

Jenna's Journal

October 24th
Late Afternoon

We drove the three hours to Austin, stopping once to pee and buy kolaches at Amber's favorite place on 290. This was my idea: a good omen, I figured. But they were out of regular sausage and just had the jalapeno variety and only the prune filling among the fruit ones. This did not bode well. We passed on the prune—for obvious reasons—splitting a jalapeno sausage one, and choked it down with ice tea.

In Austin, we stomped around the UT campus until we found the library. Here we researched for any articles that might not be on the general Internet but mentioned the events of the robbery, that day when Amber didn't exactly bite the dust. There was a total of one, from the *Daily Texan*. And there was one quote, from one of her bio professors. When we went to find him, we discovered that he had retired, moved to Bozeman, Montana, where he lived until last year when he had died of a heart attack. So we couldn't ask him if she'd had any enemies or whatever CSI-type of question I had in mind.

After that dead end, we went to St. David's Medical Center where Amber had trained as an EMT. More of the same: we convinced the lady at the ER desk to ask around, saying we were Amber's brother and sister and that we were planning a surprise birthday party for her and did anyone who'd worked with her there want to do a video birthday message. (Here I held up my cell as evidence that we could actually film). One ER nurse remembered Amber. She sang "Happy Birthday to you," into my cell and then said Amber had been a natural at EMT and how was med school going, to which we replied, great, leaving out any other details since there weren't any.

"She still with her boyfriend?" the nurse asked.

We told her no, they'd broken up.

"Shame," the nurse said. "He was always bringing her gifts." And that was all she had for us.

THE ONLY THING left was to nose around the apartment building where Amber and Terry had lived. We hiked the mile from campus, finding the street off Guadalupe with no problem. But it reminded of the last time we were in Austin, looking for Dad. We'd found him at Taco Taco Taco. Renfroe had drugged his memory, but he'd remembered most of his old life by then. Except he still hadn't come home.

I told myself: *Jenna Samuels, do not take this as a sign. Think about something else.* So I thought about tacos.

"I'm hungry," I told Casey.

"You're the one who wanted to do this."

"Yeah. Maybe we can go to Torchy's after?" (Torchy's has the best brisket and avocado tacos in the universe.)

"We'll find something, Jenna. We will."

I wanted to agree with him. I had figured we were experts after last year and the whole Renfroe/Manny mystery. But

now I was thinking we were amateurs. If there was access to all those convenient TV mystery clues like DNA and scientists who could figure out that it was Colonel Mustard in the library with the noose or whatever, even angels couldn't get there.

The manager of the apartment complex had been there five years ago, at least—which did not say much for his upward job mobility but that was the recession for you. He was a stocky guy with a droopy mustache and a belly that lapped over his belt.

"I remember Amber Velasco," he said. "Short and blonde, right?"

My heart sank again, but then he said, "Oh snap!" like a sixteen-year-old girl and amended: "No. She was the tall girl. The EMT who lived with that lab geek."

"That's the one," I said. "She's an EMT in Houston now. Spoke at our school about her job and mentioned how she'd gotten EMT care herself when her apartment was robbed. We're doing a piece in the school paper on home safety. She said, um, that she remembered you." Here I stopped, since he had not told us his name and was not wearing an ID badge.

He beamed, mouth turning up under that droopy mustache. "She remembered me? Carl Whatley?"

"Yup," Casey chimed in. "She said a lot about you, Carl."

Carl warmed up then, telling us that the "lab geek"—I assumed it was Terry, although he didn't seem to know his name—called the front office hollering about shoddy security in the parking lot. How could someone have broken in and robbed the place? His girlfriend was all traumatized and no way was he letting them keep his security deposit and wasn't it good that he had his laptop with him. He was an important guy at the lab, he'd told Carl. He was about to have some scientific breakthrough. He didn't have time to deal with a traumatized girlfriend.

"Her boyfriend was working at a lab?" I asked, not sure who I was directing it to. "I thought he was a student, like Amber." And probably a big bragger to boot.

Carl allowed that maybe he got that part wrong. But what he did remember was that Amber moved out the very next day. He saw her with suitcases and a backpack and never saw her again. He seemed eager to know what had happened to her. That made three of us. Carl could yak all he wanted, but we weren't learning anything new.

"Can't you use your Spidey sense?" I whispered to Casey.

"Tried to," he whispered back. "I got nothing. 'Cept he had the hots for Amber."

I didn't need an angel Spidey sense to tell me that.

We bid Carl adios and went to Torchy's—where we ran smack into our father, standing outside and jabbering on his cell phone.

MY FIRST THOUGHT: I should have known better. It wasn't a coincidence; it was a foregone conclusion. (Hindsight maybe the worst thing ever, second place only to unanswerable questions involving angels.) Of course Dad would come to Torchy's for lunch. He was the one who'd introduced me to the brisket and avocado tacos in the first place, when I was a kid. The guy was pretty freaking predictable, except when it came to anything that involved his own family.

"I'll see you tomorrow, Olivia," he said to whoever he was talking to, Olivia not being our mother or a name with which I was familiar at all.

Well.

Here is the thing about parents—at least this parent—who

get caught looking like they are perfectly content living a new life. A life that doesn't involve the people from their old life. Yes, even including the ones who went through hell (or in my brother's case, Heaven) and back to find him in the first place.

Here's the thing: they go on the offensive pretty damn fast.

First came the wide eyes. Then the fake smile. Then the horror. Our initial angry small talk lasted like three seconds, punctuated by my brother's, "Who the hell is Olivia?" After which Dad speed-dialed Mom and said, "Holly, do you know your children are in Austin?" After which, Casey got in his face, but I'll leave that part out because our family situation has been well-established and does not need more sad elaboration.

"Maybe Manny's guys are drugging him again," I said to Casey once we'd parted ways with our father. I realized I sounded sort of hopeful.

"Whatever," my brother said.

Needless to say, we did not stop for brisket and avocado tacos. Or even to pee. Casey and I got back in the Merc and headed home.

WE WERE PASSING the College Station exit at Highway 6, and I was staring out the window at the sign for Texas A&M. I thought briefly about Coach Collins—he wasn't worth longer thoughts—and the Aggie football philosophy he'd encourage me to adopt last year when I was in his algebra class. All that stuff about the 12th Man and being there for each other no matter what.

"It's no big deal," Casey said out of nowhere. "Maybe Bo was right. Maybe some things are better off left alone."

"He needs to come home," I said.

"What?" Casey's brows knitted together, his eyes on the road "I was talking about Amber."

"I was talking about Dad," I snapped.

Maybe Maggie sensed the ever-shifting drama of the universe, because my cell buzzed and it was her. *Crap*. I had texted her on the way to Austin. I'd told her the same lie I'd told Ryan: Dad, lunch, road trip. "Finally!" she bellowed when I answered. "Do you know how many times I've texted you?"

"Yes."

"Argh! Well listen. We have a new history teacher."

I sighed. "Oh?"

She filled me in on what I already knew, except she left out the guardian angel with a death wish part.

"His name is Mr. Shivers, but he told us to call him Bo," she said. "Said he's used to teaching college and that's how he was going to treat us."

"Awesome."

"You'll like him, Jenna."

Maggie then rattled on about how Bo had lectured to them about industrial development, and how the Houston Med Center was growing so much, especially now since foreign heads of state came there for their cancer treatments and check-ups. (Which didn't say much about the health care system in those wealthy oil countries and said better stuff about ours, not that either of us would probably ever admit it.) And all her Med Center talk started reminding me of Renfroe and Oak View Convalescent, and how Bo had recently reminded me that Oak View was up and running again and owned by some conglomerate.

Mostly her rambling reminded me that I couldn't care less

about any of this stuff. Nothing in my life was the same as it used to be. If heads of state wanted to trust the Houston medical community with their internal well-being, that was their own damn business.

I told Mags as much and hung up.

Jenna's Journal

October 24th
Later That Night

Mom's Kia was in the driveway when we pulled up. But the house was quiet when we walked in. My pulse zipped faster because it was about an hour too early for her to be home and if I'd been a gambling girl I'd bet that Dad's phone call had not done good things for her happiness quotient.

Sure enough, she was lying on her bed with the comforter, the TV blaring one of the Housewives shows, her eyes closed. Not that I blamed her. Looking too long at all that plastic surgery could make anyone want to screw their lids shut.

"You cut school," Mom croaked. "I do not need this kind of behavior from you two. I absolutely do not."

"Sorry," I told her. I actually was, although not for the reason she thought.

"I'll make chicken," my brother said.

"You don't cook," Mom said.

"Sure I do."

"He makes breakfast tacos," I said. "Remember?"

I figured Mom would lecture us some more, but all she

said was, "No, but I guess we both need to have faith in your brother. Y'all call me when it's ready. Close the door on your way out, please."

We left her with the Housewife ladies hollering. They were an excitable bunch. I figured I'd let Casey put his money where his mouth was about the cooking and hole up in my room to call Ryan—but we hadn't even made it to the kitchen when the front bell rang.

There was Amber Velasco in her EMT outfit, hands on hips.

"What the hell have you two been up to?" She pushed by me into the house, slamming the door behind her.

"Hello to you, too," Casey said.

"You recover from that hangover?" I asked, and she gave me the stink eye. I supposed I deserved it. A little.

"Bo told you?" Casey asked, shaking his head.

Amber's blue eyes flashed darker, a flush rising fast and deep in her cheeks. "You had no right," she said.

"But—" I began.

"No." Amber held up her hand. "What happened to me is my business.

Not yours. I'm going to say this once, and I don't want to say it again. I'm dead. I'm an angel. Nothing is going to change that. You're wasting your time."

"We're just being proactive," my brother whispered, glancing back towards my mother's bedroom door. "Better than sitting around and—"

"Leave it be," Amber said tightly. "Finding this out isn't gonna make you a hero, if that's what you two think. Leave. It. Be."

The front door opened again.

Bo Shivers strode in. I almost smiled. I should have expected it.

He was wearing black slacks and a grey button-down. His hair was ruffled just the right amount at the neck. His nails looked buffed and his wrist and hand scars looked faded, which was confusing because scars don't change like that overnight. At least on regular people. He smelled manly—not like Ax, but something muskier.

"Looks like I almost missed the party," he said.

Silence.

And what do you know? At this moment, Mom chose to leave reality TV, rise from her mental decline over my father's potential and current abandonment, and join us. There we were: Mom, the angel brigade, and me.

Mom nodded at Amber. She'd long ago accepted that this EMT chick wandered in-and-out of our house like she lived here. *Was* Casey keeping Mom a tiny bit forgetful still, to ease the weirdness of our lives? Without asking or consulting me or in any way discussing whether this was fair or right? But Mom's lips turned in a scowl at Bo.

"I'm Bo Shivers." He held out his hand. "Jenna's new history teacher at Spring Creek. My policy is to conduct home visits for my most promising students. I know it's unconventional, but I find that meeting my students' parents puts everyone on even ground. Those Open House nights are so rushed and impersonal, don't you think?"

My mouth gaped. Casey frowned. Amber glared.

Mom smiled. She shook hands with Bo. "Well," she said. "I only wish my son could have had you his freshman year."

"I would have loved to teach Casey," Bo announced, smiling broadly. "Perhaps I still can before he graduates. You never know. The public school system is a curious thing." He handed her a bottle of red wine. Where had *that* come from?

"You shouldn't have!" Mom exclaimed.

I turned to Casey and Amber. Casey was gaping now, too. But Amber was gazing down at the floor.

I eyeballed Casey, who frowned at Bo, who grinned at my mother, who smiled at Casey, who frowned more deeply, this time at Amber, who briefly gnawed her lower lip.

"So what's for dinner?" I asked when none of us had said anything for a few long beats. "Chicken?"

CASEY BEGAN BANGING around in the kitchen. Bo offered to help cook the meal (somehow out of our limited pantry offerings, he whipped up some sort of tangy sauce), punctuated by a lot of smiling and inappropriately flirty talk with my mom. Out of the corner of my eye, I saw our patio fire pit light up in flames even though there were no logs or matches out there that I knew of.

Casey excused himself from the cooking process at which point Amber snapped, "I've got to work a shift tonight." She gestured to her EMT outfit. "Sorry I'll have to miss the chicken. And the wine." She stomped out.

"Excuse me," I said to Bo and Mom. "I'll be right back. And maybe you should go easy on that wine."

Bo raised a brow, eyes watching darkly.

I ran down the driveway past what I assumed was Bo's vehicle—a beat-up white Ford 210 pickup that both did and didn't surprise me as his choice of transportation—and caught up with Amber just as the Camaro's engine caught and revved.

"Wait," I said.

"Gotta go, Jenna. I have to work."

I spit it right out there. "Are you afraid of Bo?"

Amber's hand was on the gear shift. "I'm late," she said. "They'll be short one if I don't show up."

"Y'all are keeping stuff from me." All of a sudden, I wasn't letting any of it go. "Y'all are scared."

She shoved the car in gear, told me to back up, and started moving—not fast, but still covering ground.

"I dreamed about you and Bo!" I shouted.

This made her press the brake and look at me more closely, but her hands stayed on the wheel. "Dreams are just dreams, Jenna."

I wanted to think she was right.

"What's wrong with knowing what happened to you?" I asked her. "Wouldn't it better?"

"No," Amber said.

She breathed in, pressing a finger to the hollow of her throat like she was checking her pulse. I saw then that she was no longer wearing Terry's necklace. This time when she told me to back up, I didn't argue. I just stood in the middle of the street, shining unnaturally in the light from the Gilroy's fake graveyard, and let her drive away.

When I heard the sound of an engine, I figured it was Amber coming back.

Instead, a dark-colored sedan careened around the corner, tires screeching. It didn't slow down. I sidestepped back up the driveway, but the car angled onto our lawn, hitting the grass so hard that the earth shook. It was coming right toward me. I stumbled, tripping over my feet, my arms pinwheeling as I tried to run, tried to right myself, tried to do something other than get squashed like a bug in front of my own house.

The last clear thought I had was this: Ryan Sloboda had asked me to Homecoming and the Bonfire and I had picked out a dress. But that was all I'd get. The universe had no plans for me to actually enjoy these things.

Bo Shivers reached me even before Casey. It was Bo's arms around me and Bo who lifted and tossed me like I weighed nothing. I landed somehow gentle as a feather on our lawn. My entire body felt warm and calm, blissful. The sedan careened away, trenching the grass and knocking over the SULLY ANDERSON fake tombstone, then sped off down the street.

My breath froze, my insides no longer euphoric. My brother threw himself at me.

"Jennajennajenna," he said over and over, his hands checking me for injury, but I knew I was fine.

"Get off me," I grunted. "I can't breathe."

"Get off her, Casey," Bo commanded.

He did.

Mom appeared in the doorway.

"Go on back inside, Mrs. Samuels," Bo called.

She did.

When I heard the roar of an engine again, my heart went crazy. But it was Amber, screeching up and running towards me without even shutting off the car.

"Jenna!" she shouted, her voice panicky-sounding, making me think of my dream.

"Did you see the car?" my brother asked sharply.

She hadn't.

Then why was she here again?

Welcome back, Spidey sense.

"She's your responsibility," Amber snapped at my brother.

"I'm fine," I said, trying not to panic.

Had someone tried to run me down? Was it a prank? Dr. Renfroe? For the first time ever, my brain admitted that I worried about him like that.

And then they were all arguing at once, their glows on a

permanent simmer—about what was significant and if this was something to worry about and were they keeping secrets from each other? Bo was looking into the air like he was scouting for fighter drones or birds and eventually I left them to it because it had been about me, but it wasn't now. I wasn't squashed. I was alive, like Mom. Hell, I was even hungry.

That sounds small and selfish and maybe it was. But once again, NOTHING was happening, not even after something HUGE. It was like when my teachers all gave me ridiculous amounts of homework and I hauled it all home in my backpack and then let it sit and hauled it back to school mostly not done. Sometimes things are so big that it's hard to break them down.

But oh how they all liked to hear themselves talk. Maybe if you're trapped being good because you're an angel, it wears on you. It sure was wearing on me.

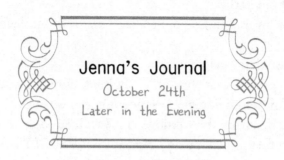

M om went back to bed before she even had a chance to eat dinner. Her cheeks bright red and a silly grin on her lips, she blamed it on the wine Bo had plied her with.

Maybe it was the wine. It didn't really matter. Bo Shivers did not want my Mom around for our little discussion about the mysterious hit-and-run attempt. And Bo Shivers tended to get his way.

Here is what Casey and Amber pondered:

Was it a random drunk?

Was it someone we knew?

Was I in danger?

Maybe that was the real reason Bo was teaching at Spring Creek High. To keep an eye me. Given what had just almost happened to me, he was doing a shit job of it.

The only thing I knew for sure? Bo was a good cook. He had not lied about that.

Amber did leave again then—insisting she really did have to work her shift, which I decided to believe since why else walk around in public wearing that butt ugly EMT get up? We were no more in the know than we had been when she'd stormed out earlier.

"Stick by Bo and your brother," she told me before she went.

"Cause that's helping."

"Things are what they are," she said. Which I guess was her way of reminding me to stay out of her business.

I watched from the window as she walked to the Camaro, stopping first to pick up and reposition the *SULLY ANDERSON* tombstone on the Gilroy's lawn. Then I stormed up to my own bedroom. When I turned the corner, Bo was waiting for me at the top of the stairs.

"Jesus!" I said, heart clattering.

"Hardly."

I narrowed my eyes.

"Your mom's TV's on loud," he said, as though that explained his stalker ways.

He rubbed a thumb over his chin. "Guarded a French chef once upon a time," he said, eyebrows waggling.

It took me a few seconds. "Like *guardian angel* guard?" I made a cheesy halo over my head with my fingers.

"Just like."

"You telling me the truth?"

"Would I lie to you, Jenna?" To his credit, he smiled. I didn't respond—obviously—and then he added, "Guarded a poet once. He drank more than I did, and the women . . ." he drifted off there, probably because my eyes got wide. "Then there was that famous inventor's wife. Really, she was the brains. But history doesn't always get it right now, does it?"

I frowned. "What inventor?"

Bo's lips pursed. "Guy named Gutenberg. Arrogant

bastard. History's filled with arrogant bastards, actually." He grinned again, teeth white and sparkly.

Was he shitting me? The printing press guy? I let it hang there because how could I tell if any of it had happened?

I started to walk around him then, because I could make up my own stories.

Out of the blue, he said, "You're a good daughter," which was possibly true but didn't make me any less pissed off at him. "It's a good thing to be. Most people do things only because they expect something in return. Another favor. Riches. The reward of heaven." He raised his eyes to the low ceiling, pressing his hands together like he was praying.

I rolled my eyes.

"Even for people they love," he went on. "But that's not you, Jenna Samuels. I think you'd do whatever it takes. No matter what."

I could have told him he was full of shit.

Instead I asked for the second time, "You lost someone, didn't you?" I felt it rolling off him somehow, this unbearable sadness. I thought of that lady in the painting I glimpsed on the wall near his bed. Was this the reason he liked to leap off balconies? Not that he wanted to move on so much as nothing mattered, because there was no one who cared if he was reckless.

My question hovered between us.

"Be careful what you wish for, little girl," Bo said. "Secrets are secrets for a reason."

Maybe it was his tone. "Screw you," I told him, turning back down the stairs. "You're not my friend and you sure as hell aren't my history teacher. I'm gonna check on my mom."

"I thought you might," Bo called after me.

When I burst into Mom's room, fists clenched at my sides,

she was watching the local news. A reporter lady was standing outside the Med Center talking about how Prime Minister of Jordan and some other heads of state—from places like Luxembourg and Bulgaria—were all coming here now for their annual physicals. And some sheik from Dubai was at MD Anderson, getting cancer treatments he couldn't get back home. Doing wonders for the Houston economy.

Just like Bo had talked about in the history class I'd missed.

Mom struggled to sit up. She blinked at me with glassy, bloodshot eyes. "Is everything all right, Jenna? You look pale."

"Want some chicken, Mom?" I heard myself ask.

"Sure, sweetie," she said. She slumped back down. "I should probably eat something, shouldn't I?"

When I went back upstairs, Bo was long gone and my brother was who knows where again. I called Maggie. I wanted to talk more about Bo's history class lecture, but she wanted to know if she should bite the bullet and ask Billy Compton to Homecoming. He played alto sax in the Spring Creek marching band. Like Ryan, he was somewhat socially awkward. That last part didn't surprise me: anyone who willingly wore a furry hat in one hundred degree Texas weather so he could march sideways while playing the theme from *Star Wars* had to have issues.

"He makes my pulse do this *thing*," Maggie said, sounding breathy. "So f-ing cute." She'd kept an eye on him at the football game—mostly his lips on that sax.

I told her I agreed, although in truth he was skinny as a beanpole, but you never knew with guys. One growth spurt and he could fill out nicely.

We hung up and I finished my homework. But all I could think was that I still didn't have my learner's permit and that if something was going to break with all these mysteries that were piling up in A-word land, then I was going to have to take matters into my own hands. Which was when I realized that there was only one person who might know the truth. One living person, that is. Terry McClain. Amber's Terry.

I could even call him. Would I call him?

Yes. No. Maybe.

He'd be traumatized by the night of the break-in, though. Maybe it wouldn't be fair to dredge up all those painful memories. On the other hand, he was smart and analytical. A lab guy. Head of stuff at Texicon now. So it stood to reason he'd want to find the attacker as much as I did, right? Geeks like him didn't like unanswered questions. Maybe that's even why he'd let Amber go, because she'd had no interest in pursuing the case. (Had he known she was dead, he might think differently, of course.) But I had to be subtle.

I picked up my phone, trying to remember his number from when he'd called Amber.

I pressed what I thought it should be. Some guy answered. Not Terry.

Tried another combination. A lady this time.

Why was I even doing this? Third attempt. No answer, not even a voice mail.

I'd give it one more chance. I pressed in the numbers. The call connected.

"Terry McClain."

My pulse did a wild hurdle.

"Terry!" Only then did I realize that I had no earthly idea what I was going to say. "Hi! This is Amber's friend Jenna Samuels. You know—the girl who was with her when we stopped at your house and drank coffee from your new K-cup machine?"

"Um, yeah?"

It didn't go much better from there.

"Well, you know how Casey's training to be an EMT, right?" I began, my armpits sweating up a storm because that particular cover story began and ended with that sentence.

"Yeah? Is Amber with you?" He sounded hopeful and also something I couldn't quite identify—nervous, maybe? It was hard to tell and that made me sweat some more.

Panicked, I launched into the same story we'd used in Austin with that guy Carl Whatley—the building manager—I was writing a story for the school paper for history on the growing crime problem and home safety.

"Amber says you might remember more than she does," I fibbed. I waited for him to start rattling on. Instead, he was silent. Probably wondering what the hell this had to do with Casey becoming an EMT. Me, too.

"You were out that night, right?" I asked, hoping to encourage him so I could stop yammering.

"What of it?" he said, and the sharp tone of his voice stopped me in my tracks. "I was studying in the library. Where I always study. I came home. We'd been robbed. But you know that already or you wouldn't have called."

Which was true.

Click.

"Hello?"

He'd hung up. I sat there with my phone in my hand. As has been well established, I was not an expert on guys. But I knew guilty when I heard it. A thought dawned on me. Maybe he hadn't been at the library. Maybe he'd been cheating on her. And maybe, five years later, he'd realized the error of his ways and wanted Amber back. He'd gone so far as to get her that necklace. And here I was, a stupid teenager from out of nowhere, about to blow everything. Either way, this was another dead end.

When my phone buzzed and vibrated again, I hoped I could apologize. Maybe Terry wasn't a brilliant douchebag with bad phone manners. Maybe he'd remembered something. But when I glanced at the caller ID, I forgot all about Terry.

"Hey, Ryan," I said, trying to sound casual and cheery. I thought 'hey' accomplished this more than 'hi.'

"Hey Jenna," he said back. "How was Austin?"

"Not bad."

"How's your dad?"

Where was this going? "Fine. Well, yeah, fine. How was practice?"

This seemed to please him, and he talked about the D-line and the coaches and how he knew Spring Creek would beat the pants off of North Ridge and that if he was lucky and kept at it, maybe Coach Collins would put him in again.

He talked and talked—about how Morris had eaten his sister's shoe this morning and boy was she steamed and how he was so excited that the Football Booster Club folks had bought a bunch of these Hulk Smash Hands that made a loud smacking sound and everyone was going to smack their Hulk Hands after touchdowns at the next game. Which of course Ryan LOVED since he was the big Avengers fan, and he liked Bruce Banner even if Iron Man, aka Tony Stark was his favorite. Good talking. The kind I wanted from a boyfriend, just shooting the shit and telling me about his day and being casual and comfortable about it.

We laughed and he told me how the varsity guys were all going to gorge on big-as-a-dinner plate chicken fried steak and mashed potatoes and gravy this week to get carbed up, and how they might have an eating contest

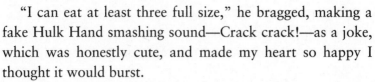

"I can eat at least three full size," he bragged, making a fake Hulk Hand smashing sound—Crack crack!—as a joke, which was honestly cute, and made my heart so happy I thought it would burst.

But here was the problem: A lot of guys, they wouldn't even notice if their girlfriend wasn't telling them about her stuff, too. They wouldn't catch on that she was encouraging them to be all chatty so she didn't have to say anything much.

"I'm sorry," he said. "You must be bored listening to all that. You shoulda told me to shut up. Tell me about Austin."

Shit. "It was fine," I said again, heart wincing.

It was the wrong thing to say.

"Oh," Ryan said. The silence was loud. I knew he was waiting for me to go on. When I didn't, he said, "Okay. Whatever. I'll see you tomorrow, okay?"

He was off the line before I could collect myself.

On the plus side, I guess Terry McClain was off the hook. Seriously. How could I blame him for being weird on the phone if I was being just as bad—to my own brand new boyfriend?

But I had to blame someone.

I tore out of my room and into Casey's. Didn't even knock. He was wearing sweats and a T-shirt and his hair was damp but still annoying perfect, and he was sitting on his bed, clicking away on his laptop. His room looked more orderly these days. Sparer, maybe, like he'd thrown stuff away—only I didn't know what. I was used to trip over dirty plates and bongs and other crap. But not lately.

"You're making Mom not worry, aren't you?" I said, without any preliminaries.

He looked up, brows knitting together, eyes curious.

"Just tell me," I said.

I took his silence as a yes.

"You suck," I told him. "You really do."

"Jenna—"

"No. It's wrong, Casey. It's just damn wrong. That's her right. To feel what she feels."

"It's safer," he began.

"No. It's easier."

"Jenna."

"Casey."

Except I knew he was right. I hated him for it, but he was.

When I got to school, Ryan Sloboda was waiting by my locker.

I was wearing regular jeans and a non-descript T-shirt and my old grey Converse. But I'd tried the khaki green eye shadow this morning and some sparkly bronzer on my cheeks and a peachy gold lip gloss that looked good with my complexion even if it did remind me a little too much of Casey's skin when he was in full angel glow.

Basically, I hadn't given up on looking good. I was feeling low, and this was the best I could do. The mustang #76 necklace was tucked into my T-shirt, but I knew if he looked, he could see the chain.

"Hey," Ryan said.

"Hey," I told him, heart tapping an SOS in my chest.

He leaned in, awkward about it, and we hugged. His chest felt warm against me. He was warm-feeling in general—not sweaty warm, but alive warm. Or maybe I noticed because I spent so much time with not-exactly-alive people. I thought of something to say, something not awkward. The seconds ticked past.

He looked at me. "I thought about it last night. I wouldn't push a guy friend to tell me stuff he didn't want to tell me. So I shouldn't push you, either. You've been through heavy shit, Jenna, you know? Your dad and your car accident and your mom being sick . . . I know it's not the same, but when my Grandpa Dale passed real sudden when I was eleven, I was pissed at the world. But I didn't want to talk about it. If someone asked how I was, I walked away. Or worse. Cause I couldn't handle thinking that someone might be feeling sorry for me or whatever."

He made his fake Hulk Smash Hands like we'd joked about last night.

My heart seemed to unfreeze. I grinned back at him, big and wide. On some level, he knew about my life— at least the parts that were public, which were more than I liked to think about. But I was so focused on the angel secret that sometimes I forgot the sum total of everything. A happy voice shouted at me: *Jenna Samuels, Ryan Sloboda is a good guy. He is the guy who hung onto that sheep during Mutton Busting and didn't let go. Stuff like that, it tells you about a guy. You like the right person. You made the right choice.*

"I get it," Ryan said then. "I really do. You went with your brother. That's cool."

The warning bell rang then, but we stood at my locker for a few more seconds, just looking at each other.

"I found a dress," I told him, figuring this would be the subtle way to check if we were still on for Homecoming. "It's a nice one." Of course somehow I'd have to get to the mall to actually buy it, but he didn't need to hear that part.

It worked: He told me he would wear his church suit and

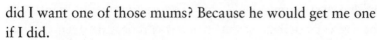

did I want one of those mums? Because he would get me one if I did.

"Doesn't have to be big," I told him.

He nodded, looking relieved.

We both knew we weren't talking ordinary corsages. The whole mum thing was an underground-cheerleader-moms-with-hot-glue-gun-skills business here in Texas. (Mum is short for chrysanthemum, for those of you who aren't local.) Even the grocery stores got in on it. The mums weren't real: You bought a huge fake white flower, hot-glued it to a cardboard backing with a big old ribbon in the school colors and then added stuff. Candy and little charms and sometimes even stuffed animals and bulbs that lit up and occasionally cow bells, which I felt was sexist, but who would ask me?

Casey's freshman year, I'd helped him make one for Lanie. We glued on a full size teddy bear with a sweater sporting his football number. The damn thing had been so heavy that Lanie had to carry it around on a hanger. But Casey said she loved it, which flummoxed me. I was not a girl who wanted a fake mum so huge that I had to drape it around my neck like a Homecoming noose.

Ryan agreed about mum size. The second warning bell rang. When we parted ways I was happy, as in really truly happy in a way I hadn't been for a long time, for about three seconds—until I spotted Lanie Phelps in the Commons Area, batting her eyelashes at Donny Sneed. Which even then I might have ignored, except my brother chose that moment to walk by. I still never quite knew when and if he'd show up for school. Often we'd arrive together, park, and then by the end of the day, I'd realize he'd gone off somewhere.

But here he was, front and center.

I knew that Lanie didn't understand what was going on

with Casey—how could she? The guy suddenly wanted to be a great Forensic scientist but was repeating Teen Leadership. Who failed a class where the big project was taking a paper lunch sack, writing your name on it in marker, and filling it with things that represented your life goals? After which everybody was required to clap and give you Positive Affirmations and then celebrate by going to the ropes course and making a circle of trust? Of course it's not like we could tell her that he was an angel now and high school diplomas weren't exactly required.

More confusing from her perspective, *Casey* had broken up with *her*.

It's true; I would never be a Lanie Phelps fan. But still. Maybe it was my romance-addled Hulk Smash Hand state. It was hard to watch.

I held my breath.

Lanie left Donny Sneed in mid-sentence. She trotted over to Casey. I couldn't help but shake my head. *Idiot.*

"I thought about you last night," Lanie told him. "That *Stay* song was on the radio while a bunch of us were driving to Sonic." Here she paused like she had imparted something earth-shattering. Across the Commons, Donny Sneed was frowning. I would frown, too.

"You eat a burger?" my brother asked, trying to smile.

Lanie goofy-grinned back at him. "Course I did. Double cheese with bacon and fries. And—"

"And extra mustard and a hot fudge sundae and a Diet Coke," my brother finished.

They both laughed.

"God, you can eat," he added, sounding like this was the most wonderful thing ever.

"But it was a diet drink," Lanie said, smiling more softly now.

"Of course," my brother said.

You didn't have to drop a house on me to make me understand that they were somehow talking in flirt-code. Would Ryan and I ever get to that point? Without the secretly dying and breaking up stuff? This is what I was pondering while Lanie and Casey googly-eyed each other and nattered on about double-cheeseburgers. Even lunkheaded Donny Sneed (poor guy) must have seen that really they were saying, "I miss you. I love you. I want to watch you eat hot fudge and kiss it off your lips."

"Take a picture," said a deep voice beside me. "It'll last longer."

I whipped my head around and found myself standing next to Bo Shivers. Right: I had almost—only almost—forgotten. I was supposed to be going to World History. Yes, where he was now my teacher. I also realized that I wasn't the only one staring at Casey and Lanie. A crowd had gathered.

"Why don't you push her off the roof, Samuels?" someone hooted. "Then you can skydive after her."

I cringed.

My brother's face went stony. Lanie Phelps blushed. Her eyes wandered, maybe searching for Donny Sneed, but he was long gone.

Mostly people didn't remember what the news had called our 'Skydiving Stunt at the Galleria Last Christmas.' But they hadn't exactly forgotten, either, even if the rumor mill had died down. Which in some ways surprised me since this was Texas. We regularly cornered the market on crazy. It was legal here to shoot feral hogs from helicopters. A little skydiving stunt shouldn't get everyone out of whack. But that was high school for you, Texas or not.

Bo Shivers cleared his throat.

"Miss Samuels," he said. "I believe we are both late for 1st period."

I HAD TO hand it to Bo Shivers: he knew how to get a class's attention.

Right off the bat, he started in about how fast food has given Americans a "throw-away mentality" because everything comes quick and wrapped in paper and inside Styrofoam. He informed us that this has devalued our sense of everything. He also wisecracked about how his own teaching philosophy might also be called "throw-away mentality," at least as far as substandard student work. The entire room burst out laughing, except me. Mags was hanging on his every word, which just made me pissier.

"But seriously??" Maggie interjected when the laughter died down. She sat up straight in her challenge-the-teacher posture. "Just because I eat a Whataburger doesn't mean I'm not environmentally aware."

That got everyone buzzing. Lots of 'yeahs' and 'Do you hate Taco Bell, Mr. Shivers, because that's just un-American' and 'Are you like from New York or somewhere?' I was glad. Bo had no business here. At least my best friend could call him on it, since she had no idea who or what he was.

Bo just smiled. The classroom door opened, silencing the growing tide of questions. One of the cafeteria ladies trudged in wheeling a huge cart with plate after plate of green chili cheese burritos all individually wrapped in tin foil, with just the tops showing so you could tell what it was.

Well, that got everyone buzzing again.

And what did Bo Shivers do? He picked up a burrito, unwrapped it, and scarfed it down.

Then he did it again.

Then he did it three more times until he'd eaten five. Five green chili cheese burritos. He didn't even burp. He stood there, wiping his lips with a brown paper napkin, looking no worse for wear, all flat-abbed and angel-perfect. Except of course for those scars on his wrists which were mostly covered by his long-sleeved button-down. But I knew they were there.

"What the F!?" Maggie said. Like always, that's exactly how she said it—just the letter 'F.' But around us, I heard the full word. Including from my own mouth. It was all I could do not to march up there and sock Bo Shivers in his full-of-burritos stomach.

"So," Bo said, giving his mouth one last blot, and ignoring the not-so-whispered f-bombs. "Get out a piece of paper. I want you to write about this."

Here there were loud groans from the class.

"Do you value burritos more or less when you can get them by the dozen twenty-four hours a day? Does it influence your behavior? Does it have an effect on the economy? On our society? On civil discourse? And if you don't know what that means, then look it up."

The cafeteria lady wheeled the empty cart back into the hallway. Bo closed the door. Sat down in his teacher chair. Watched us. Everyone kept talking. I didn't know what was flummoxing me more. That Bo Shivers had consumed five cafeteria burritos in under a minute and wasn't doubled over in pain or that he actually expected everyone to do the writing assignment. Bo's gaze shifted from some invisible point on the back wall to me.

He stood. Walked toward the door. Held my gaze, gesturing for me to follow.

I didn't move.

He gestured again. "Miss Samuels," he said, holding open the door.

"Jenna," Mags whispered. "He means you."

I wanted to hug her and punch her.

I knew I couldn't refuse. I trudged after him. We stood in the hall, him watching the class through the little window on the door.

"If you're trying to kill yourself with cafeteria food, go over to Ima Hogg. Those lunch ladies are pretty shifty-eyed. Death by burrito. Isn't that beneath you? And by the way, no one is going to do your stupid assignment. Okay, Maggie will. But she'll be sarcastic. Trust me."

"Opinion duly noted," Bo said.

"Why are you here? And don't say to teach my history class."

Bo's dark eyes glittered in the buzzing glow of the non-environmentally friendly fluorescent fixtures above our heads. "I'm starting to think your brother and Amber need assistance," he said after a few beats. "As we both know, you are quite the handful."

With that, he opened the classrom door again and held it for me. When he didn't say anything else, I took the cue. I sauntered in, looking casual and upbeat, flopped down at my desk, and pretended to write my essay.

Sometimes what people don't say is louder than what they do.

Here is what was sinking in even if I didn't want it to: *My brother wasn't lying.* Casey had died saving me. Amber had helped save me, too. Bo had plucked me from the path of an oncoming car. Three angels had all kept me from biting the dust. Why was I cursed? What was up with that?

But mostly I thought: what in the world would they be saving me for?

M aybe I was only imagining that Bo meant something significant. If Casey hadn't said anything the other night, I would have figured Bo was just talking out of his hind end because that's what he liked to do. Chaos was his favorite pastime. He'd bragged so himself. (Then again, he was a liar, but that just proved my point.) He was stuck here, so dragging everyone else into his mess made him feel superior. He had saved me, but so what? He was an angel. He *had* to do good deeds. Just like Casey. Amber, too.

Best not to think about it. And for the rest of the day, I kind of pulled the not-thinking off.

Maggie's dad drove me home from school since Casey had to go right to his shift at BJ's. He promised that Wednesday— today—would be the day we'd finally get to the DMV. When we came back tonight for the Bonfire, I could take the wheel with him in the passenger seat. Finally!

Also, Maggie's dad took us to the mall, and she and I bought our high-low dresses. There was a sale so I had enough cash left on my gift card to snag a pair of sparkly silver stiletto heels. I practiced hobbling around the store in them—feeling like an idiot mostly—but they made my legs look long and maybe even sexy, although that was probably a stretch. As long as Ryan liked them.

After that, it was home and dinner and homework. Nothing strange or unusual. Talking on the phone to Ryan. Texting Mags. Listening to Casey listen to bad music too loudly from behind his closed door.

Bo and Amber did not come over. Mom seemed cheery and neither artificially calm or too upset, just right in the middle like a normal mom. Dad did not attempt to communicate, clearly thrilled to be back in Olivia-land. I could almost pretend.

And then it was today.

WE HAD A substitute in World History, and I decided to believe this was a good thing. Caught Casey in the hallway after first period and asked him about it, and he looked at me neutrally and said, "That's Bo's business, I guess." I could tell he probably knew something, but before I could ask he directed me to meet him in the student parking lot as soon as the last bell rang.

Only when I got there—after assuring Maggie that I had a ride home and a hasty detour because I'd left my Spanish book in my locker—Casey was nowhere in sight.

Had he left without me? No. The Merc was sitting pretty as you please. But my brother was MIA. My stomach knotted, just a little.

I texted him. No response. Called. Nothing. We needed to move the car. The band members were trickling out of the band hall getting ready to practice their moves in the student

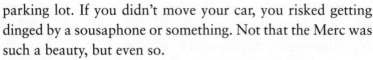

parking lot. If you didn't move your car, you risked getting dinged by a sousaphone or something. Not that the Merc was such a beauty, but even so.

When I heard my brother's voice coming from somewhere to my left, I was relieved. I whipped my head around but didn't see him. He was shouting—I couldn't make out what, but where the hell was he? Nothing over there but the practice field. The *football* practice field.

"Stay focused! " I heard him bellow. "Where's the ball?"

Shit. My stomach sank. Goosebumps rose on my skin. The tiny stomach knot expanded to a boulder. Casey had looked totally calm during that whole thing with Lanie. Not happy, obviously, but calm.

I knew that was too damn good to be true.

I flew toward the field, pressing in Amber's number. Straight to voice mail. I hung up. Maybe she was already on her way. If this (not that I knew for sure what "this" was) did not summon up that Spidey sense, nothing would. Casey was perched in the metal bleachers, about halfway up, sitting in the tangle of football-obsessed dads who came out for practices. "Don't look at your damn feet," he was hollering. "Keep your head up." Then: "You're running slow, Sneed. Get a move on."

Shit. Shit. Shit.

At least he wasn't glowing. Or maybe that should worry me. Maybe he let himself glow to remind himself of what he was. He stomped down, his feet so heavy that the metal echoed, then hopped over the last row with an easy grace. He strode, almost casual, across the black cinder track and onto the grass. Right past Coach Collins, who stopped in mid whistle-blow and grabbed my brother by the arm. On the field, practice continued. Donny Sneed kept running the ball. Only one player looked up: #76. Ryan. But only for a second.

Over on the far side, beyond the field, the cheerleaders were practicing, too. I saw Lanie Phelps stand stock-still, her pom-poms pressed against her chest.

"Casey," Coach Collins said, and I knew it was bad when I heard him use my brother's first name. "You need to leave. You are not part of this team. You're just gonna get yourself in trouble."

"Can't get in trouble," my brother told him, his voice too loud. "That's the whole point, coach. Trust me. Ask my sister. Hell, ask the new World History teacher. Mr. Bosephus Shivers. He'll tell you."

My brother wrenched his arm away and trotted onto the field, muttering, "Bosephus," which was not (as far as I knew) Bo's full name. If he'd looked drunk like Amber the other night at Wild Horses, or high, maybe I could have excused it. Or at least explained it. But I suspected he was just sad and lonely and stuck being a do-gooder for the rest of time, however long that was.

And worse, even acting like a jackass, Casey shone in a way that made my sinking stomach thump my knees. Like Bo Shivers, every attempt to make himself less than what he was now ended up the opposite. My brother couldn't destroy himself any more than Bo could.

Another coach, one I didn't know, grabbed for Casey. He ducked out of reach, flopping down on the grass. Then rolled onto his back, flapping his arms and legs.

It took me a second.

He was making a snowless equivalent of a snow angel.

I got it. This was what angry humor looked like. Bad and ugly and out-of-control. They all shared it: Bo and Amber, too. All the dead people in my life.

Casey rose then, another graceful movement, and maybe

he would have stopped too. But Donny Sneed, football tucked under his arm, loped over. My brother's hands tightened into fists.

"Son," said Bo Shivers, striding onto the field out of nowhere, but maybe I just wasn't paying attention. His voice, a full deep bass, silenced everyone else. He stood facing Casey and Donny. "I suggest you stand down and stop making a damn fool of yourself. And I suggest you do it now." He didn't say which one of them he meant, which I felt was decent of him.

I was still holding my cell and now it vibrated along with the sound of Bo's deep voice. Amber. "Bo's here," I said.

"I know," she told me, without explaining back.

I flicked my gaze to the field, trying to pick Ryan out of the pack of boys. My breath felt constricted. What kind of normal boy would keep things up with a girl dragging around so much A-word baggage that he could never understand?

Amber showed up before I could obsess too much. After that there was a bunch of hollering and bunch of people shaking their heads—including Lanie Phelps, who to her credit, looked torn about what exactly was upsetting her most.

And then there we were, on the road, the Merc left behind. Me in Amber's Camaro. Bo and Casey in Bo's truck, caravanning down the freeway towards Houston and Bo's loft.

Bo wanted a meeting. He wanted it at his place. And he wanted it now.

So much for my learner's permit. (Again.) At this rate, I'd be in college before I could learn to drive. Maybe older. I pictured myself with a cane and white hair and dentures, taking the learner's permit test.

"I need to be back for the Bonfire," I grumbled. Amber gripped the wheel, breathing deep through her nose.

I repeated myself. More than once. "Ryan expects me," I added firmly.

Amber studied me briefly, then trained her eyes on Bo's truck in front of us. "It sucks," she said. "I know that. He's nice, right? To you, I mean? That's important, Jenna. Girls always think they'll retrain a guy. Make him into something that he's not. But it never works. Not really. People are what they are. So you have to know up front. Is this the one?"

"I'm only in ninth grade," I said.

I did not say what I was thinking. Which was that I really, really liked Ryan Sloboda in a way I'd never liked a boy before and that I wanted to keep at it and see where it went. That I believed the universe was a douchebag for giving me these FEELINGS for a cute boy with spiky buzzed hair and brown eyes and a tiny dot of a freckle above his mouth and writing talent and single-minded adoration of Tony Stark and a desire to GO PLACES other than here and maybe with me. In spite of everything else that was going on, everything I couldn't explain, which he'd forgiven.

Amber's lips angled into a tight smile, but she didn't look at me.

"It'll work out," she said.

She wasn't as good at lying as she used to be. We both knew how these things went.

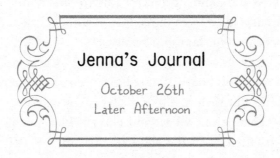

Here is what I noticed as we trooped into Bo's ridiculously fancy apartment: Two wine glasses on the grey stone kitchen counter, one with pink lipstick. And over in the bedroom area, the bed was all rumpled, the red satin sheets a tangled mess.

Eww.

"Take you from a date?" Amber asked, following my sour gaze.

"If you want to call it that," Bo said.

This was disturbing on many levels. Not the least of which was that he TAUGHT AT MY SCHOOL NOW, although this was no doubt a short-term arrangement. But why would I be surprised? Bo was beyond surprise. It was perfectly in character: cutting school during his first week on the job to do whatever it was he was doing in those red silk sheets with whomever had been drinking with him.

Someone who favored a not that attractive shade of pink lipstick. The heavy kind, not the pretty glosses in my Sephora kit.

Bo plucked a small remote from his work desk. Pointed toward the fireplace. A screen above it lowered. He clicked again, above him, and a projector turned on. I hadn't noticed it before, suspended from the ceiling. Another click and something opened on his laptop.

"You bring us here to watch a movie?" Casey asked. He sounded tired and hoarse. Must have been all that screaming on the field. But then just like that, his voice sprang back to normal. "There's a new Fast and Furious I haven't seen."

He'd been silent in the elevator ride up, not that any of us had been that chatty. Which was fine. I wasn't sure what I wanted to hear from him right now, but it didn't include snot-nosed jokes. Understanding someone's behavior does not necessarily translate into being less pissed off.

Bo said, "Sit." He gestured toward the leather couches.

I glanced briefly at that wraparound balcony.

"No worries, Miss Samuels." Bo's eyes glittered. "I have no plans to leap."

"Shame," Casey said.

Amber winced.

"Listen to me, son," Bo said, eyes darkening now. "Listen well. I am no martyr and have no need of suffering. They made me what they made me a long, long time ago. I've done my time and then some. I'm still doing it. And so will you. I get it, Casey Samuels. I understand. I feel your longings for every damn thing you will never have again. You can screw that little cheerleader—you can make her see God— but you can never love her. You can save your sister here a million times over and it's not going to change things. *They* picked you. *They* brought you back. Just like me. Just like Ms. Velasco. And all the rest of us. And we do what they tell us, by *their* rules, until *they* tell us not to. We can try to be shitheads, but

we will always fail. Always. If there's a choice, we'll pick the right side. Do the right thing."

My mouth had dropped open somewhere after the phrase "screw that little cheerleader." But here is what I realized. Casey and Amber weren't disagreeing with the last part. The angel part.

"Casey, you still toke up," I said. I wasn't sure why I even brought it up.

He sighed. "I lost my taste for it, okay?"

"No, you didn't." Even to my ears I was sounding ridiculous. I thought of his room and its new and tidy absence of drug paraphernalia. Well, shit.

"He's one of us now, darlin'," Bo said. "And he's attempting to do it the hard way."

I would have answered, but my brain was whirring in a wheel-of-doom loop. What kind of a person would still pretend to be a weed addict for his little sister? But I already knew the answer. My brother wasn't a *person* anymore.

Bo turned back to Casey. "Amber here hasn't exactly explained it all to you, has she?"

Amber's skin emitted a forbidding golden glow She was simmering inside. "You said he wasn't ready."

"I've said a lot of things. A definite error in judgment." Bo clicked the remote again. The front slide of a PowerPoint presentation appeared on the screen, one of those lame low-budget ones we have at Spring Creek. There were three words in bold.

SOMETHING IS COMING

Of course Professor Bo Shivers would have a PowerPoint.

He looked from Casey to me and then back at my brother. "You're a bit slow, son. We're not saints. Management needs us to be what we are. Bastards. Angry. Willing to throw ourselves to the lions but only so we can rip their hearts out before they can hurt someone else. If we were perfect—some Mother Teresa types, some damn Thomas Aquinas —we'd be no good to them."

Casey shook his head, his jaw tight.

"You're putting a spin on things, Bo," Amber snapped, but the glow had faded. "You're no different than Casey."

Bo just smiled. "Amber, this is for Jenna's sake. And maybe you could stand to learn something, too." He tilted his head at me, the way he did when I first met him, and his dark eyes bored into mine.

"Look around you. Your fellow humans—we're an ugly bunch. Oh we're noble now and then when it suits us. But when people talk about evil, they need to give it a name, a face, with some demon or devil." He growled, deep in his throat. "They don't see it in themselves. It never ends what we do to each other. Massacre after massacre. Men. Women. Children. Crucifixions. The Crusades. Baba Yar. Leningrad. Bergen-Belsen. The Killing Fields. Suicide bombers. Attempted hit-and-runs." Here he paused. "It never ends. Manny and Renfroe, they're just the tip of proverbial iceberg—"

"Manny and Renfroe?" I gasped. "What do you mean?"

"Pay attention," he said, and clicked the remote. Then he put his hand on my shoulder. It still hurts a little to remember, but here's what happened, in PowerPoint form:

- The second slide flashed on the screen. *FREE WILL PART I.*
- All at once, my body seized. Images rushed through my brain. A half-naked screaming boy, explosions shattering around him. A woman holding a baby, collapsing from a shot to the head. A heap of

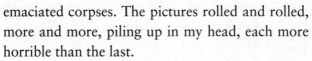

emaciated corpses. The pictures rolled and rolled, more and more, piling up in my head, each more horrible than the last.

- The third slide flashed on the screen: *FREE WILL PART II.*
- Wild bursts of color and I felt silly and giddy and dizzy. I saw Bo, wearing some colorful hippy-looking shirt and a fringed vest like you see in 60's movies and he had a glass of amber liquid in one hand and what looked to be a joint in the other.
- Somewhere in my frozen state I heard Casey and Amber shout, "Let her go!"
- There was a *FREE WILL PART III* with Mother Theresa and some ancient old man and then Martin Luther King and Gandhi and a bunch of women I didn't recognize—and I burst into tears, even though I wasn't sure why.

The next few slides were a jumble of economic flow charts and world events and drug cartels and a final thought of "good masquerading as evil but really, what was the difference?" but at that point I was too cloudy to absorb it all. When I snapped out of it, the screen was blank.

Amber and Casey had pulled Bo away from me. Everyone was breathing heavily. Bo shook my brother and Amber loose. The three angels stared at me, waiting for a question.

The only one I could manage was, "What the hell did you do in the Sixties, Bo?"

Bo apologized for putting his memories in my cranium. He rambled for a minute or two about some guy named Hunter Thompson, who was something called a "gonzo" journalist, which basically meant he made no judgments even while he put himself in the thick of things he was reporting. This seemed to include a certain amount of "experimentation" (Bo's word) with drugs like LSD. I supposed that explained how Bo's memories painted psychedelic circles in my brain.

After that, Bo explained how everyone had hated President Nixon, but that as I could see, Nixon didn't have a lock on evil or corruption. Or something like that. I was still sort of giggly from Bo's flashback. The politics escaped me. In any case, whatever was going on, it was bigger than Dr. Renfroe's poisoning of my family. And the European conglomerate that ran Oak View was probably part of it. Bo could have said just as much rather than give me a history lesson.

I was feeling a little winded. But I was ready to make nice and move on.

Casey was still full-on pissed off and in Bo's face.

"You like to hear yourself talk, don't you?" he hissed. "That's what this is, right? You talking and name-dropping and expecting us to believe it. Telling us the same old same old about something I'd see in some straight-to-video spy movie—"

"Casey," Amber said. She held up a hand. A warning.

Something dark and frosty crossed my brother's face. He kept his eyes on Bo. "I'm sorry you had to break up that shit back at school. I did it. I own it. According to you, that makes me more valuable. Well maybe it does and maybe it doesn't. But my sister needs to leave. She has a function to attend. And as I don't have my damn car, one of you will need to drive her."

I wanted to hug him. I wanted to shout hooray.

Instead, I found myself asking Bo, "If Manny and Renfroe are the tip of the iceberg, then who are the bad guys? Like, the bad guys we saw in *FREE WILL PART I*? Our family

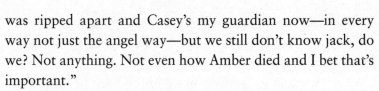

was ripped apart and Casey's my guardian now—in every way not just the angel way—but we still don't know jack, do we? Not anything. Not even how Amber died and I bet that's important."

Bo just smiled. He didn't turn away.

"You put all those images in my head, so I know you can do all sorts of things, can't you? So here's what I think. I bet you don't want Amber to know why she died. It makes no damn sense, but I think that's the truth. I know you saved me, too, but now I'm wondering if you didn't somehow make our father bump into us in Austin so we'd stop investigating. How do I know you didn't do that?"

"What would you like me to say?" Bo asked.

"I think it makes you feel like the man." Anger welled up, with images of the horrible things from that first slide. "Holding power over everybody. Over Amber." I spun to face her. "You need to stand up to him. You need to."

But Amber turned away. I felt like once I ran out of steam, we'd be where we always were. In the dark.

I turned, too, and my gaze settled briefly on one of the paintings. Then another. They were mostly his own, I realized, not just the one in the bedroom of that lady. Deep, beautiful colors. Different scenes, each of them, but in the ones I could see from here, there was always a female figure far in the background, tiny and distant, like she couldn't be easily reached. If there was time—but there wasn't—I could ponder this. Wonder about a dead man who would paint that over and over.

"Casey," Bo said. His tone was soft.

I turned, eyes flashing between Bo and my brother.

"Here's what she hasn't told you, son. This is your war. Yours. So stop feeling sorry for yourself and figure out why.

You said it yourself. I told you to follow the riches. So why aren't you doing that? Someone has tried to kill your sister. Twice. Isn't that telling you something?"

Casey made a dismissive sound in the back of his throat. "It's telling me that I need to take her and go. It's telling me she's right. You get your jollies off by manipulating us."

"Haven't you listened to a word I've said?" Bo's voice was thunderous. The loft shook. I saw—and heard—a rustling movement under the back of his shirt. Any second now, his wings would unfurl. Something inside me said that if they did, they would fill the room. My stomach knotted into a ball of concrete. "Do you know what free will is?"

"Forget free will, Bo. Fuck you." Casey turned to me, holding out a hand. "Come on, Jenna. We're going."

I didn't want to take his hand. I wanted to stay at Bo's. But what else was I going to do? Like Bo said, this was Casey's war.

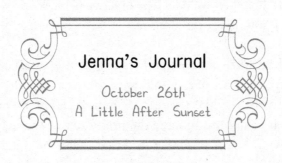

Amber caught up with us on the street while we were calling for a taxi. "I'll drive you," she said.

Bo wasn't with her, but I sensed he wasn't up there in his little sky palace twiddling his thumbs.

"Is he telling the truth?" I asked.

"I don't know," Amber said.

"He's been your boss for five damn years. How did he get those wrist scars?"

"Jenna. I really *don't know*." She sucked in a breath like she was about to say more, only she didn't. But there was something in her eyes that told me she, too, was lying. Or maybe she wasn't. Maybe . . . My head hurt from the overload.

"Whatever." My brother was looking up at the sky. "Jenna's late."

"I don't care," Amber said. "You think he's a pissant, anyway."

"Yes, you do care. And not about what I think of Jenna's boyfriend."

More frosty glares all around. (But my heart did sing a little at the word "boyfriend.") And then we did what I had wanted to do when we'd left the practice field. We drove back to school in time for the Bonfire.

LATER I WOULD believe that I was right, after all: We should have stayed at Bo's. We should have talked and hollered and cut the truth free like they do diamonds. Hack them loose from their caves and squeeze the pretty out of the ugly coal. But Bo would have probably said that that's the thing about free will. You don't always do what you need to.

I SLIPPED MY phone out to call Maggie and tell her that I was already at school. I knew she thought I was with Casey at the DMV taking my permit test.

"I won't even text you," she'd said earlier when I saw her in the hall before Spanish II. "Don't want you to freak out and fail it or something."

That only made me want to talk to her in the worst way. And that feeling grew. Now it was overpowering. I had to come clean. Tell her everything while we ate a gallon of chocolate ice cream and then let her give me one of those henna tattoos on my ankle. Or maybe somewhere more showy than that. If I could tell her, Maggie would have advice. Good advice. Best friend advice. If she believed me.

Well, that wasn't going to happen.

But there was a text from Ryan. *Are you okay? Hope you make it for Bonfire. Talk later. ~R.*

There he was again, spelling everything out fully, taking his time about it. I pictured him tapping his thumbs on the screen, making sure the message was just right for me. Was he home, maybe? Getting reading for the Bonfire, Morris

nipping at his heels? He had not run screaming (metaphorically speaking) from my brother's antics on the football field. I memorized every word after reading it four straight times. That way if it got deleted, I'd still be able to see it in my head.

"You going to stay?" I asked Casey. Amber had driven off, not saying much. What was there to say, really? Like Bo, I suspected she'd be around somewhere. But that was her business. I'd done my best. It wasn't my fault she didn't want my help.

He shrugged. "I'll be around. You just meet me at the Merc after, okay?"

We stood there looking at each other.

Then he took me by surprise and wrapped me in a hug, tight and then tighter. I wriggled my arms free and hugged him back, burying my face in his shoulder. I breathed against him, holding on until eventually it felt awkward and we let go.

"You really gave up weed?"

Casey laughed, almost a belly laugh but not quite. "Yeah. I really did." His laugh dried up. "It was easier to let you think I didn't."

I pushed him away, feeling cranky. "You think I'm a little girl still, don't you?"

"What I think is that sometimes I want things to just go back the way they were. Way back. Like to when we were little."

"So you could pick on me?"

His lips arched into a grin. "Hell, yes."

"Bo was quite the stoner back in the day," I observed. "Maybe we should introduce him to loser Dave."

Casey's smile flickered. He shrugged. "Don't think about Bo now, Jenna."

We were quiet for a while. "You'll be fine," he said. "You let Sloboda come to you, remember? He will."

I rolled my eyes.

"He's right, you know," Casey said then, looking at his feet then finally lifting his head to look at me.

"Ryan?"

Casey shook his head. "No. Bo. I think he's right, Jenna. I think he's telling the truth. He just—well, I think that's how it works. I have to get to it on my own."

My heart bumped against my ribs. "Like looking more into what happened to Amber, you mean?"

He looked up and into my eyes. "It's bigger, Jenna. That's what Bo means with his 'something-is-coming' crap. It started with Renfroe. With those memory loss drugs he developed. *Memory*, Jenna. That's big. That's what Bo's been talking about. You know what people could do with drugs like that? You could control a lot if you could control what people remembered, right? That's everything. That's what we all have. Memories."

My mouth felt dry as a bone. "But you're not a memory," I said. "You're here for *me*. Even Bo told you that. Because I was poisoned and a car almost ran me down and Dad is gone and Mom is . . . ." I swallowed over the boulder in my throat, doing my best to hold things inside. I was a tough Texan girl, but even I was not beyond crying sometimes. "You know a lot of stuff for a guy who's retaking Teen Leadership."

Casey's lips twisted into a crooked grin. "Stupid paper sack project."

"Asswipe teachers," I said, going with it.

"Douchebag principal."

I smiled at him.

"I'm going to solve this, Jenna. I know it's what I'm meant to do. And then you can be proud. And I can stop—"

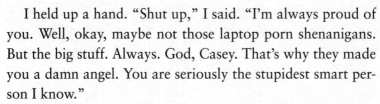

I held up a hand. "Shut up," I said. "I'm always proud of you. Well, okay, maybe not those laptop porn shenanigans. But the big stuff. Always. God, Casey. That's why they made you a damn angel. You are seriously the stupidest smart person I know."

He looked away. "Not smart," he whispered. But he held out his fist.

I turned my hand into a fist and bumped his.

"Go on." Casey gestured toward the football field. "Band's starting up. The whole shebang is about to begin. You wouldn't want to miss old Ryan waving from the football player's float would you?"

"Shut up," I said again. "He's going to be a famous screenwriter someday, did you know that?"

I hopped out of the Merc. The place was crawling with people—students and parents and teachers and people's little brothers and sisters. The parade would come down the school road and then ride into the stadium and around the cinder track. Later, after the pep rally stuff, we'd end up back on the far end of the parking lot where they piled up a bunch of wood for the bonfire. Now, the sound system was warming up. I turned to Casey and laughed because *Copperhead Road* was blaring. Same song that Amber had danced on the bar to back at Wild Horses, dragging that poor, clueless faux-cowboy up there with her.

It's before my time but I've been told/He never came back from Copperhead Road.

Casey laughed from behind the closed door and shooed me away.

Across the parking lot, Maggie was waving. She was wearing jeans and a blue Mustang Power T-shirt. I was supposed to be wearing the same thing—I'd promised her because as has been well established, Mags does not enjoy solo school spirit. I almost turned around again, but headed towards the field.

Halfway to Mags, I realized I hadn't actually said goodbye.

I t was a kick ass parade.

Someone had donated hundreds of samples of some new sports drink—*EXTRA ENERGY! Five different flavors*! Fit-looking college-age guys in matching T-shirts handed them to us from buckets as we pressed with the crowd into the stadium. I started to unscrew the cap off the tall plastic bottle.

"Those things are full of chemicals," Maggie announced, using her "my body is a temple" voice. She set hers—Sour Green Apple— on the ground and some short kid with unfortunate forehead acne picked it up.

The last thing I wanted was another fight. It was just an energy drink! And a free one at that. The really bad world stuff from Bo's PowerPoint was still roaming free in my head. Maggie needed to get over herself.

"Look," I said, pointing to the label on my Berry Surprise. "It's got vitamins. That's good, right?"

"You want another one?" one of the bucket guys asked Maggie. I took a closer look at his T-shirt. The logo over his pocket was stitched with *EXTRA ENERGY!* " and then underneath it: *Texicon.* Those Texicon folks must have buckets of money, too. Maybe one of their founders went to Spring Creek High, what with giving us free beverages along with the fancy new Jumbotron they'd donated.

Whatever. It was just a drink. That was not why we were here. Let everyone else gulp the things down. I pressed my bottle back in the guy's hand.

Maggie grinned with a little nod of approval.

"C'mon," I said, pulling her toward the stadium. I was too amped up to be thirsty anyway.

Soon we were standing along the cinder track while Ryan Sloboda—looking cute but sweaty in his football jersey—threw candy from the float straight at me. "Jenna!" he called, and my heart whirled like a top. I caught three in a row and dropped the last, then gave Mags a little frown, like: *Can I please eat this, even though it's full of chemicals?* She burst out giggling. We split the little packages of Sour Patch and Swedish Fish that I didn't even realize he knew I liked. But somehow he did.

I almost felt happy again.

Only one moment gave me a pang. The senior football players' moms' float drove by—all decked out in red boas and tiaras like prom queens, smiling and tossing Dum Dum pops and beads to the crowd. They were silly-looking that was for sure—grown women with day jobs wearing tiaras and long white gloves.

Except our Mom should be up there, I thought. If Casey was still playing, she would have been. Maybe.

Maggie elbowed me. "I almost forgot! Show me your learner's permit! Did you brother let you drive back here? Or was he all over-protective about it?"

"I, erm," I said back. The wind had changed, coming up from the Gulf, stronger and humid-feeling. Thick air. Like a storm coming maybe. I felt sticky all of a sudden, my side-swept bangs plastering to my forehead.

Mags narrowed her eyes. She twisted a strand of red plastic beads around her index finger and then untwisted it and started over. "Jenna," she said, drawing out my name. "How long are you going to go on not telling me whatever the hell it is that's going on with you? Because you know what? It's getting old. I *know* you've been through stuff. I *know*. But if you don't trust me to listen then maybe I'm going to stop asking, you know?"

Her words made my skin prickle. No matter how frantically my mind searched for the right thing to say, it came up empty. Over on the field, the football guys were lining up to do their skit. They had changed into cheerleader outfits. Donny Sneed had a blonde wig and it looked like he was aiming to mimic Lanie. (Ryan was only a freshman, even if he was on Varsity, so he was on the sidelines for this part. I admit: I was grateful.)

"You hear what I'm saying?" Mags barked.

I turned. Her eyes were serious, with something confused and hurt sitting behind them. Was this why she'd been so bossy about the Extra Energy drinks? Not because of the chemicals. But because of . . . me. I noticed now—how could I not have noticed?—that she had fixed her hair into a French braid like the one I'd been sporting the other day. Because we had planned to joke around at this thing going like two Twinkies. Best friends, dressed alike, half school-spirit/half mocking in that way we thought was funny. Maggie Boland— my backup, my bestie. My true north other than my brother.

Shit.

I glanced back at the field. The football players were prancing around in an awkward rendition of a cheerleader routine. *Copperhead Road* blared again. The opening bagpipe riffs filled the sound system and the cheerleaders joined in, wearing football jerseys with each senior's number. Nothing like some spirited cross-dressing to get the crowd all revved up. The routine gelled into the line dance, and then they were all moving together to the music. The Texicon Jumbotron flashed colors and fireworks and *EXTRA! EXTRA!EXTRA ENERGY SPIRIT!* in time to the beat.

Still it sounded mournful somehow. A chill rose up my spine.

I wondered vaguely if my brother was still in the Merc, watching Lanie wear Donny Sneed's football jersey and stomp dance with him, bending low to the beat, not realizing that the lyrics were about Vietnam and moonshine and marijuana.

"Maggie," I said. The truth bubbled up then, thick as the air, no way to swallow it back. "There's something I have to tell you about Casey. You're not going to believe it. I know that. But I swear it's true. It's a long story, so maybe now isn't best, but you're right. I need to tell you something."

Maggie took my arm. She looked me straight in the eye, curious and sympathetic and wanting to help. That was good, right? She was even ignoring Billy Compton, though the marching band had gotten into the act, stomping their sideways stomp.

"You remember last year," I began. My heart was stomping its own dance now. Overhead there was a rumble of thunder. I glanced from Maggie to the field and back again, shifting my gaze, trying to find the right words. If I was going to tell her—was I going to tell her?—I couldn't stand here all

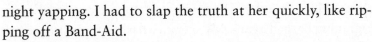

night yapping. I had to slap the truth at her quickly, like ripping off a Band-Aid.

The wind picked up, and some strands of Mags's hair came loose from her little French braid. Around us, everyone was cheering and laughing and enjoying the show on.

"It's a long story," I said, then stopped. This wasn't going to work.

"God, Jenna," Maggie said. "You're scaring me. Is this about the EMT girl? Did Casey cheat on Lanie with her or something? No—it's your parents, right? But I already know about that."

On the field, the crossed-dressed guys and girls separated. The cheer squad lined up under the Jumbotron. The video flashed on the screen. *Mustang Cheerleaders Rock It!*

We were all still down by the cinder track, a huge crowd, most of them still chugging Extra Energy like there was no tomorrow. Maybe I should have kept mine. My mouth was pretty dry now.

"Go on up to the stands, people," Principal Baker bellowed into a mic. I was surprised he hadn't made us do that earlier. It was more fun to stand down here. Fun is a dirty word in the public school system. Of course people just crowded closer toward the field.

Here's the funny thing about real life being shown simultaneously on a big screen. You don't know where to look. Do you watch the virtual version, which you can see better because it's above you? Or do you watch the real thing, craning your neck around the crowd and thinking it somehow looks less authentic even though it's not?

My eyes darted from one to the other. Next to me, Maggie was waiting for the story of a lifetime. In the sky, there was another rumble of thunder and then a flash of lightning, closer. More thunder. The storm was almost overhead now. Lightning flashed again. My memory flashed to the images of war and bombs and destruction that Bo had forced into my brain. It hadn't begun to rain yet. The air was thick and too still.

But the cross-dressed cheerleaders had begun their pyramid. I guess not even a huge storm was going to stop them from shoving Lanie Phelps into the air. The girls on the ground acted as ballast and two of the strongest ones pushed her up, their hands holding her feet while she stood tall and then lifted her leg up and up so that it was parallel to her body. I had once heard my brother tell Dave Pittman that Lanie's limberness was a thing of wonder. This had both fascinated and grossed me out, knowing that my brother had been up close and personal with her gymnastic skills.

At my ear, Maggie said, "The cheerleaders look funny. Wrong, I mean. Why is Lanie stunting? She's too tall to toss."

She did not say this in a mocking tone. But I didn't have time to process her words. Because lots of people in the crowd were acting wrong, too. Tired looking and spacy. My first thought was Dave Pittman. Was he back? Selling weed to the crowd? That made no sense. People were giggling and pointing and acting flighty in a way that seemed off, even for a football pep rally with cross-dressing. It was still early, after all. Besides, everyone had been guzzling Extra Energy. Empty bottles were scattered everywhere at our feet. Principal Baker was shouting something over the mic, but we couldn't hear him.

I raised my eyes toward the Jumbotron.

The girls pushed Lanie higher, propelling her into the air. She arched her back as she flew skyward, keeping steady so that when she fell back down, the girls could catch her and take her safely to earth.

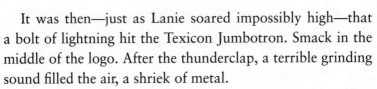

It was then—just as Lanie soared impossibly high—that a bolt of lightning hit the Texicon Jumbotron. Smack in the middle of the logo. After the thunderclap, a terrible grinding sound filled the air, a shriek of metal.

The huge letter T broke apart, pieces falling like huge daggers. The cheerleaders screamed, including Lanie. They scattered beneath her. But the screen was still working. Rain began to pelt the crowd.

"Jenna!" Maggie screamed. She grabbed my hand. The crowd pressed in tighter. I couldn't move my head. My eyes had no choice but to stay glued on the screen.

Lanie Phelps was falling.

Maggie hollered for all she was worth and all I could think was to keeping clinging to her hand so we didn't get separated. I would make it out of here with her and we would meet Casey back at the Merc . . .

And then there he was. On the screen. Casey Benjamin Samuels. My brother. My angel. Wings spread. My heart lurched. How was that possible? He'd used up his earthly flight for me. His body curved through the air, beautiful and perfect and majestic. He had been right, my brother. He was made for this.

He caught Lanie Phelps, cradling her gently in his arms, and set her down as she fell, just as he had caught me last year— just as he had in the earthly flight that had grounded him. Only he wasn't grounded now. He was swooping back up through the air. I watched transfixed as he blew an angel breath at the Texicon Jumbotron. And my heart did burst out of my chest now—at least that's what it felt like—because he blew and blew, pushing back the fire, leaving a blackened stump of a screen. And in that last instant, his eyes met mine, and he flashed me his goofy stoner smile, and then he was . . . gone.

It made no sense. It defied the laws of nature not to mention the obviously bullshit rules of Angel Management. My brother had just freaking outed himself as a heavenly being to the entire student body. But where was he?

Everyone was running.

"Did you see that?" someone said. "What the hell?" said someone else. "Is that pothead Samuels wearing wings again? He'll get himself killed!"

"Casey!" I shrieked. But he didn't reappear.

I looked up at the sky and was greeted with pelting rain. I lost track of Maggie then, let go of her hand. I had to reach Casey. I thought I heard Ryan Sloboda call my name. Maybe I did. My brain was reeling. What would I tell him? Maggie? How would I explain? Principal Baker would call Mom. How would we cover this up? Casey would have to lay hands on her for a while to make her forget this one. And a hopeful thought, even as I knew it would turn out badly: what would Dad say?

This wasn't like last Christmas at the Galleria with a bunch of strangers and an excuse that we had skydived. This was here. In front of everybody. But he had been grounded. Bo had confirmed what Amber had said. You fly once in earthly form and you lose your earthly flight. So now what? What would happen now? Would they give up on him all together? Send him to the other place? Was there even an other place?

At that moment I could have sworn I heard Bo laugh.

I froze on the field, alone.

A single white feather drifted to the wet grass.

It is hard to recall exactly what happened after that. Maybe my brain was doing me a favor.

What I do remember is this: Amber and Bo were suddenly there beside me on the rainy field.

I spun this way and that, looking for my brother. He couldn't be gone. He couldn't. Not like . . . He couldn't.

No. No. No.

"Casey!" I remember shouting. "Casey. Casey. Casey," until my throat was raw. Even after that, when Amber and Bo were dragging me to the Camaro.

"Where is he? Where is he?" I rasped. "He flew again. I thought he couldn't! Y'all are grounded. No earthly flights. But he . . . and then . . . What the hell? Where is he?"

Amber didn't answer. At some point I think Bo told her to shut up, anyway. At another point, he asked me if I needed him to carry me. And then Amber was shouting something at him and saying, "How could this happen?" And Bo was muttering something about "She wasn't his to save," and my body felt like it would stop breathing.

Footsteps and shouting from behind us as we reached Amber's car on the far side of the lot. Ryan and Maggie had caught up.

"Mr. Shivers?" Maggie was gawking at Bo. "Where are you taking Jenna?"

My heart was hammering like a demented woodpecker, but somehow I managed the thought that Bo's plan to watch out for me by teaching at our school had just backfired royally. My own angry humor. Maybe this was all some sick joke, right?

"Jenna can't talk to you right now," Amber said.

"We're going to find Casey," I said. Even to *my* ears this sounded stupid. But I said it again, because I thought: if I say it enough, it will happen. It couldn't be the other. I wasn't ready. I would never be ready. Not like this. Not now. I wasn't prepared. Casey would have prepared me.

The thought felt small and selfish. I was in that car with him last year. I saw him slumped over the wheel after our accident. I saw what he looked like. I *knew*.

Ryan's cut had stopped bleeding, the rain washing it to a thin red gash on the curve of his forehead near his left temple. Amber was telling him and Mags to leave again, but I saw him plant his feet.

"Jenna can speak for herself," Ryan said. He glared at Amber, puffing out his chest like he was on the football field. Ryan Sloboda, who would someday write amazing characters like that Tony Stark. Ryan Sloboda who had hung on to that stupid sheep. "I remember you. You're that EMT lady who spoke to us at Ima Hogg last year."

"Where's your brother?" Maggie asked. Then she swept

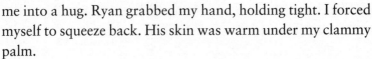

me into a hug. Ryan grabbed my hand, holding tight. I forced myself to squeeze back. His skin was warm under my clammy palm.

Even as I felt the niceness of that, my brain screeched: *Tell him to go away. He can't be here. He doesn't understand what I'm so upset about, other than that Lanie Phelps almost bit the dust and then she was saved. How could he? I can't tell him the truth. He wouldn't believe it anyway. So he can't be my boyfriend anymore. And here we had just gotten started.*

Bo Shivers laid his left hand on Maggie's arm and his right on Ryan's.

"Wait," I began.

But it was already done. Mags stepped away. Ryan's hand slid from mine.

"She'll call you later," Amber said, not even looking at them.

"Maggie needs a ride," I said, remembering.

Ryan blinked. Looked at me. Looked at Maggie. "My dad's coming for me. I'll take you home, Mags."

Here is what else I remember—and although there are many things I'd like to forget about last night—I want this one for always: Ryan Sloboda blinked again, like he was trying to reset his brain. "You should come with me, too, Jenna," he said. His lips lifted into a smile, brown eyes locked on mine. "This being our first real date and all." He shook his head, grin turning crooked. "Next time I'll ask for better weather."

Then his brow furrowed like he was remembering all the bad stuff or maybe forgetting it again because Bo had used his angel powers on him. Or maybe both at once. It was hard to tell.

"Does your brother have wings?" he asked spacily.

I let Bo clomp him on the shoulder again.

SOMETIME AFTER THAT, Bo, Amber and I stood in front of my house, the light from the Gilroy's graveyard reflecting on us.

"You can find him, right? Bring him back? Damn Lanie Phelps. Damn storm. And he flew? What's that about? I thought y'all couldn't. But he did. And now . . . I still need guarding. That's obvious. I—"

"You need to listen," Bo said.

"To what?" Impossibly, Bo's hair looked greyer. The lines on his face deeper. Not that I gave a shit right then.

I grabbed his wrist, jabbing a finger to his scars, forcing myself not to flinch at how raised and thick they felt. "Gonna include these in your story?"

"Jenna!" Amber cried.

Bo turned to her and gave her a quick headshake. His eyes went dark, darker than usual. Something I couldn't interpret crossed his face.

I expected a lie. Instead he said, "Yes."

Amber moved closer to me.

I gulped air, feeling light-headed and lost. Mom's car was in the driveway. At some point, I would have to go inside and tell her . . . something.

"Don't have all night," I said, trying to sound tough and brave. It was just me and them now. I shoved that thought down deep where it wouldn't panic me. It bounced back up.

Bo rubbed his right thumb across the scars on his left wrist.

"I need to tell you who I am. Both of you." He sighed. "Shit. Damn idiot."

I hoped he was referring to himself and not my brother.

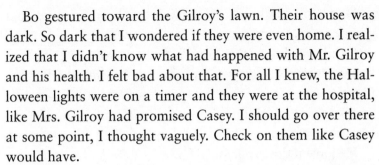

Bo gestured toward the Gilroy's lawn. Their house was dark. So dark that I wondered if they were even home. I realized that I didn't know what had happened with Mr. Gilroy and his health. I felt bad about that. For all I knew, the Halloween lights were on a timer and they were at the hospital, like Mrs. Gilroy had promised Casey. I should go over there at some point, I thought vaguely. Check on them like Casey would have.

"Let's sit," Bo said. But as soon as we settled ourselves on the damp grass by Sully Anderson's fake grave, he pushed up and paced. Amber was pale as a ghost. Funny, considering we sitting in a faux cemetery and she was dead and all. But my clenched stomach told my clenched brain that even though Bo had been her boss for five years, had been there since the beginning for her, she seemed as much in the dark as I was. *That* wasn't funny. Not at all. Plus Casey was still gone.

"There are rules," Bo began. "I know you thought you knew them." His gaze trained on Amber, not me. "I know you thought I told you. And I did. Mostly. You use up your earthly flight while in human form, and that's it. Forfeit using it again. Risk being moved elsewhere—possibly not an elsewhere you might want—which either way hasn't happened. For any of us.

"But here's what you don't know. You don't—we can't—save someone who isn't ours to save. I know how that sounds, but that's the way of it. There are patterns and destinies and organizational structures. Help the wrong person and you risk setting forth a domino effect of something that can't be controlled. You don't help someone you haven't been assigned to guard. End of story."

"But *you* saved me!" I shouted.

He shook his head. "Not like your brother saved that cheerleader."

"And you know this how?" Amber's voice was tight. I knew without her saying that she was hearing this for the first time.

"Because I saved someone who wasn't mine to save. That's how I lost my flight. That's why I'm here."

He looked down again.

"You didn't tell her that?" I shot up from the ground. "Are you kidding me? Why? Why?" In my head, I heard my brother's voice telling me I sounded like an owl again. Which was totally Casey, since I wasn't even saying *who*. But I knew I was just imagining that part. "It's that lady, isn't it? The one in the painting on your wall. The one by your bed?"

Amber was shaking her head, brows knitted. Maybe she just hadn't wanted to make the connection. Maybe she'd been too caught up in her own crap. Of course she was. She'd lost Terry. That was how people were, right?

"It was a long time ago," Bo said, voice like gravel.

My pulse picked up a notch. "Like ancient days?" I asked him, trying to be general about it.

Bo rubbed his palm over his chin. "Just like that," he said.
Amber frowned.

"How ancient?" I asked, pulse zipping a little faster now.

Bo closed his eyes. Then opened them. "I was a sculptor," he said. "King Herod was ruling Rome, if you want to mark it on the damn calendar."

"Jesus Christ," I whispered.

"About then," Bo said. "Year or so before."

I found myself sitting next to Amber. Collapsing was more like it. We both eyeballed Bo, trying to make sense of it. Was it really possible?

He told the rest then. I listened carefully. I kept my eyes on his face because I figured if I'd been lied to, I needed to watch him while he spoke. Did the best I could to hear the truth in the story. He'd been married, he said. Her name was Hadar. The word meant beautiful. He loved her. "Like a piece of my own soul," he said, tapping his chest. "Like all of it." They'd had just one child. A daughter. Shoshana. But she died of a fever and after that it had been just Bo and Hadar.

"We were sad," he said. "But that's how it went then. Babies died. People died. We would have another, I told her. I know she thought I secretly wished for a son to carry on my name. But I didn't. If a baby made her happy, then I would be happy." He sucked in a breath. "People back then . . . they didn't love each other like Hadar and I did. Couples were different. Love was different. Fathers wanted sons. I didn't give a shit about a son."

In my head, I saw that painting of that dark-haired lady on the wall by his bed, the one he had put in the background of all his paintings, far off, unreachable.

"King Herod was killing firstborn male children. It was a political thing. Power and riches, like always. I saved a neighbor's baby boy. The Romans found out. They killed me. I'll spare you the details." He ran a finger over his scars. Rubbed his wrists. Then his hands, like he was washing them.

Amber's jaw looked tight enough to snap. A muscle ticked near her mouth.

I realized I was holding my breath. I exhaled. Bo shrugged. "And then Management sent me back."

"But that's good, right?" My voice cracked. "I mean you got to go back to her then. Even if you weren't the same or maybe couldn't tell her, right?"

"Like I said," Bo said, slowly. "There are rules. Policies.

A system." He paused. "Hadar wasn't who I was sent back to guard."

The significance of this washed over me. My heart skipped again. "Then who?" Amber asked.

Bo looked at her long and hard. "You know it doesn't matter, right? You know what's coming in this story. I was such a believer," he went on, voice drifting, eyes looking somewhere far away. "I loved my Hadar, but when I came back from the dead, I thought I was lucky. I believed that it would be for the best. What a chance. What an opportunity to prove myself to whomever was running the show. But I couldn't stay in the city where we lived. Hadar had seen me killed. I accepted that. I don't know how, but I did. This is how I thought back then. You have to understand. I hid myself because I had to prepare to go where Management had sent me."

Bo laid back on the grass, staring up at the stars. "I had a boss, too, Master we called it then, although I haven't seen him since the start . . . well, you can do the math. He showed me who I had been assigned to protect, a boy in a town north of where I lived. The boy needed me, Master said. He was destined for many things and his descendants were destined for many great and important things, and without me the chain of events might be altered. I was the one for the job."

I started shaking my head. "The boy . . . did you save him?" The words came out of my mouth in a terrible whisper.

Bo clasped his hands together, lacing his fingers. "You don't know who you are, not really, until those moments come. Mine came pretty quickly. Hadar had no man to protect her. Things happen as things tend to do. But how could I watch her be hurt? Where was the justice in that? Everything changed in a minute. Less."

"Bo," Amber said. "Enough. Don't—"

"I saved her from the brutes who attacked her," Bo interrupted. "I flew without any thought that I shouldn't. Of course I did. I loved her. She was my *wife*. Felt my wings form and spread and lift me. The power—well I don't have to tell you about that, Amber, do I? Or maybe you didn't take the time to savor it. I know I've never asked you."

"You haven't asked me much of anything," Amber said, arms folded tight across her chest. I thought of what Casey said when I finally asked him. About his body welcoming the wings. How he felt like this was what he had been made for. Where was my brother now? For the first time in my life, I wondered where exactly—in the physical sense—you went . . . after. Was he anywhere at all?

Bo pursed his lips. Then he said, "I saved Hadar, and she saw me and she screamed because how could she understand? I was dead. Now I wasn't. She cried that it was a miracle. A wonder. And you know what? It felt like that. It felt good and strong and pure. I *was* powerful. I had taken to the air like an eagle, felt the rush of the world flow through me. I had done well. I had saved the woman I loved. Surely there was no wrong in that." He laughed bitterly.

"Management?" I said.

He nodded. "Management grounded me. No more flight as long as I was on earth. Reminded me in no uncertain terms that I had broken the rules. I had been chosen to protect someone else. I was jeopardizing the entire world through my choices."

This time when Bo sighed, he lit golden, like I'd seen Casey do, only dimmer somehow. Tarnished.

"You know what happened in King Herod's time if you cried miracle and the authorities didn't believe you? When you were the widow of someone who had rebelled against them? And here was my choice. Save her again and disobey the absolute rules of guardian angels. Risk every part of this new and powerful being I had become. Or do what I'd been brought back to do and protect the boy.

"You have to understand who I was back then. I was a coward. Your brother just threw himself to the lions, Jenna. Me? I walked away and did what I was told. Believed I had a bigger purpose. That the invincible power surging through me made me special. I was a guardian angel. I had a different set of rules. It never occurred to me that . . ."

Bo's eyes glittered darkly. He sighed. The Halloween lights blinked out all at once.

I sat in silence. I could feel Amber beside me, holding her angel breath.

"Until after, when I saw what the Romans had done to her," Bo finished.

"But you're still here," I said, feeling bitter. "Casey saved the right person the first time and then he saved Lanie and now he's gone. You broke the rules and here you are." I jumped up. Amber jumped up beside me. Somehow we were all standing, a circle of fury. Two of us were glowing. "You saved the wrong person, too, but here you are. Why? And there better be a good explanation. Casey *saved* me. Like he was supposed to! Casey gave up everything. He should be carried around on people's shoulders. Not gone."

I was crying now, hot tears soaking my cheeks. I didn't mean to cry. He wasn't worth crying in front of. But there I was like an idiot anyway.

"Jenna," Amber began, placing her hand on my shoulder, but I shook it away.

"You didn't save your wife. That's on *you*. But you punished my brother for it by not letting him know the rules.

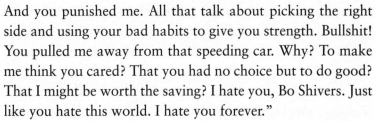

And you punished me. All that talk about picking the right side and using your bad habits to give you strength. Bullshit! You pulled me away from that speeding car. Why? To make me think you cared? That you had no choice but to do good? That I might be worth the saving? I hate you, Bo Shivers. Just like you hate this world. I hate you forever."

I stomped across the Gilroy's lawn, kicking the Bubba tombstone. I broke into a run, down the block with no particular destination in mind, just escape. Of course Bo and Amber caught up with me. I didn't have damn wings. I was blubbering and furious and probably whatever was left of my makeup was running down my cheeks with the stupid tears.

"There's a possibility that I don't know everything, Jenna," Bo said.

That stopped me. Or maybe I was just grieving and exhausted. I stood for a few beats, then finally swiveled to look at him.

Bo took Amber's hand. Held her gaze. "I should have told you what I knew. But you were angry and self-destructive. You haven't told little Jenna about those first couple years of yours, have you? I had no idea you would ever leap over that Galleria balcony to save this girl and then catch the evil doctor so her brother could get the glory. You spent an entire year . . . well, that's not important now. You can tell Jenna that part of the story. And me? I'd been brooding and drunk on-and-off for centuries. Plus honestly? Casey Samuels a self-less do-gooder? Who would have believed that?"

Here I kicked him. He pretended to wince. I pretended that I didn't know he was right.

Bo shoved his wrists in my face. "You wanted to know why I have these? Let me tell you. When I realized what a fool I'd been, I begged for them back. It was the only thing

Management ever did that I agreed with. So I could look at myself every single day after that and remember not what the Romans had done to me, but what I had done. Or rather, what I hadn't."

"And the boy?" I asked, because he hadn't said. Maybe he wouldn't say, but it felt suddenly wrong not to know. "The boy you were sent back to guard? The one who had all this great stuff in his future? What happened to him?"

Bo was quiet for a long few beats. "I did my job and pro-tected him," he said. "He married. He had children. And eventually Management said I had done what I supposed to do. They would let me know when I was needed again. Peri-odically, they have." He looked at me then, long and hard. I didn't look away. "Your brother is worthy, Jenna. You can believe me on that. And something is still coming. Big. Pow-erful. A force we need to deal with."

"Casey's gone," I drew it out long, then longer.

"Even so."

"Could he come back?" My heart didn't as much beat as flutter.

A million things I couldn't name rushed across Bo's face. "We're angels," he said quietly. "We bring miracles. We believe in them. Even me."

"Bullshit," I said, even if I wanted to believe otherwise. "You bring what suits you for the moment." I looked from Bo to Amber. "Right?"

They didn't answer. Neither glowed. They just looked like a couple of weird grown-ups I had no business hanging out with in the middle of the night.

Across the lawn, the Gilroy's front door opened, and Mrs. Gilroy shuffled out.

I ran to her. "You okay, m'am?"

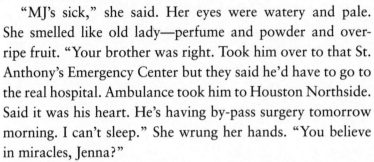

"MJ's sick," she said. Her eyes were watery and pale. She smelled like old lady—perfume and powder and over-ripe fruit. "Your brother was right. Took him over to that St. Anthony's Emergency Center but they said he'd have to go to the real hospital. Ambulance took him to Houston Northside. Said it was his heart. He's having by-pass surgery tomorrow morning. I can't sleep." She wrung her hands. "You believe in miracles, Jenna?"

My heart was too tired to flounder anymore. "I don't know," I said, not sure if I meant it. I patted her on the arm. Her skin was dry and papery. And even though I didn't want to, I thought again about Lanie Phelps, who possibly should have been dead now—but wasn't.

After that, I walked by Bo and Amber, not saying a word, and went inside to lie to my mother.

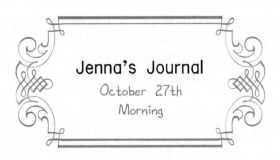

Jenna's Journal
October 27th
Morning

Here is what I told Mom: Casey had flaked out about breaking up with Lanie and run off to stay with Dave, who was living with his father up near Centerville. Dave's dad, I said, had recently taken a job running some rich doctor's ranch.

Of course, Mom cried and got hysterical and called Dad. He got less hysterical, but they both called Casey's cell like a million times. I chewed my lip until it bled and wondered if my brother's cell worked wherever he was. Or maybe it was in the cupholder of the Merc, back in the school parking lot. I realized I would have to ask someone to drive it back here for me and make up another cock-and-bull story about how Dave had picked up Casey because the Merc's engine was acting up.

At least that last part was close to true. The Merc was still a piece of crap.

I spouted lie after lie and the only thing that kept me from breaking into a thousand pieces was the thought that maybe Bo and Amber really *didn't* know shit.

Okay, I was sure Amber didn't. Bo was still a self-serving mystery. There was nothing I hated more than someone who made a bad choice and then whined about it while the rest of us slogged forward. I would never forgive Bo for convincing me to believe that my brother was just like him. If Casey was a bitter, mopey, unhappy bastard like Bo, then Casey would be here. Maybe he'd feel like an angel failure. But he'd be here.

Somewhere around three or so, Mom cried herself to sleep.

I shuffled to my room and flopped onto my bed. But I tossed and turned and ending up dragging blankets into Casey's room. I curled up on his comforter. My phone stayed clutched in my hand because I wanted to believe that some-how Casey would call. Which I know is ridiculous, but I figured I was entitled to that particular fantasy.

When I still couldn't sleep, I started nosing around Casey's room. Once I started, it was impossible to stop. I looked at it all. His old baseball trophies from when he was little. Swimming ribbons from the couple of years we both swam summer league. Movie ticket stubs from dates he'd gone on with Lanie, wrinkled up because he wasn't a girl and even though he kept it, it was just stuffed in his desk drawer with old Chucky Cheese prize tickets he'd never redeemed. My brother had been a whiz at skee-ball once upon a time.

Some framed pictures of him and me in Sea World once. Football group pictures with all the guys so tiny that I had to squint to pick him out. In his closet, I flipped through all his clothes: Jeans hung this way and that on hangers. Dress shirts and older stuff—basketball jerseys he'd outgrown, ancient pairs of New Balance sneakers with holes in them. Report cards from elementary school when he always made the high-est grades. His old letter jacket, which I put on and then took

off because it smelled like him still—sweaty and musky and somehow like the night air. Guy stuff. My brother's stuff.

He hadn't lied to me: the bongs and all the weed paraphernalia were really gone. But there on his desk, shoved half behind his English textbook so I almost missed it, was that damn paper sack project for Teen Leadership. My hands shook as pried open the bag.

Inside were the following items:

- A picture of our family at the aquarium in Monterey, CA, all wearing the same T-shirt with a sea lion on it, all smiling like we didn't have a care in the world. Dad, Mom, Casey, and me.
- A picture of him and Lanie Phelps at Homecoming their freshman year. The theme had been Hawaii and they both had these silly leis around their neck and were posing in front of a fake beach scene.
- A list of the classes that you had to take for a Forensics major at Sam Houston State.
- The football patch for the last round of playoffs two years ago. He'd gotten it and quit right after. Mom had never helped him sew it onto his jacket.

And that was it. He wasn't done, obviously. Or else he felt flummoxed, because how could he explain to the class what he really was? What he was aiming for and spending his time on? They couldn't see all that, anyway now, could they?

I lay back on his bed. I hadn't cried, not really, in a long, long time. But now I couldn't stop. I cried and cried and cried, the ugly screw up your face and send snot everywhere kind of cry. Casey was dead. No matter how long he'd stuck around or even if he came back, all these things—these ideas, these hopes and plans, even the ones he hadn't put in the stupid sack—they were nothing now. Gone.

I thought about that one white feather that had fluttered to the ground after he disappeared. The one that now sat in my underwear drawer, where you put all the things you don't know where else to hide. And decided it would be just one more useless thing to put in this sack.

DAWN WAS BREAKING when my phone vibrated. I leapt up, not even checking the Caller ID.

"Jenna?" It was Maggie. I could tell from her voice that Bo's damage control hand to her shoulder had worn off. "Do I need to come over there? You are definitely not okay, are you? Never mind that. I'm on my way. You're home, right. Stay put. I'll be right there."

"No!" I bellowed at her. "No . . . I . . . .."

"This is me walking out of my house," Mags said. And you know what she did then? Because unlike my family, Maggie's parents are COMPLETELY AWARE of their daughter's comings and goings, so it's not like she could actually leave and they wouldn't notice. But Maggie took something—probably her lace-up knee-high Converse —and thumped them on her floor so I would think she was walking.

At least that's what it sounded like.

I didn't plan on laughing ever again. But there I was, cracking up until my stomach hurt. I guess that's why the real story—shortened so that I could get it out before Christmas break—came pouring out of me. That Casey had died in that car accident last year. That he was sent back as my guardian angel. That Amber and Bo were angels, too. That yes, he had really flown tonight; did she remember this? That he'd saved stupid Lanie Phelps. That he had saved me, too, last year. We

were not skydivers. I talked fast, barely pausing, the words escaping in a mad rush.

"But now he's gone," I finished. "And I don't know if he'll ever come back."

I sucked in a long breath. I could hear Maggie breathing, too, over the cell.

I guess even for someone like Maggie Boland, who believes that the universe has a plan and that it is her job to figure it out, some things are too much to accept.

"I'm your best friend, Jenna," Mags said finally. "Do you really think you have to make up a crazy story? Your brother's a flake. Even if he's cute. You know I already know this. I've been asking and asking you if something's wrong. I can't believe you wouldn't trust me with the truth. God, Jenna. Your brother. An angel. Seriously?"

Well then. I had nothing else to say. My heart sank to my toes. I figured that's where it would stay.

We breathed at each other for a while, and then we hung up.

I curled into the tiniest ball I could and closed my eyes.

I don't remember falling asleep, only that I was thinking that I probably should just shower and get dressed and figure out how I was getting to school.

Like that other dream I'd had, this one felt real.

Casey was sitting on the side of his bed. "I washed that comforter," he told me, grinning. "You know, in case you were worried about hygiene."

"Liar," I said, sitting up.

He socked me on the arm, not hard. But I felt his warm hand on my skin. My heart lifted from my toes and danced through my body. He was back! It would be okay. He was still an angel. But he was here. Guarding me like he was supposed to.

"Jenna," Casey said. His voice vibrated in my chest, making me nervous all of a sudden because for some reason it reminded me of Bo. And I hated Bo. "You know more than you think you do. You can figure this out. You have to figure it out. I love you. I'll always love you. Just take it step by step and you'll know what to do. The pissant will help you, maybe. I think he will. And you may get in trouble, but hey, that's the Samuels way, isn't it?"

He was glowing golden, but fading in a way that made me feel cold.

"I know you think I screwed up, Jenna. But it was for the right reason. The big stuff always is. I know . . . Jenna you need to trust me. You need to trust yourself. That whole Spidey sense thing? And you? Well—"

"What about Bo?" I hated saying his name, but I did. "Is he for real with that story? His wife getting killed and all the rest of it? But it doesn't excuse what he didn't tell you. Casey, I need to know—"

He was going to tell me. I was sure of it. I could see it in his face. Which was when I woke up.

Alone.

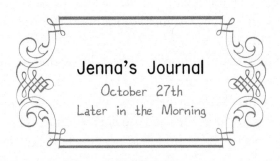

Mom was still in bed when I walked out the front door. I almost smacked into Amber Velasco.

"You need a ride to school," she said, telling, not asking.

She was wearing her EMT outfit. The Camaro was parked out front. I was wearing the jeans she'd given me because they were sitting on my desk chair—and even though I was feeling highly conflicted about the entire A-word community of which she was a card-carrying member, I refused to take that out on a pair of pants that made my ass look spectacular.

But I tossed the white shirt. I had to draw my line in the sand.

I'd also swiped on a healthy bunch of makeup. This was for two reasons: 1. I looked pasty and exhausted and I was not about to face my former best friend and my soon to be former boyfriend looking like shit. Also, 2. My brother had given me the Sephora kit. I would use every last drop of it.

"Gold glitter shadow is for night," Amber said. "And there *is* such as thing as too much eyeliner."

I sashayed past her, pretending I hadn't heard. Of course then I realized I didn't even know where the bus stop was for the Spring Creek bus. I hadn't ridden a school bus yet this year.

"Let me drive you." Amber's work boots slapped the pavement behind me.

"I'm fine," I said, although we both knew that wasn't true. What was true: I did not want to talk to her. I did not want her to help me. *My* guardian angel was gone. The reality of this was sinking in as the sun rose higher in the sky.

I ran, mostly because I had so much inside me with nowhere to go. A yellow bus rumbled past as I reached the cross street. I waved my arms. It stopped. I climbed aboard and headed straight toward the back.

"Little Samuels," drawled Corey Chambers, looking red-eyed and high. He was sitting on the aisle at the very rear. He patted the inside seat next to him and I slowed, hovering over him, deciding if it was worth it to sit.

"Your brother still friends with Dave?" Corey asked. This was Corey-speak for drug intel. Spring Creek and Ima Hogg had lost their most reliable dealer when Dave had moved. I couldn't help myself. I slapped him.

After writing me a referral, the bus driver informed me that I was banned from public school transportation until such time as the Principal Baker decided to reinstate me. I told myself it didn't matter. I was now the perfect candidate for a hardship license —least once I got that permit . . . which I couldn't get until someone drove me . . . that someone NOT being Amber. My vehicular issues were becoming legendary.

AT SCHOOL, EVERYONE was talking about last night and Lanie's fall. But there was a big chunk missing. The lightning strike, the stupidity of Spring Creek High allowing the

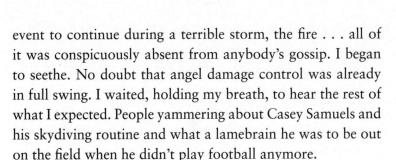

event to continue during a terrible storm, the fire . . . all of
it was conspicuously absent from anybody's gossip. I began
to seethe. No doubt that angel damage control was already
in full swing. I waited, holding my breath, to hear the rest of
what I expected. People yammering about Casey Samuels and
his skydiving routine and what a lamebrain he was to be out
on the field when he didn't play football anymore.

Instead, I heard nothing.

This one and that one—students, teachers, even my guid-
ance counselor—everyone harped on how lucky it was that
Lanie hadn't been hurt. Like she'd just landed on her feet.
Still, she was taking classes off for a spa day.

I waited again for someone (Donny Sneed maybe, that
would be good) to say something, anything, about Casey. I
was in the mood to slap another face. But no one mentioned
my brother. Not one tiny little word. Not even Donny Sneed.

I stormed to History, ready to give Bo Shivers my piece
about damage control.

I was greeted by some lady with dyed red hair, a fake
leather skirt and a V-neck floral blouse that showed a heinous
amount of tanned wrinkly cleavage. Sub again.

I turned and walked away. History would live without me,
again. Screw it. If Lanie could have a spa day, so could I. I
was halfway to the exit, in the Commons area, when Maggie
grabbed my arm.

Maybe I'd have twisted away from her too, But she held
on tight, face serious, eyes burning with something I wasn't
sure of. Plus, she was wearing baggy jeans, a generic white
T-shirt and her old Girl Scouts hoodie. Maggie had not been
a Girl Scout for a very long time. Maggie did not like anyone
knowing she had once sold those cookies. Not that being a
Girl Scout was a bad thing. Just that it was not Maggie.

"Jenna," she said, her voice low. "I believe you."

"You're wearing your Girl Scouts hoodie," I said.

The serious look did not leave Maggie's face. "It felt like the appropriate outfit for what the universe had handed me."

I stared at Maggie, assessing.

She stared back at me, wrapping her hoodie string around her fingers and then unwrapping. All of a sudden, I felt like sand was slipping through an hourglass, like time was running out, even though my brother was gone and two of the most important people in my life were dead liars with no answers. The future was just more of the same, only emptier. So why the prickle in my spine? Why the Spidey sense?

"You swear?" I asked her.

She nodded. She didn't blink. She held my gaze, eyes wide. "I was up all night. I just didn't . . . I might not believe a lot of things, but I always believe you. Believe *in* you. Which is the same, you know?"

Around us, Spring Creek High continued to do whatever it was Spring Creek High did. Inside me, hope rose and swelled. Maggie believed me. She *believed* me. I sniffed back the tears stinging my nose. If my heart had not already burst with sadness it would have exploded with relief.

"You need to tell me again," Maggie said. "Everything. From the beginning. I don't remember much. Which is the other reason I believe you. I realized something important." Here she lowered her voice even more. I had to lean in to hear her. "I always remember *everything*. You know that, right? And last night feels foggy."

"There this damage control thing," I said, trying to explain calmly. "It makes you remember it differently than it was." I put a hand on Maggie's arm. "Listen, I'm cutting World History. Bo, um, Mr. Shivers isn't there."

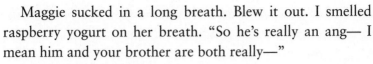

Maggie sucked in a long breath. Blew it out. I smelled raspberry yogurt on her breath. "So he's really an ang— I mean him and your brother are both really—"

"Yeah," I whispered.

The warning bell rang, and everyone was running like a noisy herd of cattle.

"Angels," I went on, hushed. "Casey, Bo, and Amber. Wings under their clothes, full-fledged heavenly beings. Although you'd never suspect it with all their bad habits. Except Casey gave up one of his, which I still have to tell you about . . . But that's the point, Mags. They can walk among us and who the hell would suspect—"

"What did you say?"

I turned to see one Ryan Sloboda. eyes popping, shoving a hand through his spiked up hair.

"Um, nothing," I said. Then, "How much did you hear?" *Did I want to know?* Still I asked.

Ryan's face flushed, but only for a moment. Mostly his eyes were on me, dark and serious. What did this mean? Had he heard it *all*? Which led to the obvious next question: was he about to stalk off and forget about me because I sounded like a looney? Calling my new history teacher an A-word. Talking about wings and damage control. Holy hell.

"That was the last bell," I said, trying for a distraction.

Ryan looked completely heels-dug-in-stubborn. Like I imagined he'd looked when he was hanging on to the Mutton-Busting sheep. "I knew it," he said quietly, but, so intense, that I backed up a step. He was going to break up with me, wasn't he? And here we'd just gotten started. "I know what I saw last night. No one seems to remember, but *I* do. I saw Lanie Phelps fall. I *saw* your brother . . . I *saw* him . . . "

He took my hands in his. My skin felt hot and cold and

then my insides felt good and bad and then I stopped trying to analyze my internal condition and just stood and waited. Maggie was still next to me. Uncharacteristically silent. Not even a peep, but I could hear her breathing.

"Jenna," he said. He hesitated, working something out. I held my breath. "I was up all night," he went on. "It makes no sense, but then I told myself that maybe some things don't have to make sense. Some things—maybe they just are. You know?"

He was still gripping my hands.

"Ryan," I said. "It's okay if you don't—"

"Here's the thing," he interrupted, like he had to get it out. "It's like Maggie told you." He glanced briefly at Mags. "I don't know what else to do but believe you, you know? Because it's you. Because you're Jenna. And just because I saw something strange doesn't mean that it isn't *real*."

Was this his comic book leanings taking over? I didn't much care. The words were all that mattered right now. They were the *right words*. Very right. Even Maggie didn't remember like Ryan Sloboda did. I wanted to kiss him again—had wanted to for a while and for a variety of reasons. But for now it was enough that he believed.

"C'mon," I said, my heart leaping like one of those salmon in a river. He *knew*. He *knew* and he was still standing here. *With me.* "We're cutting history class, me and Mags. We'll go somewhere and I'll tell you and . . . well I don't know what we'll do after that."

My brain was in a dither. In the past five minutes I had done what I'd been avoiding for almost a year: I'd told the truth. The crazy A-word truth. The truth that my brother had made me swear I would *never tell*. This was unmapped territory. What would Bo do when he found out? What about

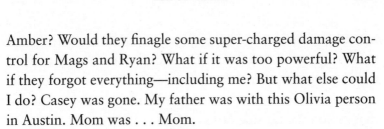

Amber? Would they finagle some super-charged damage control for Mags and Ryan? What if it was too powerful? What
if they forgot everything—including me? But what else could
I do? Casey was gone. My father was with this Olivia person
in Austin. Mom was . . . Mom.

My personal truth? It felt good to tell them. Hell, it felt
great. Scary, but okay. I was ready—more than ready—to
spill the whole can of beans. No one was in charge of me
now except for me.

"I'm in," said Ryan Sloboda.

"Me, too," said Maggie, finding her words again.

My heart did the Texas two-step. Double-time. Maybe
what Casey had told me in my dream was true. Maybe I *could*
figure out what even the angels in my life couldn't. Now that
I had Mags and Ryan on my side, two people who were actually alive, I might find out how Amber was killed. Even if
Bo knew and didn't want me to. Even if we'd met dead end
after dead end. Because now there were three of us: Mags,
Ryan, and me. We were the *living* wild cards in this deck.
We were the something unexpected. It was not my intention
to think of Coach Collins and his Aggie football philosophy
right then. But he popped in there anyway: Maggie and Ryan
were my Twelfth Men.

And if I solved this mystery with their help, then maybe
what I *really needed* would happen, too. It was a long shot,
but Texas was founded on long shots.

Then I could figure this whole mess out just like I'd hoped
when we went to Austin—just like I'd told Casey. And when
I did, Management would send him back to me.

WE SNUCK OUT a side door just as the last bell finished blaring. Hightailed it through the student parking lot, ducking

behind cars. (Including the poor Merc that I had to deal with at some point—I had found the spare key on Casey's dresser, not that it was doing me much good.) Within seconds, we were beyond the field house, at the abandoned railroad tracks that ran on the far side of the school.

Only then did we slow down. And we walked the tracks and I told them. I talked and talked and talked. The long version this time, not the short story of last night that Maggie hadn't believed. My heart galloped at first, then settled because the more I spilled the calmer I felt. Like what I had needed all along was someone who I could tell this all to. At one point the breeze picked up and my pulse zoomed. Did Bo and Amber know what I was doing? That I was outing them all word after word? If they were watching, they were hidden.

Only when I finished did I notice we'd walked all the way to Bryce's neighborhood. We were standing in front of the Chateau Hills sign. Various SUVs and pickup trucks lumbered by, but no one hollered at us to get back to school. Briefly I thought about Terry McClain, who lived over here, too. A flash of panic zipped through me. What if he drove by and saw us? Would he recognize me? Would he narc on me to Amber, thinking to get back in her good graces? I was already on his shit list . . .

It was the middle of the morning. He *had* to be at work. At Texicon, right? Probably drinking some of that leftover Extra Energy while he experimented on more mice. I had nothing to fear from Terry McClain. He was just an ordinary human. Not an angel with a hopped-up Spidey sense.

"Well, Jenna," said Ryan Sloboda. "Everything you told me makes more sense than what I was imagining. Cause you know. Zombie apocalypse is just for TV."

I started, thoughts of Terry McClain fleeing my brain.

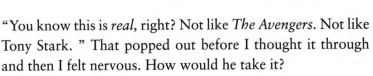

"You know this is *real,* right? Not like *The Avengers.* Not like Tony Stark. " That popped out before I thought it through and then I felt nervous. How would he take it?

"Nothing's like the man in the can," Ryan murmured, eyes dancing with both fear and resolve. He drew in a breath. "Because that isn't real life."

He was cuter than sin, that Ryan Sloboda. Once again, it took every ounce of control I had not to kiss him in front of Mags. He knew my secret. He was still standing here. He believed me.

And he *remembered.*

What did that mean? Was he stronger than Bo's damage control? Or—I hadn't thought about this at first but the more we walked and talked, the more real estate it took up in my tired brain: had Bo *allowed* Ryan to remember?

"Now what?" Mags asked.

"Well, I realized something," Ryan said without missing a beat. "Your brother and that Bo guy and that Amber chick— they're angels, right? We're accepting that as true. Let's go with that as our starting point. But here's the thing. They would *stop* a zombie apocalypse, right? Not *cause* one."

"Enough with the zombies," Mags groaned.

"But that's the point!" Ryan said. "Remember how everyone was acting last night? It was like everyone was all drugged or something. I mean I guess it's not as weird as your brother having wings, but weird, right?"

It was.

"How would they have gotten drugged?" Mags asked. "Was it in the air or something? The cafeteria food? Maybe someone could have—"

"Extra Energy!" Ryan and I gasped at the same time. I took his hand and squeezed it. In my head, I saw all those sample bottles lying empty on the ground. What better way to drug up a bunch of high school students? I mean, beyond the obvious stuff that guys like Dave supplied for a fee. But seriously: free samples of some new tasty energy drink with a cute name and multiple colors?

Only why? Had Texicon done this on purpose? Laced our drinks and studied us like . . . lab mice? Maybe a year ago, I might not have believed it. But now I knew that anything was possible.

"Did you guys drink any?" Ryan asked breathlessly. "I didn't. Coach doesn't believe in that crap. Says it's a bunch of chemicals and sugars and doesn't do what you think it does for your electrolytes."

Mags shot me an *I-told-you-so* smirk. I sheepishly shook my head. I was suddenly very, very glad she'd been so pissy about the whole thing.

But now what? For a few seconds I had one VERY DARK worry, that maybe Bo had *made* all this happen for a reason that I couldn't figure out. Could he be that bitter and sad somehow? It was possible. *You're a good daughter*, he'd told me.

No. Bo Shivers was a mystery and a bastard, but even though he hid the truth under a bunch of bullshit, he never actually *lied*. So I pushed that thought away. It wasn't like it mattered now anyway. Casey was gone. Maybe he'd come back. Maybe he wouldn't. But he had come to me in my dream and told me I had to solve this whole mess. The mess that had started with my mom's depression and my sickness. The mess that had started with Dr. Renfroe . . .

Which was when I realized we hadn't hiked all the way here by accident. We'd come to the exact neighborhood of the exact person we needed to talk to. Extra Energy was a

subsidiary of Texicon. Amber's ex, Terry McClain, was a scientific genius and a head lab guy. Just because he wouldn't talk to me about Amber didn't mean he wouldn't talk about *this*.

Plus, the way I figured it, Terry McClain was exactly the type of guy who would want to get the glory for figuring out how his *own employers* had zombied up most of the student body and almost caused fatalities. This was the guy who'd solved the mystery of my mother's memory loss, and I'd bet he was probably hoping it would be a stepping-stone in his career. Bringing down Texicon would guarantee him celebrity and a big fat job anywhere he wanted. Once he found out his company had some diabolical dealings, *no way* would he ignore it.

Okay, he couldn't answer the part about the storm and the lightning and the fire, but that was nature. (Either nature or something bigger I couldn't understand, the something Bo had warned me about. But I couldn't go there right now.) Texas had natural disasters and brush fires all the time. Point was: in answering questions, maybe Terry would spill about that night five years ago. Maybe I could kill two birds with one stone. So to speak. And then maybe Management would *have* to bring Casey back. Because not only had he saved the day, I would really need him to protect me from future drug company shenanigans.

I explained all this as best I could to Maggie and Ryan.

"I'm in," Ryan said. "I guess I have to be, if I believe you."

"Me, too," Mag said.

"It has to be now," I said. "I don't think we should wait." I eyeballed Ryan. I knew from my brother that if a player skipped school during the week before a game, Coach wouldn't let them play. But he didn't hesitate, not even for a second. "I said I'm in. I don't say things I don't mean. You need me. I'm here." He did kiss me then, his lips taking me by surprise. Not a sloppy kiss, but a sweet one. Maggie cleared her throat. "Standing right here." she said.

I stepped back and looked at them both. "You're my Twelfth Man, Ryan Sloboda," I announced, because what else did I have to lose by telling him that particular truth, too? "You, too," I told Maggie.

"Twelfth Woman," she amended. Maggie prided herself on political correctness.

"Whatever."

It was only five miles from here to the Texicon headquarters. .We could totally do this, right?

I fished the spare Merc key out of my pocket.

"Which one of you wants to drive?" I asked.

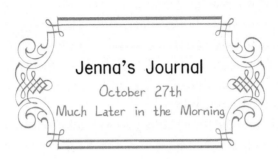

The plan was to be back by lunch. If we were lucky, Ryan could make up some excuse to his teachers and maybe Coach Collins wouldn't look too carefully at the daily attendance. I was just glad there was no sign of Bo or Amber. At least not yet. We needed to get a move on before one or both of them popped up out of thin air. My only hope (and it was a grim one) was that Casey's disappearance into the ether had put a temporary monkey wrench into that little party trick for the whole A-crew, too.

But, I reminded myself, *we* were alive. And the more important part of the plan was to present Terry with a bunch of Extra Energy bottles in hopes that he'd analyze them. We'd found a couple of unopened samples lying around the parking lot and stuck them in a plastic bag. Mags and Ryan knew that Terry had tested my mother's blood. He was the over-eager intense sort (which in my opinion outweighed his cuteness factor) but Amber had said more than once that he lived for shit like this. Who better to help us prove that someone was conducting nefarious experiments on impressionable teen-aged brains?

I ended up driving. I knew the Merc. Casey had let me practice those times in the parking lot. Plus Mags had whispered that it was best I act assertive and not too girly to counteract potential romantic fallout from the Twelfth Man comment. This was a lot to process given my emotional state, but I did the best I could.

We all sat in the front, Mags in the middle, Ryan navigating. "Stop for kolaches," Maggie said. I shot her a "you are crazy" look but then she said, "Trust me," and so I white-knuckled it an extra mile, the Merc chugging and my heart thundering.

Maggie insisted we get an entire dozen, which meant we had to pool our resources. But she pointed out that now we would have a box, and it would look like a real delivery. This sounded as logical as anything else at this point. I remembered the blog post Terry had written about his love for doughnuts, but I didn't want him to think I was stalking him. Kolaches it was.

Since it was only a prop to make us look like we had a purpose for visiting a company that tested things on rodents and researched DNA and sponsored Jumbotrons and sold energy drinks—none of which we were qualified to do—we each ate a kolache on the way.

TEXICON WAS A five-story steel and glass building in the middle of a wooded area that wasn't far off the main streets but was so tucked away that if you didn't know it was there, you'd totally drive by. I wondered if this was on purpose.

We parked. Got out and walked inside to the front desk, Ryan carrying the bag of energy drink bottles and the big white box of kolaches.

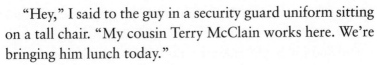

"Hey," I said to the guy in a security guard uniform sitting on a tall chair. "My cousin Terry McClain works here. We're bringing him lunch today."

It was 9:30 in the morning.

The guard gave me the stink eye, then perused a clip board. "You're not on the visitor list," he said.

"It's a surprise," Maggie told him.

We would have gone on like that for awhile. But Maggie Boland is a resourceful girl. She snagged the box from Ryan. Thumped it on the counter. Opened it and swiped up a fat kolache, one of the cheese ones. "It's his favorite," she said, then took a huge bite. "See," she said, spitting pastry crumbs, "they're still warm."

And then she crumbled to the floor clutching her throat like she was choking.

My pulse hit the ceiling. Ryan's eyes bugged out.

"Shit!" Ryan and I slammed to the floor next to Maggie. Figured I'd yank the kolache piece out of her mouth before I attempted CPR. "Open up," I hollered.

She was still chewing. She winked at us, making sure Ryan saw too, since he was new to her wily shenanigans, then went back to pretend-choking.

I gave her pretend CPR while the guard wrung his hands and Ryan counted.

Maggie sat up, red-faced.

"It's a miracle," I hollered. I leaped to my feet, dragging Ryan with me. "Please, if you could watch her while we deliver the rest of these to Cousin Terry, that would be awesome. Third floor, right?"

"Fourth," he mumbled, puzzled eyes still glued to Mags.

Before he could protest, we took off for the elevators.

My adrenaline was pumping like nobody's business.

Maggie was a badass. Ryan Sloboda was a badass. I was no longer keeping the BIGGEST SECRET EVER from my best friend and my boyfriend. Life was a shit-show, but somehow manageable, no matter what happened here.

As my brain filled fast with these exclamatory revelations, the elevator door opened. We walked out, trying to look casual. And just about slammed into Terry McClain. The look on his face was part angry, part confused, part nervous. Least as far as I could tell. It occurred to me that the guard must have called while we were riding up. I guess there was only so much recovery time Mags could fake.

"What can I do for you?" he asked. He was polite but uneasy-sounding, his voice rising more than a question-worth. On the other hand, two ninth graders had just barged into his workplace uninvited.

"Well," I said, drawing it out while my brain whirred. "As I mentioned, I'm on the school paper. So's my friend Ryan. A lot of kids over at Spring Creek were complaining about feeling sick this morning." I plowed forward, suddenly on a roll. "Belly aches and tiredness and one girl said she, um, didn't remember what outfit she'd worn last night. Which you know, with girls, is so important."

I did a mental eye roll at myself. When I lied, I sounded like an idiot. I'd have to work on that.

"Here." Ryan thrust the bag of energy drink bottles at him. Also the box of kolaches. "We brought a couple of the sample bottles. Oh. And snacks."

Terry McClain frowned. His face looked extra pale—grey actually, like he was coming down with the flu or worse—but maybe that was because he was wearing a white lab coat over his khakis. His cheekbones stood out sharper today—*had he lost weight?* Eyes on us, he unhooked the bag of

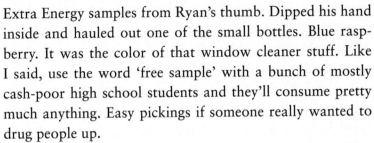

Extra Energy samples from Ryan's thumb. Dipped his hand inside and hauled out one of the small bottles. Blue raspberry. It was the color of that window cleaner stuff. Like I said, use the word 'free sample' with a bunch of mostly cash-poor high school students and they'll consume pretty much anything. Easy pickings if someone really wanted to drug people up.

That part was weighing harder on me now. Were these drinks really responsible for a chain of events that had barrel-raced into Casey saving Lanie and then . . . I shivered. Maybe it was just this building, all glass and steel and anonymous. My brain offered up a brief memory of Bo's loft. Lots of windows there too, but cozy somehow, even if Bo was sad and unpredictable and angry. This place was . . . institutional. There was no personality, no character. No emotion. As Ryan might say, It was a zombie apocalypse. .

I eyeballed Terry—studying him as he studied the gross blue drink, squinting, puckering his lips. Maybe he'd suspected something about this place, too, even though he bragged about his job. People were funny like that. Maybe *that's* why he looked so out of sorts. I suddenly wished Amber were here. If I could get Ryan and Mags to believe the truth when they'd suspected something was very wrong, I bet she could take his suspicion and turn it around, too.

"Let's go into my lab with this," Terry said. He jabbed his finger toward the hall to his right.

My chest loosened. He was going to help us. He was going to figure this out. I would finally have my leverage to get Bo and Amber make those Management angels bring my brother back. Casey had saved *me* with everyone else, hadn't he? And look at Bo. He'd saved the wrong person straight out of the box. And *he* was still here. (I felt bad about thinking that since it was the woman he loved, but *I* hadn't made up those stupid rules, had I?)

"You sure about this?" Ryan whispered in my ear. "Guy seems kind of squirrely."

"It's fine," I whispered back, distracted as his hip bumped against mine. "He's a genius." But even as I said the words, I knew it wasn't that. It was that he'd been Amber's boyfriend. He'd seen that something in her that was angelic. The same thing Lanie had seen in Casey. Even if he'd cheated on her. And I was pretty sure he'd seen the error of his ways, too. He still cared enough to give her that necklace she wasn't wearing.

Ryan blinked a few times, looking troubled. he followed along with me to Terry's lab, still toting the kolaches.

"How's Amber?" Terry asked, striding ahead of us, lab coat flapping against the backs of his legs.

"Great," I told him. I decided to leave it at that.

The lab was big, with long tables and sinks, beakers and stainless steel instruments and blank screens everywhere. He motioned us to keep following, past the lab tables and into what I guess was his office.

"Sit," he said when we were inside. He gestured to a couple of chairs in the corner. "How about some coffee?" he added, setting the Extra Energy bottle on his desk. Sure enough, another one of those fancy K-cup machines was sitting on a side table. "Y'all pick whatever you want. I have lots of choices."

Something was making my stomach uneasy, but we chose our flavors and went through the smashing of the little container so it could pee out our drink. I picked a chocolate glazed donut and Ryan picked Kahlua.

"Milk?" Terry offered. He opened the mini-fridge sitting

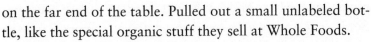

on the far end of the table. Pulled out a small unlabeled bottle, like the special organic stuff they sell at Whole Foods.

He topped off our cups with frothy white liquid. It was fancy whole milk, definitely. I usually went for two percent, but decided not to push it. Honestly, it looked delicious. I could live a little right now, given the circumstances. "Just hang here for a bit," he said, picking up the blue Extra Energy bottle and peering at it through his smudgy hipster glasses. "I'm going to look at this. So you say everybody acted 'wonky.' Tell me again what you mean by that."

So I told him, obviously leaving out the A-word parts. It came out in the same rapid-fire jumble as had a lot of what I'd been saying today. I sipped my coffee in between sentences. It *was* delicious: chocolaty and the milk made it thicker, like one of those Starbucks drinks. Texicon knew how to treat their employees.

Ryan was staring at his, so I elbowed him. "Drink some," I whispered. "Or he's going to think we're ungrateful."

He took a small sip. Then shrugged and gulped a bigger mouthful. "Mmm," he said. Which was the exact moment that my eyes started feeling heavy as lead.

I blinked hard and rubbed my eyes. Looked over at Ryan. My vision was hazy. All at once he seemed closer and then farther away and then my head swirled and I was pretty sure I was about to yak up the coffee.

"Jenna," Ryan said. A distant whisper. Shadows enveloped him.

"Drink up," said Terry McClain from somewhere that I could no longer see.

Shit, I thought, getting foggier by the nano second. *Shit. Shit.*

I rammed my shaking hand in my pocket. I was still new to

phone ownership. And my fingers felt like clumsy sausages. But I'd put Amber Velasco on speed dial as number 5. Maybe I . . .

"You're not . . ." I said, nausea rushing through me. "You son of a . . ."

"Maybe I better take those," said Terry's voice. I felt but didn't see him lift the cup from my hand as I slid from the chair.

This time I was sure I was dreaming. I wanted to wake up. I knew there was a reason I should wake up. But my eyes were so heavy I couldn't force them open.

Voices. I tried again to open my eyes. See who was talking. But I couldn't. I tried to move my arms and legs. Couldn't do that either. I could breathe. I could feel my heart beating, slower than I thought it should. I should be panicking. I should be . . . I couldn't remember. I could hear two people talking. That was it.

"You hired me to run this lab," said the first voice. It sounded familiar. Who?

"We hired you to do a lot of things," a second voice said. This one I didn't recognize. "Not litter the floor with bodies."

"But they knew about the sample drink bottles."

"And whose fault is that?"

"But—"

"Shut up. When I leave, you'll deal with it."

"But my girlfriend will be suspicious if—"

"She's not your girlfriend, McClain. You think we don't know that? We've been watching you since Austin. Five damn years, you idiot. You think we don't know the little EMT dumped your cheating ass?"

I tried again to pry my eyes open. Voice one was Terry McClain.

Was I dreaming? Was I awake? Why couldn't I move my arms and legs? Wait. I could wiggle my fingers. But my hands . . . were they behind my back? I tried to make my arms reach for my pocket. If I could get my cell out, then maybe I could at least dial 911. If this wasn't a dream.

Terry said, "What should I do?"

The other voice laughed gruffly. Why couldn't I open my damn eyes? I felt so tired. Where was Ryan? Where was Mags?

"What you should do is what we're paying you for. You saw your apartment back in Austin, didn't you? You knew then who you were dealing with."

"That was a burglary." Terry's voice was shaking.

"More or less. The police didn't catch the burglars because we caught them first. They screwed up, like you did. They lied, like you are right now. Your loyal girlfriend was home when she wasn't supposed to be. And they swore they'd taken care of it. But we all know they didn't. Because she's still here and you're still buying her expensive jewelry."

"You can't know . . . "

I faded out then. I don't know how long. But they were still talking when I faded back in. My eyes opened just a tiny slit. I saw Terry in his lab coat. The other guy was tall, his back to me. Through my squinty vision, I could see that his hair was dark blonde, and he was wearing some kind of heavy boots. My eyes glued shut again.

"The test worked," Terry said. "Every kid demonstrated the desired symptoms. I mean, there was a goddamn lightning strike. A girl almost died. *None of them remember.* But it's not like I could bring them in for cognitive testing. And that was just a miniscule amount. What I've been testing on the mice is full strength. One dose and those mice don't know what hit them. It's going to work exactly as you want it to. I've distributed the first two shipments to those addresses. Just like you directed. One dose is all it will take."

"And I should take your word for this?" said the other voice.

Terry coughed nervously. But his tone was definite when he said, "There's no one better at this than I am. You *know* that. That's why *you* came to *me.*"

A pause.

"Clean up this mess, and we'll see. And don't try calling the cops and confessing. Last time someone tried that, it didn't turn out well for him. Try looking up Dr. Stuart Renfroe, MD. See what you find. Big nothing."

And then the other guy was gone.

Terry McClain, as far as I could see, which wasn't very far, was alone. He fidgeted with something at a lab table across the room, muttering to himself. I couldn't move, but I could sense someone beside me. I willed my fuzzy eyes to shift, and there was Ryan.

Had it been real? A dream? I wasn't sure.

Here's what I *was* sure of:

- I was lying on the floor in Terry's lab, my hands tied tight behind my back.
- Ryan Sloboda was lying next to me, his eyes closed, alive. I knew this because his chest was rising and falling.

- I was a big idiot.
- Amber and I would be having a HUGE CHAT about picking boyfriends.
- This was possibly the last time I was going to wear my new signature jeans and favorite cowgirl boots.

I made sure Terry wasn't paying attention, then wriggled to my side, twisting my tied hands this way and that. "Ryan," I whispered.

He moaned but didn't open his eyes. My right hand tugged loose, just a little, from whatever was holding it. My spirits lifted. Terry McClain was a genius at manipulating pharmaceuticals, but that didn't mean he had rope skills. I mean, look at Dave Pittman. He cut stuff into his baggies of weed all the time to stretch profits, and he wouldn't be receiving any academic scholarships.

There was a chance that I could keep wiggling my hands free. Also, Ryan wasn't dead. I still had no idea where the hell Mags was, but better to focus on the positives.

My thoughts were coming hot and heavy. Was Bo right? Was this whole thing seriously part of some Battle to Come? Was Terry a power player in some huge plot? Did Amber know this? Was she corrupt, too? Did Bo know? Was all this connected to Renfroe and Manny, somehow going all the way back to crazy olden Roman days? Was that even possible?

Too many thoughts for my dizzy brain. Oddly, though, I did not feel panicked. In fact, I felt sort of unnaturally *not* panicked. Which then made me panic because I figured that the *not-panic* was from whatever drug Terry had put in that milk to knock us out for the count.

A hand touched mine. I jerked, then realized it was Ryan. "Shh," I whispered. Right at that moment, the panic kicked

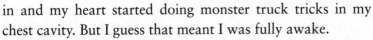

in and my heart started doing monster truck tricks in my
chest cavity. But I guess that meant I was fully awake.

Ryan wriggled right next to me. So close I could smell his
Ax. "Can you sit up?" he whispered, his breath warm in my
ear. My cheek was almost pressed against his. "If you can, I
think I can untie you."

I nodded. Yes. And quietly wriggled around until I was
sitting. Ryan did the same, scooting so we were back to back.
He also seemed unnaturally calm, but he seemed to be going
with it rather than letting it panic him, which I found impressive. His fingers began working at my plastic ties.

Unfortunately, Terry McClain started stomping around
the lab, possibly getting ready to drug us again or kill us or
drug us *and then* kill us.

I felt the ties loosen a little. Two seconds later, they went
slack. My wrists slipped free.

"Got it!" he whispered. "Now do mine."

I scooted silently backwards. Sweaty fingers fumbling,
I found it surprisingly easy to undo. I could feel *both* our
hearts thumping. But his body was still as a stone. Maybe he
was channeling Tony Stark. I realized then that pretending to
be brave was the exact same thing as real bravery.

So we were free. I was a little nauseated still. Now what?
Okay, I was more than nauseated. I made a gagging sound and
worked hard not to throw up. Terry hadn't heard us whispering or untying. But the gag he heard. He spun around. Saw
us sitting up, hands free. Let me say his eyes got pretty wide.

Turns out Ryan is an act now, think later kind of guy.

With a shout, he bull-rushed Terry, knocking him to the
floor. He kept his head up. He did not look at his feet. My
brother would have been proud.

"Sit on him!" I hollered.

"Get off me!" Terry shouted.

"You put poisoned milk in our coffees!" I shouted back, the first thing that popped into my head. I wanted to cause a scene. Because a scene would mean that we'd have witnesses. Sure enough,ther lab geeks came running. But then I had a moment of true panic. Okay, more than a moment. What if it wasn't just Terry? What if *all* of Texicon really was filled with corrupt mad scientists who kept drugged milk in their fridge?

Two guys in lab coats, khakis, and white shirts grabbed Ryan under the arms and pulled him off Terry. They were remarkably fit for science geeks who spent their days killing off mice.

"Get them out of here!" Terry shouted.

Before I knew it, two other guys had grabbed me under my own armpits. The whole crew dragged us to the elevator and held us tight until we were down in the lobby. Mostly by then I was feeling glad we weren't dead. More thoughts, hot and heavy: Terry was involved in whatever had happened to Amber that day. Was this why she'd blocked it out? Had he done something to make her block it out? Or was it Bo, protecting her? And Terry really *was* connected to everything else! The Battle to Come—*a reality!* The drugs Renfroe had developed—*a global threat! A Texas threat at least! Follow the riches,* Bo had told me. I hated that I only knew he was right long after the fact.

A-word land had swallowed me whole and had no plans to spit me out any time soon. The possibility of huge, bad things beyond just losing my family and my brother—all of this was real. Plus we were still in mortal danger. And Ryan Sloboda was probably going to run for the hills. *If we got out of this alive.*

Terry was muttering something as the guys dragged us

through the lobby. I gazed around wildly for Maggie, but didn't see her. Shit.

Fury bubbled hard in my veins. My chest was heaving. Terry McClain thought he was so smart! He didn't care if he hurt a bunch of people. If he hadn't given everyone the drugged power drinks then the stupid cheerleaders wouldn't have forgotten they tossed Lanie in the air. My brother wouldn't have had to save her. When that storm started, everyone would have run rather than milling around like lost sheep. Maybe they wouldn't have even been on the field in the first place. The fury reached a boiling point and had nowhere else to go.

"You cheated on Amber," I hissed at Terry.

His eyes bugged.

"You engineered the break-in didn't you?"

More eye-bugging. The lab guys dragged me faster across the smooth linoleum floor, preventing me from moving. Terry walked backward faster. We were almost to the big glass entranceway to Texicon.

"Shut up," he said. "Shut up. Shut up. Shut up."

"Are you working with Renfroe?" I asked. It's not like I expected him to answer, but I wanted to see the look on his face. He frowned. Puzzled. He honestly didn't seem to know what I was talking about. I wondered if he'd heard that name for the first time just now.

"Who are you giving memory drugs to?" I went on. "Who?"

Atta girl, Jenna, I heard my brother's voice say in my head. *But enough with the damn owl thing. It's getting old.*

This should have flummoxed me, but there wasn't time to worry about it. At that exact moment that the big glass doors of Texicon cracked and shattered into a million pieces.

Amber and Bo strode in, Maggie Boland trotting behind them.

In the movie version, they'd have been wearing long black duster coats flowing behind them in the breeze. Which they weren't. Even so, their entrance was a bit over-dramatic considering they were the only supernatural beings in the place—at least that I knew of. Sometimes it's about how you deliver the message. Everybody cringed. Naturally: the front doors of a major corporation had shattered and there was glass all over their nice lobby.

The lab guys stopped dragging us.

Terry McClain let go of my hands and turned around to see what all the crashing was about. I scrambled to my feet and grabbed Ryan's hand.

"You *cheated* on me?" Amber cried.

"Babe," Terry said, sounding totally confused, for which I do not blame him. It was not the accusation any of us had expected. He did not know that she had died because of him. He did not know that she was dead. And maybe I would have felt the tiniest bit sorry for him had he not added, "It's sort of your fault, you know. If you hadn't asked me to research what was in the blood sample last year, then no one would have known I was still working on this project. Then they wouldn't have . . ."

He clapped a hand over his mouth. Didn't say another word.

Bo was glowing. I saw something rustle under his shirt near his shoulders and I knew it was his wings. Any second now, I figured he'd start spouting something like, "Stand still while I smite you, dickhead!"

"Holy shit," Ryan said.

"I told you," I hissed at him. "I thought you believed me."

"I did," Ryan said. "But I—"

If he said something else, I didn't hear it. Because I was

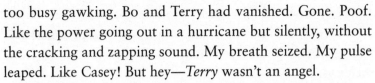

too busy gawking. Bo and Terry had vanished. Gone. Poof. Like the power going out in a hurricane but silently, without the cracking and zapping sound. My breath seized. My pulse leaped. Like Casey! But hey—*Terry* wasn't an angel.

"Jesus!" Ryan hollered and it sounded like he was mimicking my brother, who did not choose this moment to return.

I looked around wildly, glass crunching beneath my feet as I turned this way and that. The lab guy henchmen—*were they in on it? Or just duped into helping?*—whirled frantically, too. Then they bolted for the exit, scrabbling over the crunchy floor.

"Stop," said Amber. She did not shout. She did not gesture. Just said 'stop,' calm as can be.

They stopped.

She squinched up her eyes like Casey had done at the ball field, skin glowing deep golden, something simmering inside her.

"You never saw this," she said. "There was a storm. Things happen."

Mags and Ryan and I exchanged silent looks of awed understanding. *Damage Control.* My eyes flashed back to the lab henchmen. They were staring at Amber like she had just imparted the secrets to the universe.

"Walk away," Amber said. "It's been a weird day. Shit happens."

The lab guys shuffled off. My mouth hung open—just a little—as I watched them go. Even the security guy appeared calm and collected.

"*You* can do that?" I asked Amber. She didn't even look at me as she strode toward the elevator.

"Oh Jenna," she said as she passed, so quiet I almost couldn't hear her. "Of course I can."

"Holy cow," Maggie said. "Holy f-ing cow."

"Screw the Avengers," said Ryan, not whispering at all. "This is better than Agent Phil Coulson coming back from the dead."

"What the hell? Where are they?" That was me.

"Rooftop," Amber gasped. She was breathing hard like whatever she'd done had taken something out of her. "Let's go before he does something even more stupid."

I had no idea how she knew or if she meant Bo or Terry. Probably both.

HERE IS WHAT we saw when we rode the elevator to the roof and climbed up these little stairs and out the creaky metal door:

- Bo Shivers standing with his toes over the edge of the roof, balanced perfectly, holding Terry McClain by the back of his lab coat.
- Terry, toes over the edge. He did not look as comfortable with this.
- Bo's wings, fully extended—white and grey mixed, spanning so wide that he had to stretch out his arm to keep ahold of Terry. He was glowing so brightly it hurt to look at him. He was a fearsome creature, Bo Shivers.

"Don't!" Amber shouted. "Bo. No."

Bo lifted Terry. His feet dangled in thin air.

My heart ceased beating. One second. Then two. Then I exhaled sharply and it coughed back to life. I realized that Ryan was holding my hand. His fingers intertwined with mine, gripping tightly. Maggie was wide-eyed and silent.

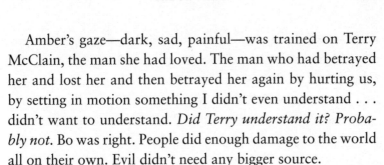

Amber's gaze—dark, sad, painful—was trained on Terry McClain, the man she had loved. The man who had betrayed her and lost her and then betrayed her again by hurting us, by setting in motion something I didn't even understand . . . didn't want to understand. *Did Terry understand it? Probably not.* Bo was right. People did enough damage to the world all on their own. Evil didn't need any bigger source.

"And now," Bo said, his eyes also fixed on the man he was holding delicately in the air thirty stories up. "You are going to tell his what you did. You are not going to leave anything out. You must be held accountable, you know. That's how this works." His voice boomed so loud that I plucked my hand from Ryan's and covered my ears.

"Put him down," I said.

"Too late," Bo thundered. He lifted Terry higher. Terry's mouth opened and closed like a fish on a line. "Put him down," I said again.

"Miss Samuels," said Bo Shivers, Texas slipping into his voice. "You're gonna have to let me do my job. I hadn't taken you for the squeamish type."

"Do what she say," Ryan told him. His hand was shaking but his voice was firm.

Maggie was crying. Maggie never cried. I couldn't blame her. Maybe Amber could work some memory healing on her, just to make this whole thing less traumatic. But even as the thought flashed through my brain, I shoved it away. The truth hurts sometimes. It *should* hurt.

"Talk," Bo told Terry, tightening his grip, his wrist scars twining darkly. "I'd suggest you spit it out there pretty fast. My hand feels sort of twitchy. And these children here are quite impressionable. I'd hate to let them see you splatter."

That, apparently, did the trick. Terry talked. He talked his head off while my heart beat itself into a frenzy, and Ryan gripped my hand and didn't let go, and Maggie seized my other hand. Amber pressed her lips together. Her eyes—dry as a bone— never left Terry McClain.

It wasn't a surprising story. I'd heard enough bits and pieces back at the lab. I'd heard other pieces when we were at Bo's watching that terrible, mind-twisting PowerPoint. It was, in the end, the same crap that things like this always are: powerful people somewhere spending money to control whatever or whomever it was they wanted to control.

Terry McClain had been in on it since Austin. He had cheated on Amber. He thought he could trade up. He thought he was smart enough to control things. He had signed on to create memory drugs for a top-secret group inside Texicon, connected to other people whose identity he honestly didn't really know. He thought he could get away with it. He thought it didn't matter. It was just chemistry, right? Just a job. He was paid very well. He moved up and came here to Texicon where he could use all their labs to create whatever he needed. He figured he was on his way. People would know him. They would remember his name. He would be important. Somebody.

But my brother and me— and Mags and Ryan—we'd stopped him. Because he'd been part of what had hurt my family even though none of us knew it at the time.

And Amber Velasco, well, I could read between the lines on that one. Management sending her here to shepherd Casey and by extension me . . . that was no coincidence. She was the only one who could have been sent because all of this was about her, too. Like me she had been in the dark. Unlike me, she'd *wanted* to be there.

But like Casey, she made a damn good angel.

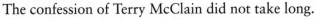

The confession of Terry McClain did not take long.

Of course, this was no Dr. Renfroe scenario. There would be no police involved. There was no one coming for Terry but us. And we were already here.

"So what do say, Ms. Velasco?" Bo asked her when Terry's voice had dried up. "What shall we do with this man? Drop him? Set him on fire? Might burn down the whole place. Could be problematic." He licked his lower lip. Cocked his head, looking for all the world like a curious bird, what with his wings still being fully extended.

A thin line of blood, dark and red, drizzled from Terry McClain's nose. His glasses were gone. I'd seen them tumble and fall.

It felt like a long time before Amber answered. From up here, I could see everything: the mall and the trees and the water tower and bunches of houses, all looking pretty much the same. The wind had picked up, and I don't think it was Bo's doing, just the weather changing—finally. A blue norther was fixing to blow through. Fall was finally here in Houston. In a few days the time would change and it would be Halloween and then Thanksgiving and then people would be putting up Christmas trees again.

"I want him to forget," Amber said. "I'd like all of them to. All of it, Bo. Every bit."

At first I didn't understand what she meant. Not the actual words of it, but the nature of the punishment. And then it drifted over me what she was saying. He would remain where he was but the rest of it would be wiped. He wouldn't know what he'd been involved in. He wouldn't know what he'd been working on or towards. He wouldn't remember the blonde man in the boots who'd threatened him back in the lab. It would all be gone. He'd be head of the lab at Texicon.

An ordinary person—not special in any way— working with his mice.

"If I take it all," Bo said, "It'll take you out, too. What you had with him, what you were to him. All of it. You understand that, Amber?" He used her first name this time, voice wrapping it gently.

She studied her feet like a great answer was written there. "Yes," she said. "Yes I do. He deserves *that*, too."

Bo nodded, one brief motion.

"And then we'll wait." Bo flicked his gaze over each of us. The world seemed to throb and thrum up here on the roof above the thirtieth floor—the tallest building in our little suburb. "We'll see what happens. Who comes to see him. Who wants something from him. What else we can find out. Maybe nothing. Maybe something. Time will tell. And if there's anything on this earth you and I seem to have, Ms. Velasco, it is time."

In the end, they did it together, Bo and Amber. Closing their eyes and using their collective angel powers and wiping Terry's memory clean. Bo set Terry down on the roof. Gently, which was a surprise.

Here was the thing about Bo Shivers, I understood then. For all his rage and badness, he was, like my brother, always at the core, an angel. He just couldn't help it. Neither could Amber.

"Go," Bo said to Terry. "Go back to your office and call 911 about the storm and the windshear."

Terry went. We watched as he stepped back through the metal door and it closed behind him.

And then Bo's gaze fell on me. Something unreadable crossed his grizzled face. He strode to me, pressing a hand to my cheek, the tips of his wings fluttering against me and

even though I was filled with something unreadable myself, I reached up and touched my finger tips to those scars he'd taken back to keep. "You okay, darlin'?" he asked, wings retracting and then gone like they had never been there.

I told him that I was.

Some other mild commotion ensued, both with the remaining lab guys and with more damage control and mentions of Management. The phrase "stupid and irresponsible" got tossed about more than once, including for the part where I had operated a motor vehicle while underage. And considerable colorful vocabulary once it really washed over Amber and Bo that I had told EVERYTHNG to Mags and Ryan.

This, Bo announced all high and mighty, was "unprecedented," and I made him swear on his wings that he wouldn't do what he had done to Terry and make them both forget. I tried to say it lightly, like I couldn't imagine he'd really do it, but my insides clenched anyway. He made no promises. And eventually I told myself that he was telling the truth. At least for now. As for the future, well, that was the future.

Turns out that Amber had gotten my emergency pocket text, which was great to know. As for Bo, I figured Amber had called him or it had been that angel Spidey sense. But he said no.

"I knew you were a you-know-what," Maggie said, flap-ping her arms like she was doing the Chicken Dance. "And I figured Jenna needed all the help she could get." Here Mags turned to Ryan. "No offense, Ry. But you were in over your head, both of you. So I decided if I called the school and pre-tended there was some kind of emergency at Bo's house near Texicon and asked did they know his cell, that one of those school secretaries would at least call him even if they didn't give me the number. Which is what happened. I knew if they told him 'near Texicon' he'd know something was up."

Here Maggie fixed her gaze on Bo. "I mean you know you don't have a house near Texicon, right?"

Bo, for perhaps the first time in millennia, was speechless. Maggie Boland was a force of nature.

There was more talk then. Ryan and I told everything we'd seen and heard, and I recounted the conversation between Terry and the guy in the boots. The two of them talking to each other had been real, not some crazy drug dream. This is what my own Jenna-sense—yes, this is what I was calling it—told me.

Memory drugs were out there. Terry McClain had helped develop them. Probably independently of Renfroe, which was strange, but as has been widely proven, strange things happen all the time. Something Big was at stake. It had started with my family, but it was bigger than that. Much bigger. And Bo's belief that Oak View was at the bottom of it, seemed to make sense now.

As for Terry McClain, it was his secrets that those men had come looking for that fateful night that Amber had been murdered. It was his fault that she was dead. He had betrayed her by cheating on her, had been gone the night she died alone and then came back as an angel. And now he didn't

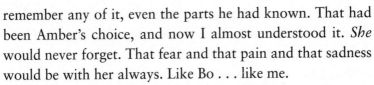

remember any of it, even the parts he had known. That had been Amber's choice, and now I almost understood it. *She* would never forget. That fear and that pain and that sadness would be with her always. Like Bo . . . like me.

Except I was luckier than most. I had Mags. And for now, there was Ryan. Who, it turned out, had not run for the hills, not even one tiny little step.

Lanie Phelps had dumped my brother and Terry McClain had done worse to Amber. Bo had chosen angel-dom over love. My father had run off to Olivia-land. It was a long list of crappy, that much was for sure.

How did you ever figure out if a person you loved was the right person? One who would stick with you no matter what? Was Ryan that type? I decided to believe he was. But I knew there were no guarantees.

Still, we had gone undercover and solved at least some of the mystery.

"We're like gonzo journalists," I informed Bo. (I had looked up that Hunter Thompson fellow to make sure Bo wasn't joking and referring to *The Muppets*.) "But without the LSD," I added.

LATER, AS WE hiked to the Merc, which Amber was going to drive home for me, Amber scrolled the news on her phone. There was a breaking announcement that at least five heads of state had suddenly cancelled their appointments to come for checkups at the Houston Med Center. City Council was bemoaning the loss of income since that meant their entourages weren't coming either.

I frowned. "Did someone tell them something fishy was going on?"

Bo looked at the sky and didn't answer.

Then he trained his gaze, inky and inscrutable, on Amber. "You should have let me drop him," he said. But there was no heat in his voice.

She didn't respond and he didn't push it—surely a first. But then Bo pulled me aside. Mags and Ryan were already climbing into the backseat. Amber slid into the driver's seat, fit the key into the ignition. I followed Bo a few cars down, still half expecting Terry McClain to pop his head out of the smashed-up Texicon building.

"Jenna," Bo said. His face was solemn, but his voice was gentle. "You need to understand. You've got something, darlin.' I don't know what it is yet, but I will. There really is a Battle to Come. A big one. You're in the show, Jenna. You know what I mean by that? Whether you want to be or not."

"I'm just fifteen," I told him, pulse going erratic then steadying.

"In my day," he said, "That was old enough."

My sizeable and colorful vocabulary aside, I had no words. Was he telling the truth? Was it possible that I—the girl who didn't even have a learner's permit—had some fancy destiny in store? Like my brother becoming an angel so he could help me and the world, this seemed a rather cock-eyed turn of events. And if I had a destiny, what did that say about free will and chaos theory and why Lanie Phelps was still alive and kicking? It made my head hurt.

There was only one person I could truly trust to tell me straight, even if he did it in his own crazy roundabout manner. But he was gone.

Was Casey watching me from *somewhere*, hoping for the best?

If he was, I still didn't know how to respond to Bo's predictions. I did not think I was particularly special.

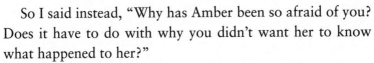

So I said instead, "Why has Amber been so afraid of you? Does it have to do with why you didn't want her to know what happened to her?"

He looked at me hard, in that way he had the first time we met, that way that felt like he was mining to my soul.

"Some things people have to come to on their own," he said. "They have to be ready." I reckoned he was very right about that.

Over in the Merc, one of them—Mags probably—honked the horn. A thought floated: Ryan was still my boyfriend. He had helped save me and I had helped save him. That was good.

Bo tilted his head, then looked at me straight on. "Sometimes I do things that make sense at the time. I told her if she didn't stop your brother and you from meddling, that Management would pull her. She's more fragile than you think. There are still things you don't know. Not everyone is like you, Jenna. Not everyone has your strength."

I gave him the stink eye. "You angels sure lie a lot," I said.

"We're an imperfect bunch. Like I told you, I think it lets us do our job. But the outcome of humanity? That we don't manipulate. Not ever."

Was that the truth? I had no idea.

We studied each other some more, Bo Shivers and I, and then he said, "I do believe you helped avert the apocalypse, Ms. Samuels. I think that's enough for one day."

He started to drop his gaze, but I had one more question.

"Could Casey come back still?" I asked.

He didn't answer.

I took that as a maybe.

F riday came and went. The coaches let Ryan play at the game, half of one quarter only, but Spring Creek ended up losing by a touchdown which was a disappointment to everyone. But it was only one game. We still had a winning record. There was always next week.

Also, Ryan brought me one of those fake mums. It was huge and gaudy and covered with little boxes of candy and trinkets and in the middle of the mum, he'd hot-glued a plastic angel.

"Seriously?" I asked him, blushing.

He grinned in that way that made my heart do handstands in my chest.

On Saturday, as planned, Ryan and I went to the Homecoming Dance. I wore my new blue-sequined high-low dress, which honestly, looked mighty fine. In a nice turn of events, Billy Compton the alto sax player and Maggie had mutually decided that they should go together. Maggie said she'd been sure he was waffling around it and she was waffling around it and finally Thursday night after being present for my near-death experience and learning that the universe had been cooking up some strange situations while most humans were looking the other way, she called Billy and said they should ask each other at the same time. Which they did. Billy Compton, it seemed, had boyfriend potential after all.

So we were going as a foursome and Maggie's mom was driving because the Bolands had an SUV and could fit us all.

"You look awesome," I told Mags as we got ready at her house.

My mother was stuck in bed again too much of the time and it wasn't pretty, but what could I do? The best I could, was all I figured. Maybe Casey *would* come back. I couldn't— I wouldn't give up hoping. Maybe my dad would start acting like a dad again and move home. Maybe Bo Shivers—who had taken over guarding me along with Amber—would stop confusing the ever-loving out of me.

Anything could happen, right? I mean look at Houston. We were a port city even though we were miles from the water. But then some optimistic types had dug out Buffalo Bayou deep enough to make ships fit.

I could do that with my life, couldn't I? Believe that I could make it anything I wanted. Even if there was hole in my heart the size of a semi.

So I did what a normal girl would do. I shared my Sephora kit with Maggie. We glittered ourselves up and even smeared the sparkly bronzing cream on our legs so they'd look tan and sexy. I tottered around in my new heeled sandals. We both did up our hair in fancy French braids. If some Big Bad wanted to take over humanity one memory at a time and I was destined to somehow help stop them, well, I wasn't going

to do it tonight. We were pretty dolled up by the time Maggie's front doorbell rang.

Who was out there, but Amber Velasco.

It's not like it took her angel powers to figure out where I'd be.

"You have a second?" she asked. I shrugged, then followed her outside, my too-high heels tapping against the walkway. I hadn't had much use for angels the past day or so.

"Don't use up all that glitter crap," I hollered over my shoulder to Mags. "I wanted to do some more of it on my décolletage." This was a new word I'd read in one of those fashion magazines. A fancy term for a woman's cleavage. Classier than saying boobs.

"You okay?" Amber said as her conversation starter.

I wrinkled my nose. "You came over to ask *that*?"

"Seemed like a plan at the time," she said.

"*You* okay?" I tossed back at her. She had said very little— okay nothing, which is less than little—about Terry and Bo and the whole shebang of crazy. Amber Velasco was still not big on Personal Revelations. Not that I blamed her anymore.

She didn't answer. An eternity ticked by. But I had a Homecoming Dance to go to with my boyfriend. I took the bull by the horns.

"I would have let Bo drop Terry," I said, but I didn't think I meant it. I only meant to let her know that she deserved better . . . more. We all did.

"Would you?" she asked, in the same even tone she'd used the other day when I understood that what an idiot I'd been about angels and their power and about her. There was a lot more to Amber Velasco than met the eye.

Lot more to me, too. "Maybe," I said. It was as close to being honest about this as I planned on getting. Would

Bo—an angel—have killed Terry McClain if Amber had told him to? Would he have wreaked angel vengeance like something out of ancient days? What would it have changed?

And me? Would I have applauded? If it was last year again, and Renfroe was leaping over that Galleria balcony, would I have just let him go?

I stepped closer, realizing I was taller than her in these heels, although not by much. "You pretend you don't care about . . . what happened. But that's a lie. You have a good heart, " I said. "I mean obviously you do or you wouldn't be a 'you-know-what.' I air-quoted it and then did Maggie's goofy Chicken Dance wing flap as a joke. "I would have kicked Terry McClain in the nuts, by the way. Let him remember *that* part."

Amber pursed her lips.

A few more seconds, and she said, "I hear Mr. Gilroy is going to stick around for awhile," she said.

I raised both brows, but I was glad to hear it.

"You know that angel grapevine," Amber said, lips twitching in what I realized was a smile.

"That a joke?"

"Maybe."

I hadn't planned on hugging her, but that's what I did. She hugged me back.

"We have some unfinished business," she said then, face serious. My heart bumped hard. Was she going to tell me the other stuff that Bo had hinted at? Whatever she'd done those first couple years after she'd come back as an angel? "I'll pick you up in the front of school on Monday after classes. Finally get you that learner's permit."

I hugged her again. It seemed only polite.

After that, I went to the dance with Ryan and Maggie and Billy—the only one in the group who did not know A-word

secrets. That made it easier to talk about other things, which was just fine with me. But I knew if something went wonky, I had my Twelth Men, even if one of them was a girl. My brother might still be MIA, but at least there was that.

The weather had finally turned. Just as the wind had hinted while we stood on the Texicon roof. Cool and dry and full of promise. I breathed it in, deep as I could. Sometimes—all the times—you need to hang on to the good stuff.

For now I let Ryan Sloboda—wearing a suit and tie and looking ridiculously handsome—hold my hand as we walked into the school cafeteria, all decorated up like a Hollywood star party. We posed for pictures on the fake Red Carpet and then walked out to the dance floor, which was the cafeteria covered in fake Hollywood sidewalk stars. The yearbook geeks were snapping pictures like paparazzi.

Someone tapped my bare shoulder. I turned. Lanie Phelps stood there, looking very pretty, the tiniest of bruises purpling her cheek—I guess from where she fell and 'no one' caught her.

I looked at her. She looked at me. Ryan squeezed my hand and cleared his throat. I thought: Casey Samuels loved you with all his heart and now he's not here and you don't even remember.

Lanie blinked. "Is Casey coming?" she asked, and my heart tightened hard and sharp in my chest.

"Nope," I said, easing the word around my stony heart. Ryan squeezed my hand again. He really was something, Ryan Sloboda.

"Oh," Lanie said. They had voted her Homecoming Queen last night. Donny Sneed—who would never be good enough for her—was King.

We'd have gone on like this for awhile, me and Lanie, but up front, the DJ got started.

"Got one I know y'all love," he said into the mic.

And what do you know, *Copperhead Road* blared from the sound system.

I might have cried then, for Casey and all of it, but I was glittered up and there was Ryan. He leaned in and we kissed. Soft and sweet. A good, solid, kiss that almost knocked me out of my high heels.

Then I kicked them off anyway, and Ryan and Maggie and Billy Compton and I joined the crowd, dancing and stomping to *Copperhead Road*. I thought about Amber and Casey and even Bo Shivers. About all the things lost and gained and still unknown. Tears welled at the corners of my eyes, but I told them to go to hell.

We kicked and stomped and turned and Ryan—who knew my secrets and was still willing to be my boyfriend—grabbed me up and even though it wasn't part of the line dance, he swung me around and kissed me again, lips pressing against mine, light at first and then deeper. A slow, wet kiss that lasted a very long time.

Sparklers set off in my brain and other places.

"Things always going to be this crazy with you?" he whispered, his mouth warm and delicious against my ear.

"That a problem?" My heart stomped half a beat off.

Ryan smiled, big and dazzling and perfect. "Nope. Just checking."

He pulled me back against him. He wasn't wearing Ax tonight, just plain old Ryan smell, which was fine with me.

"You smell good," I told him, hoping he'd register the message.

We danced some more. Kissed some more, too. Ryan was an excellent kisser.

The world was a crazy place, the A-word world even

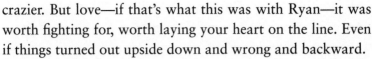

crazier. But love—if that's what this was with Ryan—it was worth fighting for, worth laying your heart on the line. Even if things turned out upside down and wrong and backward.

Was I destined for more than what I could see around me? Was that what all of this had been about? The thought fluffed my brain, leaving trails of sparkly possibility. But right now, this—the dance, Ryan's body pressed against me—was enough. I was not my father, chasing a shinier life. I was not Amber . . . not my brother, I was just me.

Here is what I decided: the bad stuff would just have to wait.

Least until Amber Velasco finally took me for that learner's permit on Monday.

Then all bets were off.

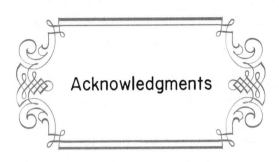

Acknowledgments

I owe a huge debt of gratitude to the collaborative awe-someness and effortless hipsterness (the non-ironic kind) of the team at Soho Press. Endless thanks to my editor, Daniel Ehrenhaft, who is never afraid to send an editorial letter that begins, "Now don't be nervous, but . . ." And then follow up with a *Spinal Tap* video to soften the blow. My craft is owed so very much to his thoughtful and always patient guidance. Also to Bronwen Hruska—publisher, author, curator of writers, mom in search of easy ways to create an Arctic wolf out of clay on short notice—and her merry band of nimble, brilliant folks including Meredith Barnes, publicist for the ages, and Juliet and Rachel and Rudy and Janine and the rest: I love making books with all of you.

On the other coast, I send sunny LA smiles to the best agent in the world, Jennifer Rofe, without whom I would be quite lost. Thank you, cowgirl!

Many, many thanks to Kim O'Brien, Bob Lamb, Dede Ducharme, and Suz Bazemore for Wednesday night critiques and cupcakes and other library contraband. And my beta partners: Varsha Bajaj, Christina Mandelski, and Crystal Allen for their wisdom and endless quest for the perfect breakfast.

Thanks to my own guardian A-words in the Texas book community: authors, readers, librarians, booksellers—including but by no means limited to bloggers Maria Cari Soto and Katie Bartow and the wonderful and career supportive folks at Houston's Blue Willow Bookshop and Murder by the Book and Round Rock's Book Spot. Y'all deserve a lifetime supply of kolaches and breakfast tacos.

Thanks mostly to my readers, including Hannah in England: I tell these stories for you! Thank you for embracing the quirky Houston world of Jenna, Casey, Amber, and of course, Bo.

To borrow a well-worn phrase, "Texas Forever!"